"That was you put on today. . . ."

"You had those people eating out of your hand," Daniel said.

"But not you."

"No. Never me."

"You knew I was faking? But you didn't say anything."

"I've warned them already. I've warned them and warned them, but they won't listen."

Cleo came closer, so she was directly in front of him. He could see the star like pattern in her hazel eyes—green shot with black. "You're not saying words they want to hear," she whispered. Her hands were at her sides, her head tipped so she could retain eye contact. Inches separated them.

What did she want? After last night, he didn't think she'd want to breathe the same air as him, let alone stand so close. "Why did you come here, Cleo?" *Cleopatra, with your red toenails, and red lips.* "Did you come here to see me?"

Cleo frowned. "I think," she began, sliding a sandaled foot between his bare feet, hooking a thumb in the belt loop of his low slung shorts, just above his hipbone in a way that seemed way too familiar. He liked it. "I'm not entirely sure, but I think I came to see you."

He smiled then, a smile that felt like it blossomed from deep inside him, a smile that was suddenly reflected in Cleo's face. "I was hoping you'd say that. . . ."

BOOKS BY THERESA WEIR

American Dreamer
Cool Shade
Some Kind of Magic
Bad Karma

Published by HarperPaperbacks

BAD
KARMA

THERESA WEIR

HarperPaperbacks
A Division of HarperCollinsPublishers

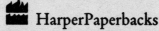

HarperPaperbacks
A Division of HarperCollins*Publishers*
10 East 53rd Street, New York, NY 10022-5299

This is a work of fiction. The characters, incidents, and
dialogues are products of the author's imagination and are not to
be construed as real. Any resemblance to actual events or
persons, living or dead, is entirely coincidental.

ISBN 0-06-101296-3

HarperCollins®, ▰®, and HarperPaperbacks™
are trademarks of HarperCollins Publishers Inc.

Cover illustration © 1999 by Danilo Ducak
Cover design © 1999 by Saksa Art & Design

First paperback printing: July 1999

Printed in the United States of America

Visit HarperPaperbacks on the World Wide Web at
http://www.harpercollins.com

❖ 10 9 8 7 6 5 4 3 2 1

For Martha, my world traveler

BAD
KARMA

1

Folks there called it Missour*a*. Daniel Sinclair used to call it Missour*a*. Now he called it Missour*ee*. That pretty much summed up his status in the small town of Egypt, Missouri.

Outsider.

His was a bigger fall from grace than most, because he hadn't always been an outsider. No, Daniel Sinclair had been born into the welcoming, nurturing arms of Egypt, Missouri, which was the only way you could ever really belong. You could live there twenty years, but if you hadn't been shot from someone's loins on that sacred soil, you were an outsider. And if you were born there and left, well, then you could add traitor to your résumé. And if you came back, nobody forgave you and everybody talked about your hoity-toity accent, which was really no accent at all, but rather the absence of one, a fact there was no use in arguing. You would never convince anyone in Egypt that he or she was the one with the accent.

In California they'd teased Daniel about his lazy drawl. In Missouri they teased him about his city talk. A guy couldn't win.

Daniel stood looking out the door of the one-story clapboard house, past the flies that clung to the screen waiting for their chance to get in, and past the gray-painted porch at his battered blue truck, which was waiting to take him someplace he didn't want to go. As a kid, he'd harbored the horrendous misconception that once he became an adult, he wouldn't have to do anything he didn't want to do. Then he'd grown up and realized what a bunch of shit that was.

"Beau!" Daniel shouted over his shoulder, preparing to announce his departure.

Knowing his brother, Beau would still be in the bathroom going through the ritual of combing his hair until not a strand was out of place and shaving so carefully and thoroughly that his face took on a baby-smooth sheen.

"See you in a few hours!" Daniel put a hand to the door. The flies stirred, then resettled, their very sluggishness seeming to mock the heaviness that seemed so much a part of him these days.

It was going to rain, Daniel told himself. Flies always wanted in when it was going to rain.

"Wait!" Beau's shout came from the dark recesses of the house. "Wait for me."

Daniel's shoulders sagged. He'd been afraid of this.

Beau hurried as much as Beau could hurry, which

meant it was a full three minutes before he stepped out of the bathroom, every hair in place, his striped polo shirt tucked snugly into neatly creased jeans.

"You can't come," Daniel told him.

"Why?" Beau's blue eyes held surprise. "Aren't you picking that lady up at the train station? I love trains. You know I love trains."

It wasn't that Daniel didn't want to keep Beau from seeing the train; he wanted to keep him from seeing the "lady," the psychic. To Daniel's supreme irritation, the town of Egypt had hired a damn psychic. The only reason Daniel had agreed to pick her up was so he could give her his personal welcome, which he hoped might just end with their guest purchasing a ticket back to the voodoo land she'd come from. The encounter wouldn't be pleasant, but somebody had to do it.

"The lady's name is Clara," Beau stated with authority.

"Who told you that?"

"I heard you talkin' to Jo about her. Said her name was Clara. Clara Voiyant."

Daniel laughed. "Her name's Cleo Tyler, although I think I like your name better."

"Cleo. That's a weird name."

"Maybe it's short for Cleopatra," Daniel joked.

"That's even weirder."

"No shit."

Beau shifted his weight from one foot to the other. "What key is she going to find?"

Oh, man. Daniel had hoped to keep the key business quiet. "You haven't told anybody about it, have you?"

Beau looked down at his feet. "Maybe Matilda."

"Matilda?"

"You know. The girl at Tastee Delight."

Shit, the whole damn town probably knows by now. It was so stupid, and unfortunately so damn typical of Josephine Bennett. When her husband, the former chief of police, had died two years ago, Jo took over— which would have been fine except that at the same time she went on a spiritualism kick, and now she thought rocks and cards and candles were the answer to everything. What was next, séances at the police station?

Jo had read about Tyler's involvement in a kid- napping case in California. But Daniel had heard that Cleo Tyler hadn't had anything to do with it, that she'd been brought in just as the police were ready to rescue the victim. An opportunist, Tyler hadn't wasted a second in taking credit for solving the crime and saving a kidnapped child's life. Daniel had tried to tell Jo that Cleo Tyler was nothing but a fraud and a con artist, but Jo wouldn't listen.

"I've consulted my cards," she'd told him, "and they say she's the one."

"The one what?" he'd asked. "The crackpot?"

"When did you get so serious?" Jo had replied. "You need to lighten up. What's happened to you, Danny boy? When you were little, you were always laughing. I never see you laugh anymore."

"Nothing's funny, Jo."

And that was the truth. Nothing was funny.

"The patrol car's being worked on," Daniel told Beau now. He'd deliberately taken it to the garage the previous day so he'd have the excuse of not enough room. "There won't be enough room for all of us in the truck. I'm sorry."

"We can fit. Three people? We can fit. Three people have fit before. Is she fat?" Beau thought about that for a while. "Even if she is fat, we can fit. I'm skinny, and you're . . . I don't know, you're regular."

"She has a dog."

"What kind of dog?"

"I don't know." Daniel felt an impatience growing in him. He fought it and failed. "A dog," he said sharply. "Maybe a big dog. Maybe a take-a-bite-out-of-your-ass dog."

Daniel instantly regretted raising his voice. It wasn't Beau's fault that the town of Egypt had hired some wacko to come and read tea leaves.

Beau was good-natured, but he knew when he wasn't being treated fairly.

Daniel had been told that, even as a baby, Beau had been good-natured. That he hardly ever cried and hardly ever stopped smiling. Daniel wouldn't know, because Beau was two years older.

Beau was a little slow. He'd come into the world in the front seat of their parents' '57 Chevy. That was before Lamaze, before fathers were allowed in the delivery room, and before mothers really knew a lot about what was going on. The two inexperienced parents had tried to keep Beau in the birth canal, where they thought he belonged, until they could get to the hospital; consequently Beau had been deprived of oxygen for several minutes.

Funny thing was, Beau didn't consider himself cheated in any way. No, he was one of the happiest, most contented people Daniel had ever known. And wasn't that what life was all about—if not happiness, then at least contentment? So what if your pockets weren't lined with gold and you didn't know the difference between Mont Blanc and Bic—did any of that really matter in the end?

Daniel had thought it would be easy, moving back from LA, but living in Missouri was just a different kind of hard. As a kid, Daniel had pored over travel books. He'd soaked in everything he could about places he feared he might never see. Sometimes he thought that if he hadn't read those books, he'd be like everybody else in Egypt: complacent, almost smug in that complacency. The people in Egypt didn't think about what was going on in the rest of the world, what they might be missing. *They* were the world. If it wasn't happening in Egypt, it wasn't happening.

Daniel envied their complacency.

People were always reaching for more. Maybe the secret was to reach for less.

Daniel watched as, wordlessly, Beau plopped down on the couch, picked up the remote control, and clicked on the television. He was pissed.

"I'll see you later, okay?" Daniel said, needing to reassure himself as well as Beau.

No answer. Beau didn't take his eyes from the TV screen.

"Tonight we'll cook those steaks I got yesterday."

How did things get like this? Daniel wondered in frustration. He wanted to be Beau's friend, his brother, not his parent. The enormous responsibility was turning him into some grumpy-assed old man, somebody he didn't like, somebody he wouldn't want to hang around with.

He let the flimsy door slam shut behind him. Through the haze of green mesh, he saw Beau staring at the television, arms across his chest, his body rigid. On the screen was a talk show, most likely about some sordid, sensationalistic topic.

Daniel sighed and stood there, hands on his hips, and contemplated his sandaled feet. Here he was, denying his brother the pleasure of a ride to the damn train station. That was small of him. Really small. Maybe Jo was right. Maybe he was taking life too seriously.

He lifted his head. "On second thought," he said through the screen, "I really could use some company."

A man transformed, his anger forgotten, Beau jumped to his feet.

"We don't want to be late," Daniel said, even though he knew it was useless to try to hurry his brother. As with his morning ablutions, Beau had a certain procedure he had to adhere to before leaving the house.

He checked to make sure everything was in place—his shirt tucked in, his belt through every loop of his jeans. Then he grabbed his Velcro running shoes.

Beau loved Velcro. He often lamented the fact that not every pair of shoes in the world fastened with Velcro.

One time when Beau and Daniel were out walking through the woods and had gotten cockleburs stuck to them, Daniel had shown Beau how the burrs had tiny hooks all over them, just like Velcro. "That's what gave the guy who invented Velcro the idea," Daniel had told him.

Beau had examined the cocklebur closely, as amazed as only someone as unjaded as Beau could be. While most people over the age of ten had lost the capacity to wonder at uniqueness, Beau had retained that perception into adulthood. Daniel often thought that Beau represented the ability to embrace life—an ability that people lost as they got older, what he himself had lost.

"TV," Daniel reminded him now.

"Oh, yeah." Happy as a puppy, Beau jogged back, clicked off the television, then followed his younger brother to the truck.

2

With a firm grip on Premonition's harness, Cleo Tyler adjusted her dark glasses and grabbed the train's metal handrail.

"Watch your step there, miss," the conductor said, his strong fingers grasping her by the elbow. "There are three steps down. One, two, three."

Her feet made contact with cement.

"There you go."

Three days. It had taken three unholy days to get from Portland, Oregon, to Clear Lake, Missouri. Heat blasted her from all sides—from the murky sun above, from the cement below her feet, from the train behind.

"Station's straight ahead," the conductor said, still gripping her arm, obviously reluctant to turn her loose.

"I'll be fine," she said, flashing him a movie-star smile.

He released her arm. She heard his voice, muffled now because he was turned to help the next passenger. "Watch your step. Watch your step."

My God. It's so hot, was all she could think. Was it

always like this? It couldn't be. This had to be something abnormal.

Maybe she should have listened to Adrian. But no, part of the reason she'd come to Missouri was because she'd decided that Portland was too close to Seattle, too close to her brother. He'd rescued her from herself, probably saved her life, but that didn't mean he owned her. He couldn't seem to understand that she was okay now.

"Where are you going?" he'd asked when she called to tell him she was leaving. "Do you know anybody there?"

"No. That's why I want to go. And it's money. It's a job."

"Prostitution's a job, but you're not doing that." There was a long silence. "Are you?"

She should have been mad. Instead she laughed. "Not yet."

"Shit, Cleo."

"I'm kidding. I'm not that desperate."

"Cleo, look. Why don't you come to Seattle? We'll talk about this. Maybe I can get a loan so you can go back to school."

"Adrian, no." He had a wife, two little kids, a second mortgage on his house, and a recording studio that was just barely staying afloat, Adrian having jumped into the business at the tail end of the Seattle grunge era. "Really, I'm okay."

"I worry about you falling in with the wrong people."

She laughed again. "Brother dear, I *am* the wrong people. You should know that by now. I'm the person our mother always warned us about."

He laughed—it was a sound she never got tired of hearing.

"I'll call you when I get there."

"You'd better."

"Love you."

"Me too."

Adrian. He was the only person she could be herself around, but even with Adrian she knew she could only reveal so much. It would scare him and worry him if he knew how hardened by life she'd become.

Premonition tugged at his harness, reminding Cleo of more immediate concerns. The yellow Lab put his nose to the ground and made a beeline for the train station, hiking his leg on the corner of the building.

It wasn't easy traveling with a dog, especially a big dog. You could put a caged cat in the baggage compartment; it would most likely be miserable and hysterical, but better off than it would have been traveling in the open. Dogs were different. Dogs were social. Whereas cats might love cramped, confined, dark places, dogs hated them. A place like that could really screw up a dog's psyche. For that very reason, Cleo had spent three days on a train when she could have flown.

That was why, in these situations, she put Premonition in his guide dog harness and pretended she was blind.

She didn't like the idea of exploiting a handicap,

and she hated the deception, but for the sake of Premonition she was able to justify the ruse. It was simply part of the scramble that was called life. At the animal shelter where she'd gotten Premonition, she was told that he'd been so mistreated by his previous owner that he'd never be able to adapt to a new life, but that had made Cleo all the more determined to have him. And except for a fear of confined places, he was now a well-adjusted dog.

Done with his business, Premonition pulled her to a grassy area where he could get off the baking cement sidewalk and rest his paws in the cool grass. Behind her, the train chugged away from the station, taking with it the noise and steam, but not much of the heat.

Looking out through dark glasses, Cleo saw but pretended not to see two men moving toward her, both about six feet tall, one with dark hair, the other light.

"Daniel Sinclair's an Aries," the police chief had warned Cleo over the phone. "With more of that sign's undesirable traits than desirable ones."

Aries. A fire sign. The most energetic of the fire signs. Aries used that energy to bring about change. So what undesirable traits did Daniel Sinclair harbor? Was he intolerant, a poor judge of character, impulsive, or all of the above? But then there were the positive traits. Aries individuals were the risk takers, daring and aggressive.

Neither man looked like a cop, she decided. And

they both looked rather . . . well, *unusual*.

The dark-haired man was tidy to the point of seeming obsessive, while the light-haired man was sloppy in an almost equally obsessive way. The tidy one was dressed in a striped polo shirt tucked neatly into creased jeans. On his feet were Velcro sneakers.

She didn't know anyone over four years old who wore Velcro.

As they closed the distance, she could see that the Velcro man's face was shiny, as if someone had held him down and given him a good scrubbing. In the back of her mind she thought, *There's something a little slanted here.*

While the Velcro man was soft around the edges, his friend was rough. He wore khaki-colored cargo pants. Leather sandals, no socks, and a camp shirt that had probably been black at one time but was now a soft gray. Were those pink flamingos? And palm trees?

Yes.

He hadn't even bothered to shave. The whole look shouted, *I don't give a shit what you think.*

A shock of hair that was genetically brown but had been bleached and streaked by the sun fell over unflinching eyes. Direct eyes. Bold, Aries eyes. Eyes that held irritation. At her? Or the heat? Or both?

She'd expected someone older. She didn't know why. Maybe because to her a police officer was an authority figure, and authority figures were always supposed to be older, no matter what her age. If she was eighty and got pulled over by a cop, he would have to be at least eighty-five.

"You Cleo Tyler?" the sloppy one asked in an authoritative way that immediately set Cleo on edge, that immediately had her wanting to respond with something childish, like *What's it to you?* Instead her voice said, "Yes."

"I'm Daniel Sinclair."

She read him so easily. A complete skeptic. She didn't mind skeptics. In fact, she was one. She'd spent the last several years trying to prove to herself that psychic phenomena didn't exist.

She could see that Daniel Sinclair had come prepared to dislike her, but the sight of a blind person had sent him into a tailspin. Now he felt guilty for disliking someone who was handicapped, but he still thought she was out to take the town of Egypt, Missouri, for a ride.

Which could be the case. But it wasn't her fault that they'd come begging for her help. It wasn't as though she was in the business. She'd been working in a coffee shop, for God's sake. Lately she'd been toying with the idea of going back to school, but when the Egypt police chief called for the third time, Cleo found herself considering their offer. Her life had fallen into a rut. And when she was told she'd get paid whether she found the master key or not, well, it was an offer she couldn't refuse.

The man in front of her was looking at her as if he knew her inside and out. What arrogance. He knew *nothing* about her. And at that moment she decided she didn't want to know anything about him. Let him wallow in his smug narrow-mindedness.

"You don't look like a policeman," she stated, implying that people weren't always what they seemed. Her comment also let him in on her harmless deception.

At first his expression was one of surprise. That was instantly replaced by one of self-satisfaction. He'd expected deception from her. "You're not blind."

"What about you?" she asked, sending the conversation volleying back. "Are you who you pretend to be? I'm sensing a man out of his element."

"Don't use that mind-reading crap on me. I'm in my element. I couldn't be more in my element."

"How do you define element?" she asked, suddenly realizing just how tired she was, wishing she hadn't started this word game.

"I'm the small-town cop who can do whatever he wants."

His eyes were an intense Paul Newman blue, so dark they were almost artificial-looking. Contacts? No, he wasn't the type. He wouldn't bother with clear contacts, let alone tinted ones. "You mean you run the town?" she asked.

"If I ran the town, you wouldn't be here."

"Now why doesn't that surprise me?"

"Did you ever think you might be tempting fate by pretending to be blind?"

Maybe he wasn't such a skeptic after all. She

wouldn't bother to explain *why* she pretended to be blind. Let him think what he wanted. Let him think she was a manipulative con artist. She didn't care. To try to explain would mean she cared what he thought of her, and she didn't. Let him think she was the fraud he wanted her to be.

"Are you saying you believe in fate but not in psychic ability?" she asked.

"That's a good one."

The other man, apparently growing restless and fearing he'd never become part of the conversation, jumped in, unintentionally defusing what was fast becoming a hostile situation. "I'm Beau."

"My brother," Daniel added as explanation.

Beau eagerly extended a hand, his arm straight, his posture perfect. His hand was soft but warm, his grip firm. She smiled into the most beautiful pair of eyes she'd ever seen. "Hi, Beau." There, in front of some godforsaken train station in the middle of some godforsaken state, she'd found a good heart. And good hearts were rare. So blissfully rare.

"What sign are you?" she asked.

"What?"

"Zodiac sign."

She could see that he didn't understand. For a moment she regretted having asked. But then she forged ahead, hoping to repair the damage. "Pisces. I'll bet you're a Pisces."

"Oh, yeah," he said, finally getting it. "I am."

She introduced him to Premonition. It was love

at first sight. Beau began to play with the dog, running a few steps away, then waiting for the dog to catch up. She'd never seen Premonition take to someone in such a way.

"Is it always so hot here?" Cleo asked Daniel, still unable to fully grasp the smothering heat.

"No, sometimes it's even hotter." He seemed to take a sadistic pleasure in telling her that. "This yours?" Daniel asked, indicating the only bag around.

"Yes."

He picked it up, groaning in surprise at the weight. "Guess those pyramids and crystal balls weigh a lot."

"Actually, it's the portal to my time machine."

His sun-bleached eyebrows lifted and he actually smiled. "No shit."

Enough words had fallen from his tongue for her to detect a soft burr. "What kind of accent is that?" she asked, trying for small talk as they walked in the direction of the parking area. "Not Missouri." She really didn't care, she told herself. She hadn't a shred of curiosity about the man.

"LA, maybe."

"That's not LA I'm hearing."

Daniel shifted her bag to his other hand. He figured she must have been picking up on the slight accent left over from his Scotland days. He'd been so hot to see the world that he'd worked his butt off to save enough money to spend his junior year of high school in Scotland. He'd always planned to go back, but then he fell in love and his life had been a downward spiral ever since. He'd never completely lost the accent, though.

"I spent some time in Scotland. The accent's easy to pick up, hard to get rid of." He had to give her credit. Most people didn't notice it.

She took off her dark glasses, as if trying to see him more clearly. "It's a long way from Scotland to Missouri."

Her eyes were green—green and a little puffy. She was one of those people who perpetually looked as though she'd just gotten up. The sleepiness gave her face a softness he didn't trust.

"We can't always choose the roads we take," he said.

Understanding, her gaze went from him to Beau and then back.

Daniel knew what she was doing: milking him for information so that later she could amaze people by saying things like, "I see bagpipes . . . I see a kilt." And everybody would be so impressed with her extrasensory powers. Everybody but him, that is. He should just feed her back a bunch of bullshit.

Her top was white and sleeveless, with a row of tiny buttons down the front. Around her neck were three necklaces, two shorter ones of hemp and beads and a longer chain that disappeared down the front of her top. She had dangly earrings in her pierced ears, earrings that kept getting tangled in her long, curly red hair. She wore an ankle-length skirt of a million different colors. On her feet were brown sandals; on one toe was a silver ring. As they walked toward his truck he kept catching a glimpse of a tiny tattoo on her ankle. A rose?

She was by far the most exotic thing Egypt had ever seen.

Daniel had expected Beau to like Cleo, because Beau liked everybody. But the dog was a surprise. Daniel didn't know Beau liked animals so well. They'd had a dog when they were kids, but then most kids had dogs. It didn't necessarily mean they were crazy about them.

Beau lowered the tailgate of the truck, and Daniel heaved Cleo's suitcase in, sliding it across the bed. Beau scrambled in after the suitcase.

"Sure you want to ride back there?" Daniel asked. "You don't have to."

Beau plopped down with his back to the cab's sliding window, then patted one leg. The dog jumped gracefully into the truck, collapsing on Beau's lap.

Daniel slammed the tailgate shut. "Okay, but when you get tired of it, let me know."

There had been an unusual openness in her reaction to Beau, Daniel thought as he eased behind the steering wheel. People usually reacted to Beau in one of two ways. The most common was embarrassment. They would look at him, then look away, deciding to ignore Beau and talk in an intense way to Daniel, fast and desperate, with a kind of pleading in their eyes. And then there were the people who treated Beau like a baby. That irritated Daniel almost as much as the people who ignored him. Because Beau wasn't a baby. He had more on the ball than a lot of people. Hell, he had more on the ball than Daniel. Beau was happy and kind—and what people didn't get was that Beau was perceptive, a lot more perceptive than most.

Cleo had treated him as an equal. She'd taken his hand. She'd looked him in the eye, never shying away. She saw him as a person. In that moment Daniel had decided he might have to cut her a little slack. But then he had to remind himself that he hadn't picked her up to sweet-talk her.

"I know all about you," he announced.

She snapped her seat belt into place and looked up at him with those big sleepy eyes of hers.

"But then I guess you would already know that, because you can read my mind, right?"

"It doesn't take a mind reader to pick up on hostility. Why don't you just say what you've been wanting to say for the last five minutes?"

He started the truck, gave Beau and the dog a final check, then pulled away from the curb, heading in the direction of Egypt. "I know how you took credit for finding that kidnapped child in California when it was really the police who did all the work."

She gave him a strange, self-satisfied smile, as if he'd said exactly what she wanted to hear.

"Guess you pretty much have me figured out. But what you're forgetting is that people need to believe in something. They need to believe that magic stones keep them safe and that cards tell the future. That they have *control*. Because the alternative, that life is random and nobody is in control, is just not acceptable."

"So are you saying you consider yourself an opportunist rather than a con artist?"

"You could say that." She crossed her arms over her chest, scooted down in the seat, and closed her eyes.

End of conversation.

Ten minutes later she was asleep, breathing through her mouth—or maybe she was just a damn good actress.

Why the hell did she take a train and not a plane? he wondered, noticing the faint purple smudges under her eyes.

At that moment something hit the windshield, drawing his attention back to the road.

Rain.

It came on fast. By the time Daniel pulled over and stopped, rain was pouring down, creating a deafening roar inside the cab of the truck.

With the rapid cognizance of someone who'd spent a lot of time watching her back, his passenger awoke. She looked around, quickly grasping the situation.

Before Daniel could jump from the truck, she flung open her door. "Come on!" she shouted. At the same time, Beau and the dog scrambled out of the back. Cleo scooted over. They jumped in, with Beau slamming the door behind them.

Ah, nothing better than the smell of a wet dog, thought Daniel sarcastically.

The dog shook, spraying water against the inside of the windshield, then struggled for space in total disregard of people's legs and how wet he was. Cleo tried to hold him down, but he was too excited.

"No, Premonition. Sit. Sit." With both arms around him, she finally forced him into temporary submission.

Smashed against the passenger door, Beau sat there giggling.

Daniel squeezed his arm past the dog and flipped the defrost to full blast. While waiting for the fogged-up window to clear, he tried to wipe some of the water from the inside of the glass.

"Here."

Cleo fished in a leather purse that looked like a small version of a backpack, and handed him a Kleenex. He took it, swiped a little at the window, then tossed the wet, mangled tissue to the floor. He flicked on the wipers, then reached for the gearshift, finding a knee instead. Her leg was wedged against the lever.

He jerked his hand away. "You wanna shift?" he asked.

"Sure. Ready?" She put it into first gear.

He let out the clutch, checked for traffic, then pulled back onto the two-lane road.

The truck's engine hummed higher and higher; he put in the clutch. It took her a moment, but she found second gear. By that time they'd lost some momentum. The engine lugged, then gradually smoothed out as the truck gained speed.

They finally made it into third; and Daniel pressed the gas pedal until they were cruising at a good clip along the wet pavement.

It was then that Daniel noticed that her bare, wet arm was stuck to his. And her hair, her long, curly hair, was stuck to him, too. With the rain had come even more humidity, causing her hair to take on a life of its own. It had been curly when she stepped off the train, but now it was corkscrewing around her face. Tendrils of it were reaching out and grabbing him.

"What are you looking at?" she asked.

"Your hair. It's doing weird shit."

She made an attempt to pull the strands from his arm, but they kept latching back on.

"I have all the C. S. Lewis books," Beau announced out of nowhere.

"Oh? I love his books," Cleo said. "Especially *The Chronicles of Narnia.*"

"I'm waiting for a new one," Beau said. "I've been waiting for a long time. I'll bet the next one is going to be really good, too."

Daniel elbowed her, hoping she wouldn't tell Beau that Lewis wouldn't be coming up with any new masterpieces. He shot her a look of warning that said, *Beau doesn't take death well.*

"You might have a long wait," was all she said.

"I can't read very good," Beau told her. "But Daniel can. He can read like crazy. He's always reading stuff. Like the paper. And cereal boxes. Sometimes at breakfast, I'll ask him, 'Daniel, what's that word?' And he knows it. He always knows it. Even if he doesn't know it, he can say it. That's because of phonics. They tried to teach me phonics, but I just couldn't get it. That's when Daniel said that some people were made for reading and some for listening. So he's the reader and I'm the listener."

"And the talker," Daniel said. "Don't forget that."

Beau laughed, getting the joke. "And the talker."

All three laughed until Premonition decided to shake again. Then all three yelled. Or at least Daniel and Beau yelled—Cleo's shout was more of a scream.

An hour after leaving Clear Lake, they arrived at their destination. Egypt, Missouri, didn't live up to its exotic name. It looked like a million other cookie-cutter towns that stretched from sea to shining sea.

It was pure middle America, with tree-lined streets and two-story bungalows built at a time when wood was thought to be an inexhaustible resource. Driving into Egypt was a little like rolling back the clock several years. It was a place where Cleo could imagine women gave Tupperware parties and sold Avon door to door.

She'd always thought of Missouri as hilly, but Egypt was flat. The town fathers had taken advantage of the lack of contour and laid out the community in a grid, with everything of importance, such as the four-story courthouse made of stone that had darkened over the years, smack dab in the center of the grid.

Along with the old-fashioned feel, there was a strange, carnivalesque atmosphere—a consequence of the campaign signs, complete with publicity photos, that were everywhere. Clusters of them stood in yards; nearly every storefront window boasted at least one. Most of them seemed to be promoting the same handsome, smiling man.

Reelect Mayor Burton Campbell. Burton Campbell for mayor.

"Important guy," Cleo commented.

"He's running unopposed," Daniel said. "The prick just likes having his name plastered all over town. Will you?" he asked, indicating the gearshift.

It was more of a command than a request, but she obliged just to keep the peace. It didn't seem worth arguing over.

"I call him Burt the Flirt. He's also the only dentist in town, so if you have a cavity you want filled, I'm sure he'll oblige."

What an ass Daniel Sinclair was, Cleo thought. "If I need a cavity filled, I'll wait till I get out of here."

"Good idea."

She peered through the streaked windshield down the empty, glistening street. "Doesn't look like there's a lot for a policeman to do in this town."

"I keep busy."

"Yeah?" she asked, not believing him.

"Getting cats out of trees. Parking meter violations. Breaking up the occasional keg party. Stuff like that."

"Sounds exciting."

Beside her, Beau coincidentally let out a huge yawn.

"Better than zipping up body bags," Daniel said.

She'd have to agree.

The place where she was staying turned out to be a motel on the edge of town. From the outside, it looked like everything a traveler would dread. She'd stayed in some dives in her life, but even before seeing the room, she guessed that this place would have to rank near the bottom. It was called The Palms, but it might as well have been named the Hyatt Regency, for all the reflection the name bore to the actual place. The Palms was just past the outskirts of Egypt, the owners apparently expecting the town to expand and eventually catch up with the twelve-room eyesore. It had been new once, Cleo had to remind herself. And probably nice once, something that was even harder to believe.

By the time Sinclair pulled up in front of the lobby, the rain had slowed to a drizzle. Beau and Premonition bailed out, and Cleo went inside to register. The guy behind the counter had slicked-back black hair, a goatee, a lot of turquoise-and-silver jewelry, and an attitude.

She signed the guest book, got the key, and

stepped outside to find that Daniel had already unloaded her suitcase and was waiting on the cracked, weed-infested sidewalk.

Cleo dangled the key with the plastic number that was almost worn off. "Six."

Daniel Sinclair carried the suitcase to the door and put it down. "Beau and I were just talking," he said in an unenthusiastic voice. "How would you like to eat supper with us? We could pick you up later."

Why was he asking when it was so obvious he didn't want her to come? Then she looked at Beau, who stood smiling and nodding, Premonition leaning heavily against his leg. There was the answer to her question.

"I don't know." Cleo unlocked the door and swung it open. Her nose was assaulted with the scent of ancient body odor. She swallowed and stared into the darkness, then turned back to the two men.

Daniel was silently begging her to say no. Beau was silently begging her to say yes. Once again, she was struck by how perfect Beau and Premonition seemed together.

She smiled. "I'd love to. Oh, and Beau, would you mind taking Premonition with you for a few hours? He could use a little exercise."

"All right!" Beau shouted. He dropped to his knees and put his hand up so Premonition could give him a high five. Premonition, who had already known how to shake when Cleo got him from the pound, lifted one paw. Beau laughed in delight.

"Yeah. We're a team. We're a team." Beau jumped to his feet and ran for the truck, the dog close behind.

Cleo looked up to see Daniel glaring at her. "You can't mind-read worth shit," he said.

"Oh," she said, smiling, "but I can."

3

The motel room was like something from a Quentin Tarantino movie. Twenty dollars a night, it was the kind of place where prostitutes rendezvoused and alcoholics slept off their latest indulgence.

Worse than that, everything was orange—the curtains that sagged from ceiling to floor, the threadbare chenille bedspread, the shag carpet with a trail worn from the door to the bed and from the bed to the bathroom.

Cleo hated orange.

Why not a nice avocado green? she wondered ruefully. *Anything but orange.*

She crossed the room and jerked open the curtains to reveal a breathtaking view of a solid brick wall. She tugged the curtains shut again. Several hooks were missing, making the curtains droop in an out of synch way.

Things weren't any better in the bathroom. The

floor was made of tiny, one-inch tiles with grout that had accumulated years of scum. The shower seemed to have been an afterthought—one of those square fiberglass jobs with a trampoline floor and metal trim that could give you a good case of tetanus if you weren't careful.

She discovered that the toilet flushed only if you held down the lever. Actually, she was surprised and quite pleased that it flushed at all. There was a hole in the wall where the toilet paper holder used to be. Now the half-used roll was perched precariously on the back of the tank. Beside the toilet was a plunger. An omen, a sign of things to come?

On the rust-stained sink was a drinking glass. It had the same opaque, water-stained quality as the shower curtain. She made a mental note to pick up some disposable cups.

She regarded her reflection in the mirror above the sink. Under the weird glow of the flickering fluorescent light, she looked like a corpse. Her face was pasty and mottled. There were deep lavender circles under her eyes. Her lips looked grayish, almost blue.

This sucked.

Cleo pulled at the tiny chain, turning off the light, then left the bathroom to lie fully clothed on top of the bedspread. She wasn't yet brave enough to pull down the covers. Exhausted, she soon fell asleep and dreamed a dream she hadn't had in years. . . .

She was back in college, dressed up for Halloween, wearing a bright orange pumpkin outfit that was made of some cheap polyester fabric she'd picked up at Kmart. It was stuffed with newspaper that crinkled when she walked. She would have preferred to use batting for filler, but she was a college student and didn't have that kind of money to spare. The fabric for the pumpkin had been enough of an expense.

Jordan was there.

In the dream he was still alive, even though she knew he was dead. He kissed her, saying he'd always wanted to make out with a pumpkin. She hadn't told him yet, but she was pregnant.

Jordan was a pumpkin, too, although he was so tall that his pumpkin wasn't round, but long and narrow. He laughed his bright laugh and said he was more like a squash.

And then the scene changed, the way things did in dreams. Suddenly they were at the theater, watching *The Rocky Horror Picture Show*, tossing dried toast, laughing, having a blast.

Then came the bad part of the dream, when they were crammed into Jordan's little car, rain pouring down, Halloween lights from a lone house casting strobelike patterns on their faces.

Suddenly the car was skidding, then, just as quickly, it hit something and came to a bone-shattering halt. After the crash, Cleo was instantaneously outside the car; the rain was beating down on her, but she couldn't feel it. There was something she must see, something she had to look at, but she was afraid. So afraid . . . .

Don't look, don't look.

But she had to look. She couldn't keep herself from looking. That was what the dream was all about. Looking. Seeing something she didn't want to see.

She looked.

Why, it's okay.

She let out her breath. She relaxed. What had she been so afraid of? It was only a pumpkin. Only a smashed pumpkin.

She stepped closer in order to get a better look at the pumpkin lying in the middle of the black, rain-wet road. And suddenly she saw that it wasn't a pumpkin at all, but Jordan. Broken. Smashed.

She stared and stared.

Close your eyes, she told herself. *Don't look.*

She closed her eyes, but she could see right through her eyelids.

Turn away. All you have to do is turn away.

But she couldn't move. Couldn't make the dream stop. She opened her mouth to scream, but no sound came out.

Jordan! Jordan!

Cleo came awake with a feeling of joint anxiety and relief: relief that the dream was over, anxiety because the dark mood of it lingered in her mind like an insidious poison.

She hadn't had the dream in almost two years. She'd thought all that was behind her. She lay there staring at the ceiling for a few minutes, and then her gaze tracked around the room, finally falling on the offensive curtains.

She jumped from the bed and pulled down the orange monstrosities. She wadded them into a ball, looked around, then finally stuffed them under the bed. Next she pulled the bedspread free, wadded it up, and put it under the bed along with the curtains.

There.

Better.

What time was it?

The room actually had a bedside digital clock.

Damn. Daniel Sinclair would be picking her up in twenty minutes. That wasn't enough time. Not nearly enough time. She couldn't pull herself together by then. She held out her hands. They were shaking. Her hair and her clothes were soaked with sweat.

Oh, God. She'd thought all of this was behind her. She'd been well for two years. Four, if she counted the years she was in therapy. So why now?

She shoved herself from the bed. On wobbly legs, she went to the air conditioner, which was clanking like a dishwasher, and turned it to high. Then she dropped to her knees in front of her suitcase.

She unzipped it, flipped back the top, and began digging, finally retrieving a plastic zip-seal bag. She opened it and pulled out a brown prescription bottle, quickly unscrewing the cap and dumping the contents into her palm. Vitamin C tablets. A couple of aspirin. That was all.

She'd known she wouldn't find anything else. It was like wishing for that birthday pony when you were little. You knew it wasn't coming, but you still had to look for it the next morning—just in case.

She checked the refill date on the brown bottle. The prescription had expired two years ago.

She plopped down on the bed, grabbed the phone, and put in a call to her shrink's office.

"I'm sorry," the receptionist said in a soothing voice. "Dr. Porter is practicing in Texas now. Would you like to make an appointment with one of the other doctors?"

"I have a prescription I need to get refilled."

"One of the other doctors would be glad to see you."

"No, you don't understand." Panic was rising, rising. "I can't come in to see anybody. I'm in Missouri."

"Then you'll have to see somebody there. I'm sorry."

Cleo hung up, wondering what she was going to do. Then she grabbed the skinny, tattered phone book, found Daniel Sinclair's number, and dialed. She would tell him she couldn't come. Tell him she had a headache.

Beau answered. And said Daniel was on the way to pick her up.

4

Daniel pulled up in front of room six and cut the truck engine.

Too bad she had to stay in such a dive, he thought, allowing himself to feel a little sorry for her. Not her in particular, he told himself. He'd feel sorry for anybody who had to stay at The Palms. But she had no choice, since it was the only place in town.

At one time it had been a nice mom-and-pop establishment, and while the rooms had never been luxurious, they'd been clean and safe. Daniel knew for a fact they weren't either one anymore. There wasn't a lot of crime in Egypt, but when there was, The Palms was usually involved. There had even been a homicide there once, before Daniel had moved back, an ugly deal where a prostitute from St. Louis had been murdered. The case went unsolved, the few clues they'd had leading the police to believe that both the prostitute and perpetrator had been passing through and by chance had stayed at The Palms. It was something Jo liked to pretend had never happened. According to her way of thinking, the murder didn't really count because the people involved hadn't been from the circle that constituted Egypt, Missouri.

Daniel had hung out at The Palms when he was little. He didn't remember how he and the original owners, Millie and Babe Johnson, had become acquainted, but on hot summer nights he'd sometimes ride his bicycle past the edge of town to where The Palms sat by itself. It had been new then, and to a child it had held the hint of the exotic, the promise of far-off places. Daniel had never seen an actual palm tree, but he'd often imagined climbing one, planting the soles of his bare feet against its curved bark.

Millie and Babe had always talked about retiring in Florida. So when they'd opened the twelve-room motel, they'd named it The Palms. Even when he was little, Daniel used to think, *Why do you keep talking about it? You're getting old. You're running out of time. Why don't you just go?*

He didn't want them to leave. He knew he'd miss them. But still, it kind of irritated him, because even as a kid, he knew they were wasting precious energy *talking* instead of *doing*. Old people only had so much gas. It wasn't until he himself got older that he realized people had to have dreams, even if they never had any intention of fulfilling them.

Out there at The Palms, he and the Johnsons would shoot the breeze. They'd sit in brand-new white metal lawn chairs under a brand-new neon sign that glowed like the future. But then Millie died, and Babe had a stroke and was moved to a nursing home. Daniel had been to see Babe a few times, but Babe hadn't recognized him, having already moved to a place where nobody could follow. The Palms was sold and it had been nothing but downhill ever since.

Danny got out of the truck and stepped up to the door, weeds brushing the legs of his pants. It had quit raining. The sun had even come out a little, creating what Daniel referred to as "the fucking steam-bath effect."

He knocked. Nobody answered, so he knocked again.

He finally heard the sliding of the safety chain. Then the door opened.

Her eyes were kind of puffy. Had he gotten her up? But then he reminded himself that her eyes had been puffy before. Instead of stepping outside, she kept the door partially closed, so all he could see was her face and her hand against the door.

"I'm not going to be able to make it," she said.

She's backing out, he realized, astounded, anger beginning as a tiny spark in his brain. *So Miss Clara Voiyant isn't coming.* It didn't surprise him. Not one bit.

Daniel thought about how excited Beau was, how he'd been working on some special secret dessert all afternoon, something made with Cool Whip and ice cream from a recipe their neighbor, Mrs. Abernathy, had cut from a women's magazine. Everything was a big deal to Beau, but for some reason Cleo Tyler's visit was an especially big deal, sort of like a visit from the president. Or Captain Kirk—Beau was a real *Star Trek* nut.

The spark of anger flared, ignited.

Daniel shoved open the door. She took a few steps back, a hand to her chest, her eyes wide, her mouth open in surprise and indignation. He followed her in, slamming the door behind him. The room was dark. Worse than that, it smelled of mildew and an ancient stench he associated with locker rooms.

"Listen here," he said, pointing at her. "I would be thrilled to find out that I don't have to put up with your presence. Unfortunately, Beau didn't come equipped with a bullshit indicator that detects people like you, people who might not be good for him to hang out with. Beau likes everybody. He likes you. He's been working his ass off for the past two hours, so you're not going to disappoint him. You're going to go, and you're going to act like you're having a good time and like you're enjoying the food, no matter what kind of strange concoction he's put together."

He stopped to catch his breath. Man, where had that come from? What was the matter with him? It didn't take him long to come up with why: The responsibility of taking care of Beau was getting to him. He felt trapped. Claustrophobic. And thinking about the Johnsons, about people getting old and dying without fulfilling their dreams, had bummed him out.

Even so, he couldn't believe he'd just lost it like that.

Now he turned his back to her so that he was facing the door. Hands at his waist, head bent, he took a deep breath and said, "I'm sorry. Forget about it." He waved one hand to demonstrate the insignificance of her joining them, or to try to erase the tantrum he'd just had. "Just forget about the whole thing." He had his hand on the doorknob, ready to step out into the Missouri heat, when her voice stopped him.

"Wait. Give me a minute."

He turned in surprise to see her rummaging through her suitcase. She dug out a brush and began tugging it through her hair. She should have left it alone; brushing it only made it wilder, puffier. She had a lot of hair. Then she found a black stretchy thing and pulled her hair back into a ponytail. She grabbed something else out of the suitcase, a small cloth bag and what looked like a shirt. Then she hurried to the bathroom, shutting the door. Two minutes later she was back out, wearing a black T-shirt and bright red lipstick that stood out starkly against the paleness of her skin. It made her look even more foreign, even more exotic—like a whisper of the life he might be missing. Still wearing the crinkled skirt she'd had on when she got off the train, she slipped her feet into her sandals, then followed him from the room. And he kept thinking that her toenails were the exact same color as her lips.

●　●　●

Cleo felt much better after getting out of the dismal motel room. How was she going to stand that place for the rest of her stay?

They cruised through town, moving down tree-lined streets where a little blond kid fresh from his bath, wearing print pajamas, pedaled furiously down the sidewalk on his Big Wheel, looking as cool as a five-year-old in pajamas could look.

An old woman sat out on her porch swing, all bundled up in a sweater even though the temperature was still above eighty. It was a pleasant town, a sweet town, Cleo decided.

Daniel and Beau's house wasn't anything like what Cleo had expected. It wasn't the kind of place where two guys lived. In fact, it was something a person might term a "widow house," one of those cute little houses where things had just gotten out of control—where vines grew wildly, and flowers grew wildly, and before you knew it, the yard and house kind of became one.

The first thing she noticed when Daniel pulled the truck to a stop in the dirt driveway were the red roses cascading around the porch, some of the blooms hanging so low that they had to duck their heads to get in the door.

Inside, the living room had shiny wood floors covered with throw rugs. The overstuffed chairs and couch were decorated with doilies. There were blooming African violets in front of windows with lace curtains. A faint scent of lavender hung in the air. On the wall near the door, a cuckoo clock ticked softly.

It was a wonderful house. A comfortable house. Not a man's house. Cleo looked around, expecting to see an older woman appear at any moment. Instead Beau showed up, his face shiny and smiling, Premonition at his heels.

"The charcoal's ready." He seemed proud of that announcement.

"I told you to wait until I got back," Daniel said.

"I can do it. I did it. You worry too much."

Daniel apparently had no answer to that. "Wanna beer?" he asked Cleo.

"No, thanks." It probably wouldn't be a good time to mention that she was a vegetarian, she decided.

Daniel grunted and moved toward the refrigerator. She heard the hiss of a bottle cap.

"Come on," Beau said, taking her arm and pulling her toward the patio doors, leading her outside.

Beau had done the decorating—she could tell. He'd strung up plastic lights in the shape of cowboy boots and red chili peppers. In the center of the wooden picnic table, four candles waited to be lit.

Over the solid wood fence, dark clouds skittered. The sky had turned a brilliant pink, casting a warm glow over everything. Out past the covered patio, a brick path wound through a perennial garden to end at a small shed that might have been a hothouse. Near the shed, not far off the path, was a blue ball—one of those shiny glass orbs found in country gardens.

"Who takes care of all of this?" Cleo asked, trying to picture Daniel Sinclair knee deep in lavender, but failing.

"I do mostly. Danny helps me sometimes. But he's not very good at it. When my mom gets home, she can take care of it again."

"Where is she?"

"Park Manor."

"Oh." A nursing home, she assumed.

"Before Danny came back, I took good care of her."

"I'm sure you did."

"Come on. I'll show you the gazing ball."

The brick path was only wide enough for one person. Beau insisted she go first, not with a motion of his hand, but with an easy shove, until they both stood admiring the blue globe, as shiny and out of place as a cheap Christmas ornament.

"I spray it with window cleaner and shine it."

She'd seen a lot of them in her life but had never been able to figure out what purpose they served—unless being an eyesore was a purpose. Kind of like a plastic pink flamingo, she supposed.

"At night you can see all the stars," Beau stated, still staring reverently at the globe.

Cleo looked up from the globe. "Stars?"

"Yeah. You look in the ball and see the stars."

"Oh."

What a beautiful, simple concept. She was stunned by her own ignorance. All along she'd thought the globes were worthless, only to discover they were something remarkable. How could she not have known? How could she not have noticed something so remarkable? Were there other things she was missing? Other things that, on the surface, looked ordinary but upon closer inspection were a wonder?

People always complained that there was nothing new under the sun, but they never stopped to appreciate what *was* there, Cleo being just as guilty of that as the next person. And then there was someone like Beau, who saw the beauty of the everyday, not only saw it, but recognized it.

Cleo smiled at him. "I'd like to see those stars sometime."

"You can see them tonight."

She looked up at the watercolor sky. "I'm afraid it might be too cloudy."

Behind them the patio door opened and closed.

She turned to see Daniel heading toward the grill with a plate of raw meat. She heard a sizzle. Smoke and flames flared, then died back down. A feeling of nostalgia washed over her, the smell of the charcoal and seared meat reminding her of childhood cookouts on the Fourth of July.

"Sometimes my mom would go for a walk and she wouldn't come back," Beau said. "She would forget how to get home. Isn't that weird? I never get lost. I know every street in this town, and every store. And not just in town. I know all the country roads, too. When the mailman takes a vacation, me and another guy deliver mail, because I know the roads and I know where to go."

"That would be wonderful, to have such an amazing memory."

"They said I couldn't take care of her anymore, but I could. I really could."

"I'm sure you did a great job. Is that why Danny came back? Because your mother was forgetting things?"

"No . . . he just wanted to come back. He likes it here. He'd rather be here than anywhere."

It seemed as if Beau was trying to convince himself of Daniel's contentment as much as he was trying to convince Cleo.

They began walking back in the direction of the patio. "I heard Danny talking about you bein' here to help find a key. I lost a dog once. His name was Fido. Do you know where he is?"

Oh, boy. The direct question. How could she sidestep this one? "How long ago did you lose him?" she asked, stalling.

He squinted and looked brainward. His expression cleared when he found what he was looking for. "I was eight."

Cleo relaxed. *Years* ago. Nobody would expect her to find a dog that couldn't even exist anymore. "How old are you?"

"Thirty-six. I'm always kidding around, calling Danny my little brother, even though he's bigger than me." Beau laughed, and the sound was so infectious that Cleo joined him.

"What's so funny?" Daniel asked.

Beau hadn't allowed himself to be detoured from his original question. "I asked Cleo to help me find something."

Intent on his cooking, Daniel said, "I'm sure Cleo can help you find anything you lost. Isn't that right, Cleo?"

"Not a dog that vanished over twenty-five years ago."

"Oh, Fido. No, I don't think Fido's coming back."

"He might," Beau said, for the first time giving Cleo a glimpse of stubbornness.

"Do you have a Frisbee?" she asked, trying to distract Beau from the Fido problem. "Premonition can catch Frisbees."

"Yeah. Wow. I'll go get it." Beau loped into the house, with Premonition following.

"Nice manipulation."

"Apparently drinking makes you even more sociable." She indicated the new beer in his hand. "What happens after a couple of six-packs? Do you get all giddy and giggly, or do you just pass out?"

"You should know the answer to that. In fact, I can't see a need for you to ever ask any questions."

"You're overreacting. I never claimed to be omniscient." And then she got to the real issue. "Why do you hate me?"

Her direct question caught him off guard. He searched for an answer. Perhaps it was too much for him, because he didn't answer her.

"People like me are marketing hope," she informed him, poking a finger in his direction for emphasis. "And hope is something everybody needs."

He finally found the words he was searching so hard for. "That's a bunch of shit."

"Are you an ass with everybody, or is it just me?"

She could tell by the you-got-me twist of his mouth that he knew there was no way he could win this argument.

And then she found herself staring at the dark roots of his sun-bleached hair, the dark roots of his sun-bleached eyebrows. It was that same striking combination that had made Peter O'Toole so mesmerizing in *Lawrence of Arabia*.

He took a long swallow from the brown bottle in his hand. "What are you doing? Reading my aura?"

"Maybe."

"Is it black?" he asked blandly.

That was funny, but there was no way she would reward him with a smile. Instead she looked up at him and said, "I see a man who feels trapped by circumstances he believes to be beyond his control."

"You've been talking to Beau."

"I've been keeping my eyes open." She'd had enough arguing. She looked around, searching for a new subject. "The garden—it's beautiful. It's nice of you and Beau to take care of it until your mother comes back."

Behind her hung a heavy silence. She turned. For the first time that evening, Daniel looked uncomfortable. "She's not coming back."

"Oh?" She didn't understand. Did they feel they couldn't take care of her?

Daniel cleared his throat. "She died two years ago."

"But Beau told me—"

"I know what Beau told you. The same thing he tells everybody. For some reason he won't face the fact that she's gone. He refused to go to her funeral. He said he was going to stay home and keep her company instead. Sometimes I hear him whispering to somebody, and when I ask him who he's talking to, he says it's Mom."

"Wow."

"Yeah. Wow."

She stared at him, wondering what to say. It was on the tip of her tongue to say she was sorry when Beau and Premonition returned with the Frisbee. "I had trouble finding it," Beau said, out of breath. He handed her the Frisbee, then stood there, expectant.

"Premonition. Here, boy. Go get it." She tossed the Frisbee at an angle, so that it would get enough height for Premonition to track it with his eyes while at the same time gauging where it would descend. When it seemed he'd outrun it, he jumped, his body twisting. He caught the plastic Frisbee in his mouth, his teeth clamping down hard. Beau laughed and clapped, and even Daniel stopped messing around at the grill to look impressed.

Premonition came running with the Frisbee in his

mouth. He dropped it at Cleo's feet, wanting her to give it another toss.

"Let me try!" Beau shouted.

Cleo handed the Frisbee to Beau. "You have to toss it high enough so he can have time to figure out where it's going."

Beau tossed it straight up. It came down like a rocket, almost hitting Cleo in the head. Premonition danced at their feet as if to say, *Hurry, hurry.*

This time Cleo stood behind Beau, her hand on his wrist, showing him how to toss it.

It was a perfect throw.

And a perfect catch.

Cleo, Beau, and Premonition played and ran and laughed for ten full minutes before Daniel interrupted them. "Come on, kids. Time to eat."

The meal was baked potatoes, steak, and iced tea. Cleo managed to secretly feed her meat to Premonition, who sat patiently waiting at her feet under the table.

Then came dessert. Pumpkin pie.

"It's cold pumpkin pie," Beau said. "Made with ice cream."

Cleo stared at the neatly cut piece of pie in front of her, topped with a baseball-sized glob of whipped topping. That was good, because underneath, the pie was the color of the motel rug and the color of the curtains.

The color of a broken, smashed pumpkin.

She spread the whipped cream all over the pie,

trying to cover every bit of orange. Then, with the edge of her fork, she sliced a bite-size piece and lifted it to her face. The orange of the pumpkin peeked out from under the white of the whipped topping. She closed her eyes and shoved the forkful in her mouth. She quickly found she couldn't swallow it. She chewed and chewed, but the pie had taken on the consistency of stained orange shag carpeting. She gagged a little, hoping nobody noticed. There was no way the piece of dirty carpet was going down. Then she jumped to her feet, her fork clattering to the patio. She had a brief glimpse of two surprised faces before she turned and ran for the garden, throwing up next to an azalea bush.

As she stood there hunched over, waiting to make sure she was finished, she became aware of someone she assumed was Beau standing not far behind her. "It's not your cooking," she said, straightening, her stomach seeming to have settled. "My stomach's been upset for a couple of days."

"I guess you weren't just trying to get out of a visit to our house."

It wasn't Beau behind her but Daniel. He handed her a glass of water. She took a few cautious sips. When her stomach didn't protest, she drank half the glass.

"I'll take you back to the motel."

Thinking about the motel brought back the feeling of queasiness. Sweat broke out on her forehead. She wiped at it with a trembling hand. "Yeah, I should probably rest up for tomorrow." She looked across the yard to see Beau and Premonition playing together, and again she was struck by how well they got along. Premonition had been full-grown when Cleo got him from the animal shelter. He'd been long past the puppy stage and the all-important time when those strong loyalties were formed, so she'd always assumed he would never be able to really bond with anyone.

Beau and Premonition came running up.

"Would you like Premonition to stay the night?" Cleo asked, immediately wishing she hadn't offered. It would have been nice to have Premonition's presence at the motel.

"Oh, yeah. Like a sleep-over!" Beau laughed at his own silliness, then took off, dropping to his knees several yards away and rolling onto his back, with Premonition pouncing on top of him, tail wagging furiously.

"What'd you do that for?" Daniel asked angrily.

"What do you mean? I just thought—"

"I know you're trying to suck up to us, but don't use Beau to do it. He gets attached easily. I don't want him getting hurt."

She stared at him a long moment, then quickly said, "I'm ready to go."

"I'm taking Cleo back to the motel," Daniel shouted to Beau while still glaring at her.

"Get some dog food on your way home," Beau said, not looking in their direction.

A fresh flicker of irritation crossed Daniel's features.

Cleo smiled blatantly into that irritation. "He likes the soft kind, preferably beef flavored."

As they were leaving, Cleo spotted a stack of magazines on an end table. "Can I take one of these?" she asked, picking up the top one, not bothering to look through the stack. It didn't matter what they were about.

"Suit yourself."

"And a pair of scissors. Do you have a pair of scissors I can borrow?"

Back at the motel room, Cleo began cutting out pictures, then remembered she didn't have any glue. Damn. She ended up going to the sleaze at the front desk and asking to borrow some glue. He finally came up with a gross bottle of clear stuff, the kind with the rubber cap that you had to press down on, forcing the glue out the slit.

The man smiled at her in a knowing way, as if she now owed him sex for the glue, or at least a performance in his next porno flick.

Back in the motel room, she took a shower, all the while trying not to touch anything, making a mental note to pick up some flip-flops. Afterward she sat cross-legged on the bed, cutting out pictures and gluing them on the yellowed motel stationery she'd found under the Bible in the drawer beside the bed. It was something her shrink had taught her to do whenever she couldn't relax, when she couldn't shut off her mind. For some inexplicable reason, she was drawn to pictures of barns. Nothing but barns . . .

5

Cleo didn't fall asleep until dawn, not until reassuring sunlight began to filter its way in around the outer door. When the alarm sounded at eight o'clock, she'd barely managed two fitful hours of sleep. Unfortunately, her inability to sleep was part of an old, familiar pattern, one she'd almost forgotten until the events of the previous day. First there had been the nightmare, then the little problem with Beau's pumpkin pie, then being unable to sleep when she was exhausted.

It's this room, she tried to convince herself. *It's not me. It's this creepy room.*

She got out of bed, found her sandals, and slipped then on. Without bothering to brush her hair or teeth, and still wearing the knee-length gray tank top she slept in, she left the room and marched to the lobby, where she rang the bell over and over until her buddy from the day before showed up, a jelly doughnut in his hand and in his teeth.

"I want another room," she demanded. He wasn't the only one with an attitude.

His eyebrows lifted in surprise. "You got the best room in the place."

"I want a different room. There's something wrong with the one I'm in."

· "What? What's wrong with it?"

"It's too orange."

"They're *all* orange." Nevertheless, he checked the keys that hung on the pegboard behind the counter. "Lemme see . . . that's storage. That's storage. Ceiling fell in on that one. That room's got a standing reservation. That leaves us with number three. It's got a broken air conditioner. Number eight's got a broken toilet."

"What about nine or ten?"

"Remodeling them. Tearing out the wall in between the two rooms to make one deluxe suite with a Jacuzzi. How's that sound?"

"Like I'll be staying in number six." She didn't even want to know about the room with the standing reservation. The rendezvous point for some seedy affair, no doubt. "Is there anyplace to get something to eat around here?" she asked, resigned to the fact that she wouldn't be moving anytime soon.

"Gas station two blocks down the street. Got pop and juice. Here." He shoved a box of doughnuts at her. "Knock yourself out."

Amidst the jelly and powdered sugar, she found a plain doughnut. She took it. "Thanks." And went back to room six.

She couldn't remain there another night. She had to leave. She would tell the chief of police that she couldn't stay.

But then reality hit her. What excuse could she give? That the motel gave her the creeps? What a baby. And *how* could she leave? She'd spent her last dime getting to Egypt, Missouri. Oh, God. Adrian had been right. She shouldn't have come. What had she been thinking? She'd thought she was well, thought she'd put her past behind her, but it was still there. It had been there all along, waiting.

She found herself staring at the barn pictures she'd cut out the previous night. Perhaps it was slightly obsessive-compulsive, but she wanted the pictures out of her sight. And not only out of her sight, but hidden away somehow. She finally shoved them between the mattresses and immediately felt better. Not great, but better.

At 9:00 A.M. sharp a knock sounded on the motel room door, bringing Cleo back to her immediate problem—Police Chief Josephine Bennett and Cleo's psychic commitment.

Chief Bennett pretty much fit the mental image Cleo had gotten while speaking to her over the phone. Her hair was short, gray, and tightly permed. She was large around the middle—not fat, but the shape that unfortunately sometimes went with postmenopause. Unlike Daniel Sinclair, who chose to go completely in civilian clothes, with no hint of a uniform, Josephine appeared to be regulation from her tie to her holstered gun and her shiny black oxford shoes. On the pocket of her crisply pressed shirt was a silver badge that read Chief of Police.

For a moment Cleo recalled when she and her brother, Adrian, had gotten badges like that out of a cereal box. They were shaped just like the one in front of her, and if you didn't look too closely, they could have been real.

Josephine stuck out her hand and introduced herself, insisting that Cleo call her Jo. "Everybody calls me Jo."

She had one of those voices that fell somewhere between male and female. She sounded either like a slightly effeminate man or like a masculine woman. The masculine woman extended her hand. Not surprisingly, her grasp was warm and strong.

"Have you eaten breakfast?" Jo asked.

Cleo nodded. She had been able to get half the doughnut down before it began to taste like moldy grout. The last thing she wanted was for Jo to swing by some greasy spoon where they could both load up on bacon and undercooked eggs. "Stuffed," she said, grabbing her purse and closing the door, the smell of the room following her.

"Ignore the mess," Jo said as they got into the squad car.

It was a little hard when the floor under Cleo's

feet was littered with paper and what looked like opened and unopened mail.

"Coke?" Jo asked, flipping the lid on a small cooler that sat on the seat between them.

"No, thanks." What was she doing here? *Tell her you have to leave. Tell her you got an emergency call and you have to leave,* urged part of her mind. But another part of her countered, *Don't be a baby.*

Cleo rolled down the window and took a deep breath. It seemed as if she couldn't get away from the smell of the motel room. She sniffed her hair. It was in her hair. And on her hands. Even her hands smelled like some stranger's body odor.

"So, what do you think of our little town?" Jo popped the top of the Coke , took a long swallow, then settled the container in the weighted cup holder on the dash. "I run on these things. If I don't have my third Coke by nine-thirty, I get a killer headache."

"It's nice," Cleo said, answering Jo's question. *Leave.*

"It was ranked one of the best places of its size to live and raise kids. Safest town in the country. Bad things don't happen here."

Cleo wanted to believe that. But she didn't. Small towns were never as innocuous as they appeared.

"Do you like calliope music?" Jo picked up a cassette tape. "Come on. Be honest."

Cleo felt too many things were being thrown at her at once. "I always thought there was something a little sinister about music that is so perky."

Jo let out a laugh and refrained from pushing the tape in the player.

On the way to the police station, she filled Cleo in on what she knew about the loss of the key, going into a little more depth than she had over the phone. "There's only one master key, of course. It unlocks every public building in town: the schools, the courthouse, the police station, the fire station. For a long time the fire chief's been after me to let him have the key. Says it's more important for him to have the key than me. And he has a point. But what if there's a break-in in progress? The police department needs that master. So after two years of debating the issue, I decided to let Harvey have his way, but when I went to get the key, it wasn't there."

"Do you have any idea how long it's been gone?" Cleo asked, forcing herself to focus on the problem.

"Could have been weeks. Could have been months." Jo smoothly executed a turn. "That's the thing about a master key. It's not something you use every day. We've never had a situation come up where we needed the master. But you never know. A town's gotta have a master key."

"Have you got any clue as to what could have happened to it?" It had all seemed so easy in Portland. A missing key. What could be less threatening?

"I think that sneak fire chief took it and won't admit it. He acted funny when I told him he could have it. Looked like a little kid with his hand caught in the cookie jar. 'Don't trouble yourself to get it now,' he told me. And I said, 'Better get it before I change my mind.' And then, of course, it wasn't even there."

"Why wouldn't he come forward if he had the key?" The whole thing was so ridiculous. Cleo had gotten herself in the middle of some petty little squabble. They needed a negotiator, not a psychic.

"Because Harvey Jamison is spineless and doesn't want anybody to know he took it, that's why. He'd rather the city pay a hundred thousand bucks to have all new locks put in than admit he took it in the first place. That's the kind of person he is."

"So you basically want me to prove that Harvey Jamison took the key?"

"That's right. I tried myself. You know, clairvoyant stuff." She waved her hand at the unseen. "But I couldn't come up with anything. Guess I just don't have it. I've been taking correspondence courses on reading runes and on telepathy. I know I can learn everything there is to learn, but if a person doesn't have a sixth sense the way you do, it doesn't mean anything."

"Sometimes even with it, you can't find an answer." Cleo needed to clarify that right away. "I'm not promising you anything."

"Oh, I know. I may not have what it takes, but all the same, I just had a feeling about you after I read what you did in California." She took a long sip of Coke, then settled the can back in the holder. "When did you first realize you were able to do things most people couldn't do?"

A simple question. A straightforward question. One Cleo should have been able to answer. Should she tell her that she'd first studied psychic phenomena because she wanted to prove to herself that she had *no* ability? Because if she had that kind of power, then she should have been able to save Jordan.

For a while she'd been able to convince herself that she was nothing special. During her brief stint on a psychic hotline, she'd been wrong more often than right, garnering some unsatisfied customers. *I'm a fraud,* she'd thought gleefully. *I don't have a shred of power.* But then there had been the child in California.

A dream. A horrible dream. A vision. Of a little girl bound to an iron bed in a dark, damp basement. There had been more. A house with plywood over the windows. A huge, misshapen tree. A street.

She'd told the police about her dream. Using her descriptions, they were able to find the house, find the child.

Cleo had begged them not to mention her involvement to anyone, but when the little girl was found in the spot Cleo had described, somehow her name was leaked to the press. The police department scrambled, trying to honor Cleo's request for anonymity, but somehow everything got turned around and soon her integrity was being questioned—which was better than being hailed as the next Jeane Dixon.

She thought of a line from a Victoria Williams

song: "What you fear the most will meet you halfway." It was true. It met her and kept meeting her. And Cleo so wanted to be the fraud Daniel Sinclair accused her of being.

Chief Bennett repeated her earlier question. Cleo sidestepped it the way she always sidestepped it. "I think everybody has psychic ability. They just haven't learned how to tap into it."

That seemed to be the answer Jo was looking for, because she immediately switched subjects—from psychics to Daniel Sinclair.

"He was the head of a hostage negotiation unit in California," Jo explained, as if Cleo had asked about him. For some reason—maybe it was the small-town way—Jo seemed bent on filling Cleo in on things that had nothing to do with the missing key and were really none of Cleo's business.

"He was good at what he did. One of the best, and I'm not just saying that because his mother was my friend. Not every hostage situation can go the way we want it to." Jo slowed for a turn, waving to a group of kids waiting to cross the street. "Danny had a high success-to-failure ratio. One of the highest in the country, I believe. But then one time—I don't know the details—two kids and their mother got killed."

Jo turned down Main Street. They moved past barrels of red geraniums and park benches painted dark green to match the canvas awnings lining both sides of the street. Two young mothers stood talking in front of the post office, one with a baby on her hip, the other pushing a stroller.

It's so insulated here, Cleo thought. And it came to her that this was the kind of life people like herself and Daniel Sinclair would never have, because their lives had already been deeply imprinted by the outside world, by harsh reality.

"But being Danny, he blamed himself," Jo continued.

Cleo didn't want to hear any more about Daniel Sinclair. She didn't want to know any more about him. Not because it was too horrible to bear; she'd seen horrible things, had lived through horrible things. No, it was because she didn't want to know about him, about his personal life, his triumphs, his pain. She didn't want to know *him*.

"Just shortly after that, Lucille died. Lucille once told me she wasn't afraid of death, but she was afraid of what would happen to Beau if she died. So Danny moved back home to take care of Beau. But if you ask me, it was the other way around half the time. Danny was drinking. A lot. He'd stay drunk for days, and Beau would take care of him. So I offered Danny a job. It keeps him out of trouble most of the time, but he still goes on the occasional bender. Beau keeps me informed."

Cleo hadn't asked for the intimate details of Daniel Sinclair's life. She didn't even want to know the basic stuff, like where he'd gone to school, his favorite color, his favorite sport. She certainly didn't want to know what was under his skin.

To Cleo's relief, they finally arrived at the police station, a one-story white building that was located next to the courthouse and across the street from the fire station. Jo swung the squad car into a parking place reserved for the chief of police. Then they made their way along a wide sidewalk, up a few steps, and through heavy double doors.

Inside, Cleo was introduced to Parker Reed, the secretary. "He keeps this place running," Jo said.

And it was quite a place. In one corner was a potted palm that had grown all the way to the ceiling, had taken a turn, and was now heading toward a nearby window. In another corner was a recliner, a lamp, and a table with two potted and profusely blooming purple African violets. Underfoot were woven throw rugs similar to the rugs Cleo had noticed at the Sinclair house.

"I make these rugs in my spare time," Jo said. "I take old clothes, old sheets, old blankets, even old plastic bread wrappers, and cut everything into strips, then weave it. I'll show you my loom sometime."

"Okay," Cleo said vaguely.

Was it her lack of sleep that was making things seem so weird? First the creepy motel room and the bad dreams, now Jo and her police station that looked like an old lady's living room.

"Danny's office." Jo flung open a door, revealing a cramped room with a single small window, a desk, a phone, and not much else—and, thankfully, no Sinclair. Next was Jo's office, which was a more lavish and personal version of the front room. Mixed in with the clutter on her desk were some small, cheap picture frames, the kind you could pick up at a discount store for a couple of bucks. On the wall were more photos, many of Jo herself shaking hands with this person or that person, none of them anybody Cleo immediately recognized, but then Cleo didn't get near enough to really examine them. Something told her if she showed the slightest interest in anything in the room, she would end up getting a monologue about the item in question.

Jo crossed the room to a wall safe, dialed the combination, and opened the thick door. "Here's where I kept the key," Jo said, standing to one side in case Cleo got the notion to peer into the darkness.

"Does anyone else know the safe's combination?" Cleo asked.

"You aren't here to launch an investigation," Jo said, seeming surprised by the direction Cleo's mind had taken. "The obvious questions are my job. I just want you to concentrate on that key. I don't want your head cluttered with extraneous details."

"I'm simply trying to get an idea of what's going on."

"I want you to get some vibes from this vault, then we'll go across the street and talk to Harvey to see if you pick anything up there."

Never in her life had Cleo picked up anything from an inanimate object. There had been the missing little girl, but it had never required a conscious effort on her part. She'd never actively tried to get information. It had just come, unbidden.

Leaving the safe ajar, Jo went to her desk, sat down, pulled out a huge black ledger, wrote a check, and handed it to Cleo.

Five thousand dollars.

"Five thousand in advance, ten if you come up with the key. Fair?" Jo asked.

Cleo carefully tucked the check into a pocket in the side of her purse. "Fair." Oh, God. Why had Jo paid her now, when there was nothing more Cleo wanted than to get far, far away?

Cleo moved closer to the safe, until she stood directly in front of it, the dark, deep pit level with her face. She reached up and touched the cold metal of the door.

"Feel anything?" Jo whispered from just beyond Cleo's shoulder, inches from her ear.

Startled, Cleo jumped, her heart racing.

Peering into the darkness, Cleo put a hand on either side of the safe and closed her eyes. Careful to keep her expression blank, she stood there and silently counted to twenty, all the while thinking about the five-thousand-dollar check in her purse. Five thousand dollars. In her mind's eye, she pictured a home. Nothing lavish. She didn't ask for much. Just a tidy room with waxed floors and sparkling windows that let the sun in. In her imagination there were no cockroaches or creepy landlords or crackheads living in dark hallways. In her daydream the sun was warm on her face.

She turned the corner and found herself in a kitchen. There, above a stainless-steel double sink, was a potted geranium, its red blooms cascading happily down the green tiled backsplash. Near the back door, sweaters and jackets hung from pegs.

Five thousand dollars would get her such a place, at least for a while.

Cleo let out a heavy sigh and slowly opened her eyes.

"Well?" Jo asked expectantly.

"I'm not sure."

"Did you feel anything?"

"I need time to digest the images."

Jo shut the heavy door and gave the lock a couple of spins. "Let's go talk to Harvey. Maybe you'll pick up on something there."

They found Harvey polishing the fire truck. On the surface, he seemed like your average middle-aged guy. But when he began talking, it quickly became apparent that Harvey Jamison wasn't ordinary.

With Harvey, there was no sidestepping the issue. His lazy drawl might have been southern, but his unblinking, no-time-for-bullshit attitude was pure New York City.

"I didn't take your damn key," Harvey said, wiping his hands on a towel. *Damn* was pronounced "dai-yum." *Key* was pronounced with a long *a*.

Jo went on as if he hadn't even spoken, introducing Cleo and explaining her position in the entire conundrum.

"Howdy," Harvey said grudgingly. Cleo was fairly certain he would have been halfway polite under normal circumstances.

After the reluctant hello, he turned back to Jo. "You know I don't believe in that bullshit."

"You don't have to believe. She's going to do all the work. I want her to pick up any vibes you might be giving off."

"Like a human lie detector."

"You could say that."

"You're pissing off the whole damn town," he told Jo. "You know that, don't you?"

"That's your opinion. Cleo?" She motioned for Cleo to step closer. "Stand in his aura." She sniffed and made an arrogant face. "If he even has one."

Take the money and run.

Cleo stepped closer.

Harvey wasn't an especially tall man. Not much taller than Cleo, which would put him at about five-eleven. His eyes were very brown.

Jo put a hand to Cleo's shoulder and shoved. Cleo took a stumbling step, and she and Harvey stood nose to chin. "Um, okay." Cleo closed her eyes and counted to twenty, once again thinking about the five-thousand-dollar check in her purse.

When the time was up, she opened her eyes and stepped back.

"Well?" Jo asked in a repeat of their earlier performance. "Get anything?"

"I don't know," Cleo said, putting a limp hand to

her forehead. "I'm suddenly feeling very tired."

"I've heard that can happen. That clairvoyance takes a lot out of a person."

"I'm going to have to rest and absorb the information."

"I understand." Jo gave Harvey a final glare, took Cleo by the arm, and led her gently from the fire station.

Cleo looked back to see Harvey shake his head and return to his polishing.

They were crossing the road, heading back to the police station, when someone in a blue sport utility vehicle honked and waved, the vehicle swinging into a parking space in front of the courthouse.

"There's Dr. Campbell."

"Burton Campbell?"

"You met him?"

"I saw his signs."

"Burton's done a lot for this town. Got a good head on his shoulders." There was respect in Jo's voice. It was the kind of likable awe reserved for those special few people who were just a little bit better than everybody else. It was the kind of reaction you saw in small towns. It was the kind of reaction Cleo's mother had cultivated.

"He'll want to meet you." Jo flagged him down, even though it was obvious he'd stopped to talk to them. But then, common people often got flustered when faced with royalty.

Dr. Campbell was dressed in an expensive-looking

suit, his teeth bleached, his hair cut to perfection. He was a man selling himself with his Dale Carnegie handshake and his smooth, practiced greeting. Handsome and perfect, he was the kind of guy women had a tendency to drool over. He was the kind of guy who made Cleo sick.

"Hello, Miss Tyler. Welcome to our little community of Egypt." He held out his hand. Cleo had no choice but to take it.

His grip was just right, not too firm, not too limp, his fingertips like smooth, cool stones. And while he gave her arm a little pump, he looked directly into her eyes and smiled his winning smile, a smile that had poor Jo smitten even though he had to be fifteen to twenty years her junior.

"Burton is not only the mayor, he's best dentist in town," Jo said, proud as punch.

The *only* dentist in town, Cleo recalled.

While praise for the good doctor rolled off Jo's tongue, a black car cruised past. The vehicle was fairly new. Four doors, with "Egypt Police Department" stenciled on the driver's side. At the wheel was Daniel Sinclair. He gave them a lazy wave, his bare arm and elbow hanging out the open window. There was a smile on his face—or was it a smirk?—as he took in their cozy little chat fest. Cleo gave him a feeble smile in return, wondering if he was thinking about the cavity thing.

Jo didn't miss a beat. "Burt's initiated so many new things in Egypt," the police chief continued. A few minutes earlier she wouldn't stop talking about Daniel. Now she was waving to him as if he were a distraction she resented. "He's brought a new vitality to the town with his Revitalize Main Street project, and the Downtown Business Organization, and the KKOD."

The black car stopped at the stop sign, then moved on. "KKOD?" Cleo asked, trying to sound interested but failing. Was Daniel on patrol? she wondered.

"Keep Kids Off Drugs. We hold meetings at the youth center where people bring the entire family and we talk to the kids and the parents about keeping kids busy so they won't turn to drugs. Yep, Burton's brought a sense of pride back to Egypt."

Dr. Burton Campbell was basking in her praise, smiling with an aw-shucks attitude. "I didn't do it by myself," he said. "Sometimes people just need to be pointed in the right direction." Then he turned to Cleo. "So, are you free for lunch?"

"Actually, I thought I'd start trying to piece some things together."

"You have to eat," he said, still smiling. "There's a little place about five miles from here where they have the best catfish. You can fill me in on your plans for finding the missing key."

"Thanks, but I'd really like to just jump right in if you don't mind."

His smile didn't change. "Certainly. Maybe we can do it another time?"

"Yes. Maybe so."

Give the guy a break, Cleo tried to tell herself. The only reason she disliked him was because he was a guy her mother would have adored. Which was reason enough to dislike anybody.

6

Cleo sat on the edge of the bed, hands between her knees, staring at the fingerprint-smudged wall. She wasn't the damn queen or anything, but they could have put her up somewhere other than this cockroach-infested hole that was giving off twenty years of bad vibes. It had her karmic balance all out of whack.

To hell with it. She was getting out of there.

Cleo left the offensive room in search of a just-as-offensive manager. She found him outside in the smothering heat, sweat glistening on his forehead as he contemplated the murky, trash-filled pool. He was wearing a black nylon tank top and a pair of gray polyester shorts.

"Could I bum a ride to town?" Cleo asked. "I need to go to the bank."

"I don't know." He scratched at his belly through the tank top. "I'm pretty busy."

"I'll pay you. How does twenty bucks sound?"

Like a done deal. That was all it took to pull him away from the pool. And anyway, it seemed as if the mere contemplation of cleaning it had already exhausted him. That's how it was with lazy people. They could wear themselves out before they ever began.

He'd apparently put all of his energy into his car—it was as immaculate as it was tacky. It was one of those revamped jobs, where something had been cut here and changed there, and then on top of the new paint job he'd added some pinstripes, a lot of chrome, and a pair of fuzzy dice hanging from the rearview mirror.

And she'd hoped her trip back into town would go unnoticed.

She got in, sliding onto the clear-plastic-covered passenger seat. In the back window, a crown-shaped deodorizer wafted the heavy scent of patchouli in her direction. She could almost imagine wavy stink lines coming from it.

"My name's Willie," her driver said, pulling the boat of a car onto the two-lane that led into town. He popped in a CD. Sly and the Family Stone blared out from every direction while Willie slapped the red steering wheel and sang along.

Unfortunately, when they got to town, he pulled up right in front of the bank before Cleo could stop him. While Cleo ran inside, he left the engine running, the bass from his stereo rattling the car windows. Cleo cashed the check, relieved that she hadn't seen anybody she knew—she could count on one hand the number of people she knew in Egypt—and hurried back out.

"Is there a fast-food place around here?" she asked, sliding back into the passenger seat. She handed Willie a twenty-dollar bill. He took it and stuffed it into the pocket of his shorts. "Something with a drive-through window?"

"I can hook you up with that."

Five blocks away he pulled up to the speaker at the Tastee Delight.

Nothing on the menu looked good. Cleo finally decided on a vanilla shake and an order of fries.

"That's cool," Willie said. "You could use some meat on your bones." He placed Cleo's order, yelling over the tunes, which were still cranked up all the way, then added two Superburgers, a large order of fries, and a Big Thirsty for himself, snickering a little when he said "Big Thirsty."

The guy might be repugnant, but Cleo had to give him credit for not being afraid to be himself. At least he wasn't a Dale Carnegie clone. Cleo gave him another twenty and he paid at the window, flirting as the girl gave him his change, which he stuffed into his pocket along with the twenty Cleo had given him earlier. Then he was passing her the cardboard carrier with her shake and his Big Thirsty. He piled the white sack on top of that, put the car in gear, and pulled away.

The smell of cooked meat, along with the overpowering scent of patchouli, made Cleo's stomach heave. Luckily, they didn't have far to go, and a few minutes later they were squealing to a stop in front of her motel room. Cleo bailed out, taking in huge gulps of air, hoping to chase away the nausea.

"I've got some great porno flicks." Willie leaned out the open window to hand her the french fries she'd forgotten. With his other hand he grabbed his crotch.

"Here's a little advice," Cleo said. "When you're coming on to somebody, try to be a little less offensive."

He seemed momentarily shocked that his moves hadn't impressed her. Then he laughed, a ton of silver fillings showing. What a guy.

In the motel room, Cleo got half the shake and five fries down before she threw up.

This place is bad.

I have to get out of here.

Now. Right away.

Before she could change her mind about leaving, or before something happened, such an unexpected visit from Daniel Sinclair, she put in a call to Beau. When he answered, she quickly told him that she needed to come by and get her dog.

"What?" he asked, his voice conveying shock and panic and a number of things she didn't think she could deal with at the moment.

"I need to get Premonition."

There was a long silence. Then Beau said, "Does

he have to go? I thought he could stay with me for a while. He likes it here. He sleeps on the end of my bed—and yesterday I bought special dog dishes for his food and water, and even a mat to put underneath, with paw prints on it."

As he spoke, Cleo's heart kept sinking. Daniel had been right. She shouldn't have let Beau keep the dog, but she'd had no idea they would become so attached to each other in just a day or two.

"He's happy here," he said simply.

He's happy here. It was true. Premonition *was* happy there. He'd taken to Beau immediately.

"Can I keep him? Just a few more days?"

Can I keep him?

"Can I?"

Cleo swallowed and gripped the receiver tightly. "Yes," she said, her voice tight, tears threatening. "Yes, you can."

She hung up, then sat on the edge of the bed staring at nothing. Beau and Premonition adored each other. And Cleo lived a nomadic, unstable life, with never really having anyplace to call home. At Beau's, Premonition could have a home, a routine, a big backyard, and all the attention he wanted. And Beau would have a friend who would return that unconditional love.

They were made for each other.

Outside, a whistle blew.

A train. Train tracks. She would leave her suitcase behind and follow the tracks to the nearest town where she'd catch a ride to . . . somewhere. She'd figure that out later.

If she sat there another second, she'd change her mind about Premonition. She got to her feet. Then, in a flurry of activity and no deep thought, she stripped down to her black bra and panties, then slipped on a black knit top and pulled on a loose pair of jeans. Over that went flannel shirt.

While she knew nothing of covert operations, she'd seen enough movies to know that if she wanted to leave town without causing a stir, she would need a disguise. She didn't want to attract attention; she just wanted to slip away without anybody noticing.

Worried that her hair might give her away, she tried to tuck in under a green University of Oregon cap. It wouldn't fit. She remembered the scissors she'd borrowed from Daniel.

She grabbed the scissors and rashly whacked off her hair just above the shoulders, trying to pay no attention to the huge chunks dropping to the floor. When she was finished, she stared at her reflection in the murky bathroom mirror. The ends of her hair were ragged, the left side a couple of inches shorter than the right.

What had she done?

First Premonition, then her hair. Was she losing her mind?

Don't think, she told herself. *Just act*. She shoved what was left under the cap. In the bedroom, she rolled up a black skirt and stuffed it, along with a bag of makeup, into her purse.

Before leaving the room, she opened the door a crack and checked to see if anyone was around, then she slipped from the room. Jamming her hands deep into the front pockets of her loose jeans, she adopted a head-down posture, walking with long, loose strides, so that anyone seeing her would think she was just another teenager bumming around during summer vacation.

She headed straight for the train tracks, intending to follow them to the nearest town.

As she walked, the parallel tracks disappeared into shimmering heat waves. Hot sun beat down from directly above, baking her inside the flannel shirt. She took it off and tied it around her waist. Her scalp, under the cap, was beginning to sweat and itch like crazy.

It took less than an hour to reach a town called Shanghai City, and in that time Cleo didn't see a soul. Fortunately the tracks ran behind a gas station on the edge of town, and she could see what looked like rest rooms on one side. She left the tracks, sliding down a graveled incline. Ducking under the welcoming shade of some trees, she crossed the blacktop parking area and slipped inside the door marked Women, locking it behind her.

It was a small square room with a single toilet and a deodorizer that was so strong it burned her eyes. At the sink she splashed cold water on her hot face, then cupped her hands for a drink.

While in college, she'd done a study on how people are treated according to the way they dress.

Ninety-five percent of the time, the nicer the clothes, the more respectful the treatment—a sad commentary on the human race. Never one to let it be said that her college days were a total waste, Cleo changed clothes.

She turned off the water and quickly kicked off her sandals and shed her baggy jeans. With the cement cool under her hot, bare feet, she wiggled into the black skirt, then slipped her feet back into her sandals. Then came makeup. Finished, she removed her cap, pulled her hair back in a black scrunchy, and checked out her reflection in the cloudy mirror above the sink.

Not great as far as she could tell, but okay. She left the discarded clothes in a pile in the corner. Then with her purse slung over her shoulder, she left the rest room.

"I'm looking for someone to give me a ride to the St. Louis airport," she announced.

The only people in the gas station were three teenage boys. And from the way they were looking at her, she guessed they would have done it for nothing, but she made them an offer anyway. "I'll pay a hundred dollars, plus expenses."

All three clamored for the job.

"Somebody has to stay and work," one of them said.

They ended up drawing straws plucked from a broom.

"I could close it up for a few hours," the one who'd

drawn the shortest straw said forlornly, not wanting to be left out.

"You lost," one of the other kids said. He jingled his keys and grabbed his can of pop and cigarettes in preparation for departure. Then the two winners scrambled first to open the door for her and then to open the car door, shooting each other dark looks that they thought Cleo wouldn't catch.

It turned out the driver's name was Chad; his friend's name was Jed. Unfortunately for Cleo, but fortunately for the boys, Chad had an El Camino, which meant no backseat. Sitting in the middle, with the air conditioning blasting between her legs, the cigarette smoke choking her, Cleo asked, "How far is it to the airport?"

Daniel banged on the door of room number six.

No answer.

He gave up and walked to the lobby to find Willie.

Willie didn't like Daniel. That was because Daniel had gotten him a couple of times for running a prostitution ring out of his motel. Daniel might have been a little hard on him, but two of the prostitutes had been underage, and the idea that Willie had so defamed The Palms had driven Daniel a little wild.

"Cleo Tyler. The woman in number six," he said. "Know where she is?"

"Nope."

"Have you seen her recently?"

"Nope."

"Gimme a key to her room."

"I can't do that, man."

"Gimme a key."

"You got a search warrant?"

"Just give me the fucking key."

"Okay, man, but I don't like doing anything illegal."

"Yeah. Sure."

Daniel strode back to her room, unlocked the door, and stepped inside. He was hit by the stench of greasy french fries and body odor. What a dive. Near the door, under the window, the air conditioner was clanking away as though it were taking its last breath.

No Cleo.

Her suitcase was on the floor, where it had been the day before. There was a long gray tank-top kind of thing at the foot of the bed that he figured she slept in.

He went to the bathroom and turned on the light. On the floor, under the sink, was a pile of red hair. He picked it up. He moved it between his fingers. It was soft. Really soft.

Why would she chop off her hair? Did she just have a hankering for a new do, or was it an exercise in desperation?

Back at the lobby, he drilled Willie.

"You say you haven't seen anything of Tyler today?"

"Yep."

"That's funny, because I could have sworn I saw both of you downtown at the bank."

"Oh, yeah. I forgot about that."

"After you came back, did you see her leave the motel?"

Willie pointed over his shoulder. "She headed that way. Up the tracks. Dressed like she didn't want anybody to know it was her."

"What was she wearing?"

"Flannel shirt. Jeans. A cap."

"You wouldn't be shitting me, would you?"

"No, man. Why would I do that? The bitch pissed me off. I hope you lock her up or something."

Daniel had already started to leave when Willie shouted after him. "Hey, if she's in some kind of trouble, I had nothing to do with it. You hear that, man?"

Daniel's cop car wasn't flashy like Jo's. In fact, you wouldn't even know it was a cop car at all unless you were close enough to read the lettering on the driver's door. But with an eight-cylinder 350 under the hood, that baby could really cover ground.

Daniel turned on the radio. Before "Take a Walk on the Wild Side" was over, he was in Shanghai City.

There was only one business in Shanghai City—and that was a gas station. Daniel stopped to ask if anybody there had seen Cleo.

There was one kid inside, and he looked bored as hell. He slowly got to his feet, hands splayed on the countertop.

"Have you seen a woman around here in the last hour or two?" Daniel asked.

The kid shrugged. "I dunno."

"She's about—" Daniel thought a moment and held up one hand, remembering where she'd come up to on him. "About this tall. Around twenty-five." He almost said *long* red hair, but then he remembered the hair he'd found in the motel bathroom. "Red hair."

"I don't think so."

The kid looked nervous. Daniel could tell he was lying. He sighed and reached into the back pocket of his jeans, pulled out his billfold, and flashed his badge. That got the kid's attention. Under normal conditions, Daniel never took out his badge. It was just something he didn't like to do. Seemed too dramatic.

"There was a lady here," the kid said. "She wanted a lift to the airport in St. Louis. My friends gave her a ride."

"What are they driving?"

The kid gave him a description of the vehicle.

"When'd they leave?"

"I don't know." The kid thought. "Half hour ago, maybe?"

Daniel began moving toward the door. The kid came around the counter, following him. "My friends didn't do nothing," he said, talking fast, staying a few steps behind Daniel. "They just gave her a ride. What'd she do? Escape from jail?"

Dylan thought about her room at The Palms. "Something like that."

"Wow."

The kid was impressed. And it was hard to impress kids nowadays.

Daniel caught up with them about an hour outside of St. Louis.

There weren't that many El Caminos on the road anymore, so when he spotted the ugly maroon truck/car combination, he figured it had to be them.

He ran a license plate check and found out that the owner was a seventeen-year-old male named Chad Donald with a couple of speeding tickets, nothing more.

Daniel dropped back, allowing several cars to fill the gap between them. He almost lost them when they suddenly cut across a lane of traffic and exited without warning.

It was close, but Daniel managed to exit, keeping his distance as he tailed them into a service center.

As Daniel watched, they pulled up to an island for gas. Still keeping his distance, Daniel coasted into the truck and trailer area, parked, and waited.

One of the kids jumped out and began pumping gas. The other two occupants went inside.

Time to move.

Daniel slipped from the car and walked in the direction of the convenience store. Inside, he gave the place a quick once-over, his gaze tracking down the food aisle, over to the glass refrigerators lining one wall, and finally to a hallway with a plastic Rest Rooms sign above it. He ducked under the sign into the short hallway and went over to the door marked Women. Without hesitation he opened the door and went inside.

There was only one person in the room. A woman, wearing a tight black skirt. A woman with a rose tattoo on her ankle.

He hadn't made a sound, but for some reason she turned off the water, then slowly lifted her head. In the mirror he could see that she was wearing a lot more makeup than she'd had on the day before, or even that morning. She had dark stuff around her eyes. Her lips, instead of being red, were a deep purple.

Those eyes grew wider. The purple mouth dropped open.

He smiled. He just couldn't help it. "Howdy, Cleopatra."

7

"Let me guess. Queen of Scams, right?" Daniel said mockingly, speaking to her reflection.

Without taking her eyes from the mirror, Cleo slowly straightened.

"Nice look for you, Cleopatra."

She watched in the mirror as he stepped closer. "My name is Cleo." Afraid he was going to grab her and slap her into a pair of cuffs, she swung around to face him.

"Tired of me already?" he asked.

He didn't look angry. No, he looked slightly amused—and oh so smug, as if he'd known all along that she would run out on them, as if she'd just confirmed every bad thing he thought about her. Before, his opinion had been based on nothing more than speculation. Now she'd given him fact.

"Are you here to give me your blessing?" she finally managed to ask, thankful that her voice didn't betray her nervousness. "Since you wanted me out of Egypt all along."

He just stood there watching her for a moment. Then he let out a gust of air, looking at her as if she were some damsel in distress who'd just asked him to change her flat tire on a hot day.

"Oh, I want you out of town all right," he said conversationally. "But I don't want you to publicly humiliate Jo in the process. That's not part of the package. No, you're coming back to Egypt to read your tea leaves or whatever bogus crap you do. *Then* you can be on your way."

"You know as well as I do that Jo lost the key and won't admit it," Cleo said, playing for time, her mind racing. "Why should I go back and pretend to be looking for something I'll never find? They need to see what's in front of their eyes and get the damn locks replaced."

"What about your dog?"

Why had he brought up Premonition? She didn't want to think about Premonition. Should she try to explain? No, it would be too difficult, and he would never believe her. Let him think she was hard. *And I am hard. I am unfeeling,* she thought, trying to convince herself. *Believe it.* She had to believe it, otherwise how could she go on? How could she survive?

"You're everything I thought you'd be and more," he said.

From anyone else, the line could have been taken as a compliment. From Sinclair, it could never be misconstrued as anything but an insult. He hadn't mentioned the money. He must not know that Jo had paid her already. She hoped he didn't find out. If he did, he'd never believe that she planned to pay it back. "Glad I lived up to your expectations," she said levelly, her rapid heartbeat beginning to slow. "I'd hate to disappoint you."

He was starting to say something—a stinging comeback, she imagined—when a knock sounded on the outer door. "Hey, you okay in there?" A young man's voice. A teenager. Chad. "Charisse? You okay?"

Daniel's eyebrows lifted. "Charisse?"

"It seemed appropriate."

"Is there anything about you that's real?"

She thought about that a moment. She didn't know. She honestly didn't know.

The door opened and Chad stuck his head inside, surprised to see Daniel, almost as surprised as Cleo had been. "What's going on? Is this guy flashing you?" The kid was all flustered, nervous bravado. "I've heard about you wackos, hanging out in public rest rooms, attacking women."

Jed showed up behind his friend. They both pushed their way into the room, braver as a team. "Get the hell out of here," Chad told Daniel. "Yeah, leave her alone, you pervert," Jed added.

Daniel stared at Cleo. "Tell them," he said to her.

She didn't say a word.

When it became apparent that she had no intention of speaking, Daniel let out a sigh of resignation, looking more annoyed than alarmed. He started to turn. Chad lifted his arm. Cleo's first thought was that he had a knife. But it wasn't a knife—it was a bottle.

Before she could shout a warning, Chad brought it down against Daniel's skull in one swift motion.

Cleo screamed.

Glass shattered. Brown liquid exploded. Daniel sank to his knees, hitting the floor hard, his eyes rolling back in his head.

"Come on!" Chad motioned for her to hurry. "Let's get outta here!"

Cleo looked from Chad to where Daniel struggled to stay conscious, blood dripping from his scalp, running down his face.

"Don't do it, Cleo," Daniel mumbled, not looking up. "I'll have the kid's ass for assaulting an officer."

On one hand, she was relieved that he was able to speak; on the other, she was afraid that he would carry out his threat.

"He didn't know you were a cop," she argued. No one could look less like a cop than Daniel Sinclair.

"I can do anything I want."

"He's a cop?" Chad asked.

Cleo could see Chad struggling to change gears, at first not believing it.

"Yes," Cleo said.

"Oh, shit."

"You'd better go." Cleo motioned for them both to leave. She didn't want them dragged into her mess. They'd only been trying to protect her. "I'll be fine. Just go. Get out of here."

They scrambled away, the door swinging shut behind them.

Daniel crawled to the nearest wall, turned, and sat down, leaning his back and head against the tiles. He wasn't bleeding as badly as she'd thought. She could see that some of what she'd thought was blood was actually cola, or blood mixed with cola.

She poked around on his head, separating his hair until she found a bump. In the middle of the bump was a small gash.

She wet a paper towel and dabbed it around on the wound, not sure what to do.

Daniel pulled the paper towel from her hand. Holding the towel against his head, he got unsteadily to his feet. He stood there a moment, then reached for Cleo, putting one arm around her for support. His body was rock hard, and as hot as a furnace.

"Let's get the hell out of here," he said.

Cleo had no idea where Daniel was parked, so she let him lead the way through a maze of trucks until they came to the black car she'd seen him in that morning.

While the air was by no means fresh, the hot breeze, with its fuel and exhaust fumes, seemed to revive him a little. He let go of her and rounded the car, moving fairly well. Before he got in, he unbuttoned his shirt—this one had a Hawaiian flavor—and peeled it off, then used it to wipe his chest and neck and finally his face.

His chest was smooth, beautiful flesh with the

same rippling muscles she'd felt pressed to her side just moments before. He was beefcake and didn't even know it.

He looked across the top of the car at Cleo, squinting his eyes against a sun that was getting low in the sky. It would be dark soon. It was a good five hours to Egypt. Plenty of time to figure something out, plenty of time to get away if she decided to.

"I'll drive," she said. It was a way to let him win without losing face. "You're not in any shape to be behind the wheel." She held out her hand, expecting him to give her the keys.

He ignored her hand, circled the car, and opened the passenger door. One hand on the hood, one on the open door, he said, "I'm not giving you the keys until I'm belted in my seat."

8

"Pull off at the next exit," Daniel said after they'd been driving for about an hour.

Cleo assumed he had to use the rest room, but after she pulled off, he kept telling her to turn here and turn there, until they were in front of a huge hotel called The Towers.

She checked the clock on the dash. 9:00 P.M. "What are we doing?" If they kept going, they could be in Egypt by one o'clock.

"I'm tired and I'm hungry, I'm sticky, and my head hurts like hell."

A hotel? With Sinclair? Christ, could this get any worse? She knew one thing—she had to ditch him before he found out about the money. He harbored enough hostility toward her that he might just toss her in jail. She could end up doing time. How had she gotten herself into such a mess?

Under normal conditions, she would have flat-out refused to stay at a hotel with him, but stopping might buy her the time she needed.

She guided the car up the smooth drive and pulled to a stop in front of a set of automatic double doors.

"Go in and get the room." He reached into his back pocket, pulled out a billfold, and opened it. His badge was there, in plain sight, as he rummaged in the wallet and then handed her some bills. "*One* room. I'm not letting you out of my sight. Then swing through the gift shop and get me a shirt and a toothbrush."

Yeah, she'd swing through the gift shop and out the back door.

She was getting out of the car when he caught her by the arm. "Oh, and Cleo? Don't try running out a back door or anything. If you do, I'll catch you and toss your ass in jail."

He meant it.

The back door probably hadn't been a good idea anyway, she thought as she made her way to the reception desk. It wouldn't have given her much time. No, she needed to get away that night, when he was asleep. That way she could put some distance between them before he woke up and found her gone. Maybe she could even make it to St. Louis. She would leave his car at the airport and be on a plane before he even woke up.

She ended up getting a room with two queen-size beds. As she was signing in, she remembered that she hadn't given Chad the hundred dollars she'd promised him.

Damn.

She hadn't meant to cheat the kid. It was just that in all the confusion, she'd forgotten. Even so, it was going to nag at her conscience until she figured out what to do about it.

At the gift shop she picked up two toothbrushes, some toothpaste, a small can of deodorant, a disposable razor, and the perfect shirt. Across the front, in black letters, it read: My Kids Went to the Ozarks and All They Got Me Was This Stupid T-shirt. Perfect.

"Room four forty-three," she told Daniel, sliding behind the wheel, dropping the bag of purchases on his lap, and handing him the white plastic card with the magnetic strip.

"The money," he said, palm up, fingers wiggling.

At first she thought he meant *the* money. But with relief she quickly realized he was talking about his change. She shoved the crumpled bills and coins into his hand, then pulled away from the lobby entrance, winding up a parking ramp to finally find an empty spot on level two. Once there, they took a stuffy elevator to the fourth floor, winding through a maze of twisting hallways to their room.

She leaned against the wall and watched as Daniel inserted the plastic card in the slot, got the green light, and opened the door for her to go in first.

She inhaled.

The room was so clean. So wonderfully *clean*. And cool. So blissfully cool.

Maybe this hadn't been such a bad idea after all.

She dropped her purse on the bed. The room smelled like potpourri instead of BO. And the colors: not a speck of orange, or even anything remotely close to orange. It was all deep greens and purples.

She kicked off her sandals and sank her toes into the plush green carpet. Then she pulled two pillows out from under the spread, plopped them against the headboard, threw herself onto the bed, and picked up the remote control.

She flicked on the TV and began surfing through channels.

"Just out of curiosity." Daniel crossed the room, reached behind her, and, before she could stop him, pulled the scrunchy from her hair.

"Oh, my God," he muttered.

Cleo had been staring deliberately at the TV, but his horrified comment drew her attention to him. He was standing over her, his mouth hanging open. As she watched, the surprise on his face slowly bloomed into something that looked to her like open-mouthed delight.

"What?" Her hair couldn't look that bad.

He was laughing. The son of a bitch was laughing at her.

"Stop it."

"Christ," he said, a hand to his stomach, clearly unable to stop the guffaws. "Look in the mirror," he gasped. "You've gotta see this."

All she had to do was lift her head a few degrees to see her reflection in the mirror across from the bed. "Oh, my God." She put a hand to her ragged hair.

The freak in the mirror did the same.

"You son of a bitch. Stop laughing." She flew off the bed and started shoving at him with both hands, pushing at his bare stomach. He dropped the scrunchy and grabbed her by the wrists. "Okay, okay," he said, laughter still thick in his voice. He scooped up the black fabric hair band and handed it to her. She quickly slipped her hair through it, then dropped down on the bed, picked up the remote, and began pushing buttons as fast as she could.

Just you wait, Sinclair. As soon as you fall asleep, I'm out of here. When you wake up in the morning, I'll be long gone, along with the money and your car.

Finished laughing at her, Daniel sat down on the other queen-size bed, pulled the phone over and balanced it on his thigh, pushed a series of buttons, and waited.

"Hey, Beau. It's me. I wanted to let you know that I'm not going to be home until tomorrow. I'm staying at a hotel tonight. Grab a pen and I'll give you the number." He paused and waited, then gave Beau the hotel and room number. "What? No, I don't know. . . . Yeah, there's a pool. . . . No, I won't be swimming. I know it sounds like fun, but I'm working."

Cleo rolled her eyes.

"Yeah, maybe next time. Remember, Disney World next spring, bud. I've already got the reservations. . . . Yeah. . . . Okay. See you tomorrow. Bye."

He hung up and turned to her. "What about pizza? Sound all right to you?"

"Yeah. Fine." She resented the fact that he was suddenly acting as though holding her against her will were perfectly normal. It wasn't normal at all. There was *nothing* normal about it.

"How about a movie?" he asked. "Wanna watch a movie?"

She shrugged. From the corner of her eye, she could see that he was holding the movie guide. "No." Was this how he made his move? Pizza and a movie? A little white-bread, if you asked her.

"How about this one?" He held up the movie menu. "I heard it was supposed to be good."

"Who says?"

"I don't know. Some reviewer."

"You can't trust reviewers." She tossed the remote control on the bed. "Do whatever you want. I'm going to take a bath."

She took her purse with her—just in case he got any ideas about digging through it. In the bathroom, she stood in front of the mirror and pulled her hair free of the elastic band.

She tried to tell herself that her hair looked so hideous because it had been smashed under the cap all day. She tugged at the chopped ends, then dug her fingers into her scalp, trying to fluff it up. There was a comedian with a haircut like this, but she couldn't think of his name. His hair was supposed to look like he'd chopped at it with a pair of scissors.

Emo Phillips. That was the guy's name. She had a haircut like Emo Phillips.

It didn't matter, she tried to tell herself. It was just hair.

All her life people had told her what beautiful hair she had. And now it was gone.

It doesn't matter. It's just hair.

But it did matter. It mattered a lot.

The hair she'd cut away and left lying on the floor of the bathroom in Egypt was hair Jordan had touched, hair Jordan had loved.

The room came with packets of soap, shampoo, and bubble bath. Cleo filled the tub and sank into the bubbles. She soaked for a long time, until her toes and fingers wrinkled, until Daniel banged on the door and asked her if she was ever coming out.

"Maybe not!" Maybe she'd just stay in there. Maybe she'd keep the door locked and never come out.

Then she washed her hair twice, sliding down into the tub to rinse.

Daniel rapped on the door again. "Pizza's here," he shouted.

Why did people think pizza was the answer to everything?

She pulled up the drain lever, got out of the tub, dried off, then wrapped a towel around her head. Rather than put on the clothes she'd been wearing all day, she slipped into one of the fluffy white robes that also came with the room, tying the belt at her waist.

When she stepped out of the bathroom, Daniel was lying with his back propped against the headboard, a slice of pizza in one hand, a beer in the other, watching CNN. She crossed the room and opened the white box with red lettering.

"Ham and pineapple on one side, anchovies on the other," he said.

The sauce was a reddish orange, more orange than red when she really looked close, especially where it pooled thinly around the chunks of pineapple. "They both look so good, I can't decide," she said sarcastically, a sarcasm she was sure would be lost on him.

She settled for the pineapple, grabbed a beer, and sat down on what she already considered her bed. She could be very territorial.

"What the hell are you doing?" he asked a minute later when her slice was finally ready to be eaten. He was staring at the neat pile of ham she'd placed on a napkin near the alarm clock radio.

"I'm a vegetarian."

"You're full of shit."

She took a sip of beer. Surprisingly, it didn't make her gag. "Why is it so hard to believe that I'm a vegetarian?"

"Because you abandoned your dog, for chrissake. How can you be an animal lover if you abandon your dog? And you ate steak at my place."

"Fed it to Premonition." She examined her pizza slice with a critical eye. The sauce was definitely orange, the same rusty orange as the shag rug at The Palms.

Stop, she told herself. She stared harder at the pizza. Was that a hair? God. If it was a hair, then there was no way she could gag any pizza down.

She pulled at it. It was cheese. Hardened cheese. But maybe it was hardened cheese wrapped around a hair. Without looking at the pizza, she forced herself to take another bite, a huge one. She chewed and chewed, feeling the hair adhering to her throat. She swallowed, grabbed the beer, and kept drinking until the bottle was empty. Then she tried a test swallow. She couldn't feel anything weird, but there was no way she could eat another bite. The meal had been ruined. And next time she ate pizza, she would remember the hair.

"Aren't you going to have any more?" Daniel asked, seeing that she'd put the piece aside.

She shook her head.

"If you don't like it, order something else."

"No." She wiped her mouth with a napkin. And then she found herself lying to him the way she lied to everybody else. It was easier than trying to explain to someone that something as harmless as a slice of pizza or a piece of pumpkin pie could suddenly taste and look like a hair ball or a musty rug. "Actually, I ate earlier today. I'm not really hungry."

She got up, went to the bathroom, and brushed her teeth for a full two minutes. Then she removed the towel from her head and shook out what was left of her hair. Wet, it didn't look as bad. Uneven, but not freakish, at least.

When she came back out, Daniel announced that he was going to take a shower.

She'd thought to leave when he was sleeping, but this could be almost as good. "And just in case you have any bright ideas, I'm taking the car keys with me."

"Did I ever tell you my brother taught me how to hot-wire a car?" She smiled to herself, imagining Daniel's discomfort. At the moment he would be wondering if she was lying or not.

"Did you come from a bloody band of thieves?"

"My brother and I were always in trouble."

The truth was, they were the best kids in the world, always trying to please. But anytime anybody asked about her family, Cleo always came up with an evasive answer. It was a lot less painful than the truth.

"Gimme your robe," he said.

"What?"

"Your robe. Give it to me. I want to make sure you don't leave."

"I could wrap myself up in a sheet."

"That might be a little conspicuous."

She thought about how far it was from the room to his car, about how many people they had passed on their way there.

"Don't tell me you're too modest to drop the robe."

She took that as a direct challenge. Slowly she undid the belt and let the robe fall open. Then, with her eyes never leaving his, she slipped the fabric from her shoulders until she held the robe in one hand.

He just stood there, staring.

"Don't you want it?" She lifted the robe higher, her arm outstretched. "Here. Take it."

He took three long steps toward her, snatched the robe from her fingers, and disappeared into the bathroom.

"Have a nice shower," she said, smiling.

Inside the bathroom, Daniel leaned against the door, his eyes closed, his heart beating in his ears. Damn. Why the hell had he done that? Why hadn't he just used a set of handcuffs? He had a pair in the car. But he hated to handcuff a woman. He hated to handcuff anybody, if the truth be told. And son of a bitch, he hadn't known she was naked under there. He'd figured she was wearing underwear.

Oh, God, he thought, unable to stop seeing those full, rounded breasts, those sweetly curving hips, that triangle of red-gold hair that he imagined sinking his fingers into. The boldness in her eyes. The dare. The challenge.

What was she after? A trade? Sex for her freedom?

This hadn't been a good idea. What had he been thinking? It was going to be a long night. A helluva long night.

He pushed himself away from the door and turned on the shower, not even bothering with the hot control. Ten minutes later, when he'd gotten all the blood and cola out of his hair and off his skin, he stepped out of the shower, grabbed a towel and dried off. Normally he would have just slept in the nude, but there was no telling what Cleo Tyler would do next. A man had to be prepared. He slipped back into his jeans and stepped from the bathroom.

From his perspective, it looked as if Cleo was either asleep or pretending to be asleep. Probably pretending. She was lying in bed, covers up to her chin, one bent arm against the pillow. Her hair was partially dry, falling across her face so that all he could see were her full, slightly parted lips.

Relieved that there would be no round two—or would it be considered round three?—he pulled the mattress off the bed nearest him, covers and all. It was against the fire code, but it was the only way he was going to get any sleep. He dropped it to the floor directly in front of the door so that there was no way she could get out without waking him. Then he grabbed a couple of pillows and eased himself down on the mattress.

9

It was the dream again.

This time Cleo stood alongside the road, watching as the car came closer and closer. She tried to move, tried to shout, but even though she was there, she had no control over what was happening, no control over herself. It was like watching a movie. But unlike a movie, where you could turn away or leave the room, Cleo could do neither of those things.

Not again. Dear God. Not again.

The car floated around the corner to head directly at her. The headlights were blinding. She lifted a hand to cover her eyes.

And then suddenly, somehow, she was inside the car, and she could see herself outside, wearing jeans and a white long-sleeved T-shirt.

"Look out!"

She heard Jordan's cry of alarm. She felt the weight of the car shift, saw a cement wall hurtling toward them.

Some parts of the dream changed, but this part was always the same. The slow motion. The silent crunch of metal. The silent shattering of glass. Then her own screams.

Don't look. Don't get out of the car.

But she did. She always did.

With the real accident, nobody knew how she'd gotten out. It was speculated that she crawled through the broken front window, because glass shards were found embedded in her knees. But in the dream, she was always just *out*. Just standing beside the car looking in. But the car was empty.

She turned around, the way she always turned around.

And bumped into herself, into her wild-eyed self.

"You're a bad person," the Cleo in white said. "Come and see what you've done."

"No."

"Come and see what you've done." Cleo in white reached out and grabbed her arm. And Cleo was amazed, because she could feel the deathly chill of the other Cleo's skin, the pressure of her fingers. "Come and see what you've done."

"I didn't do it, *you* did it," Cleo said, hanging back, planting her feet on ground that kept slipping away. "You killed Jordan. You did it. I hate you. I hate you. I can't look," Cleo sobbed. "Don't make me look."

But suddenly she was in the middle of the road, staring at the broken, smashed pumpkin.

Why, she thought, the way she always thought with false confidence, *it's only a broken pumpkin*. But then the pumpkin moved. And the pumpkin cried out for help.

Jordan.

Jordan's voice. Full of pain. Full of beseeching, imploring *pain*.

Cleo came awake with a start.

She lay in bed, trying to get her bearings.

At first she thought she was back in the room at The Palms.

No. Not The Palms. A hotel, but not The Palms. She'd tried to get away from The Palms, but Daniel Sinclair had caught her. Sinclair. She was in a hotel with Sinclair.

Had she cried out?

She lay there, listening.

Silence, except for a steady, even breathing coming from the vicinity of the hotel room door. No, she hadn't cried out. That was good. Very good.

Outside, beyond the window, she could hear transports roaring down the interstate. Reassuring artificial light cut in around the curtains, casting the room in layers of shadow.

The pillow under her head and the mattress beneath her were damp with sweat. Fear covered her body like dew. Trembling, her legs weak, she got to her feet and made her way through the darkness to the bathroom. Once inside, she turned on the heat lamp, then the shower, and stepped inside.

• • •

At first Daniel couldn't place the sound.

Rain?

Yeah, rain. He liked the sound of rain. There was something comforting about it. But little by little, reality filtered in until he realized it wasn't rain at all, but the sound of a shower. A shower?

Still groggy, he struggled to put it all together.

Cleo had already taken a shower.

He went from half asleep to wide awake in a fraction of a second. He jumped from his makeshift bed. Son of a bitch. She'd gotten away. Somehow she'd gotten past him. Somehow she'd stepped over him without waking him, leaving the shower running to throw him off.

Adrenaline pulsed through him. He shoved the bathroom door open so hard it banged against the wall. He ripped aside the shower curtain, intent on turning off the water.

He froze.

What the . . . ?

Cleo sat in the tub, her knees drawn up to her chest, her arms wrapped around her legs, shaking and rocking.

Daniel reached in and shut off the water. "Cleo?"

Where earlier she'd boldly exposed herself to him, this time she grabbed the edge of the shower curtain and pulled it to her, wrapping it around herself as best she could. She wiped at her nose with the back of her hand. "C-Can't a p-person get a l-little p-privacy around here?"

He straightened. "I just thought—" What he'd thought was that she'd gotten away. This hardly seemed the time to explain the reasoning behind his intrusion. *Withdrawal*, he suddenly realized. *She's going through withdrawal.*

He pulled a fluffy white towel from the rack on the wall and handed it to her.

"What are you addicted to?"

"What?"

"Crack? Heroin? I can hook you up with some people who can help you."

Wrong thing to say. He saw that immediately.

Slowly her head came up. And when her eyes connected with his, they were glittering with anger. "You son of a bitch."

She quickly stood up, the towel forgotten, the shower curtain forgotten. She stepped from the tub and lifted her hand, ready to smack him. He stopped her by grabbing her wrists and quickly pinning her to the wall, her hands locked above her head, the soft globes of her breasts smashed against his bare chest. Above his head, he could feel the heat from the overhead lamp burning into his back. Near his right ear, he could hear the timer ticking away.

Ticking . . . ticking . . .

The next thing he knew, he was kissing her, kissing her as though she were the drug and he the addict.

She stiffened.

And then she began kissing him back.

He moved his mouth over hers, sucking at her lips, pulling away, turning his head, finding her again. He plunged his tongue deep inside her mouth, and she met him, thrust for thrust.

He released her hands and she immediately wrapped her arms around him. Her leg curled around his thigh. With her back braced against the wall, he grasped her leg and lifted it higher, his throbbing erection meeting her hot, secret place, a layer of denim the only thing keeping him from sliding deep inside her.

She let out a cry of frustration, fumbling for the button on his pants. She undid it, then unzipped the zipper, freeing him into the heat of her hands.

"You're beautiful," she whispered against his mouth. "I want you." She guided him to her.

"Wait," he said, holding back. "We need a rubber," he said in a breathless voice. "You got a rubber?"

"No. Come on. We don't need one."

"Yes, we do."

"Why? Are you afraid of me?"

"I'm looking out for both of us."

"But if either of us were tainted, it would be me, wouldn't it?"

"I didn't say that."

There was a click. The heat lamp went off, engulfing them in darkness. He reached behind him searching for the wall switch.

"Leave the light off," she whispered.

"I want to see you."

"I want to pretend you're somebody else."

"You're pissing me off."

"I'm just being honest."

"Honest? You don't know the meaning of the word."   •

"What about you? You said you were tired and hungry, but this is what you really wanted, isn't it?"

"And you don't?"

He cranked up the heat lamp. The red filaments came on, giving the space around them a weird, dark-room kind of glow. He bent his head to kiss her. She turned her face away. She was still cradling him in her hands. She let him go and pressed both palms to the wall.

He still had a hand to her thigh, her leg wrapped around him. "Look at me," he said, his voice smooth and low.

She kept her face turned away.

He slid a finger inside her. "Look at me." She was hot and wet. So wet.

He began to slowly stroke her. "Look at me."

Her face came around. Her eyes were half closed, her lips parted, her breasts rapidly rising and falling.

His strokes became faster and faster, until her entire body tensed, until she threw back her head and cried out, until she went limp and they both slid to the floor.

"It's too bad you don't have a rubber," she said, her voice thick and slurred, still lost in a euphoria he couldn't achieve. He rested his forehead against hers. "No shit," he said, his voice tight and strained.

Another minute passed with just the sound of breathing. "You could get one," she suggested. He sensed that she was holding her breath, waiting for his response.

"I don't trust you."

"You think I'll leave while you're gone?"

"Let's put it this way: I'd be surprised if you didn't."

She shoved him away. He just kind of fell back. She stepped over him and left the bathroom. Two second later he heard the bed creaking, heard the sound of covers being pulled up.

No, he didn't trust Cleo Tyler for a second. And the last thing he needed was to have her accuse him of rape. Of course, she might do that anyway. And even though there hadn't been any penetration, he'd be lying if he said they hadn't been intimate. And he'd be lying if he said he hadn't known any better.

Cleo fell asleep almost instantly. And this time she didn't dream the pumpkin dream. Instead, she dreamed something that was disturbing in a new kind of way. She dreamed that she was pregnant—with Daniel Sinclair's baby.

Cleo woke up to find bright sunlight streaming in the open curtains—and Sinclair, fully dressed, the Ozarks T-shirt stretched tightly across his chest and bunched under his armpits, going through her purse.

She bolted upright, pulling the sheet over her breasts. "What are you doing?"

"Trying to figure you out."

She pulled the bottom of the sheet free of the bed and got to her feet, the white fabric twisted around her.

"A little bit late for that, isn't it?" he asked, indicating the sheet.

She took a sweep at her purse. He lifted it out of her reach, then lowered it, letting her have it.

"I've already seen everything there is to see," he said. "And I'm referring to the purse, in case you wondered."

"Go to hell."

"Money. I should have known. Jo paid you yesterday, didn't she? That's why you took off."

It would do no good to state her case. And it certainly wouldn't do her any good to tell him that she'd planned to give back every last cent. He wouldn't believe her. She knew he wouldn't believe her.

He scratched at the day's growth of stubble on his cheek. It sounded like sandpaper. "I ordered some breakfast from room service. As soon as we eat, we can hit the road. That'll get us back in time for you to spend the afternoon with Jo and have your voodoo session, reading those tarot cards and shit."

There was a knock on the door.

Daniel's eyebrows lifted, and he looked at Cleo as if to ask, *Are you staying or are you going to be modest and make a run for the bathroom?*

She ran for the bathroom, closing the door behind her.

10

Inside the bathroom, Cleo immediately checked the side zipper on her purse. The money was still there. Reassured, she brushed her teeth and scrubbed her face, then put on the clothes from the day before, which she'd left in a pile under the sink. She detested having to wear the same panties two days in a row, but she could hardly go without, since she had nothing else to wear but the black skirt. Of course, Daniel had seen every inch of her, but she didn't want to pull a Sharon Stone.

What had gotten into her?

She was humiliated. Ashamed. And yet, just thinking about how he'd touched her—

Stop.

Just forget it ever happened. Or at least pretend it never happened. Yes, she could do that. She was good at pretending.

She dug in her purse and found her makeup bag. She applied a little foundation and lipstick, tied her hair back with the black fabric-covered rubber band, then joined Daniel for breakfast.

She stared at the huge tray, hoping to find something that wouldn't make her stomach heave. And if she didn't, well, she'd become proficient at pretending to eat.

The crescent rolls were a possibility. Coffee, yes. Orange juice, no. Not only was it orange, it probably had pulp in it. Oatmeal, definitely no.

Knowing she had to eat, she sat down on the bed, poured herself some coffee, and picked up a crescent roll.

"Something wrong?"

"What?" She pulled her gaze away from the roll to where he sat at the requisite tiny round hotel-room table, a plate of scrambled eggs and sausage in front of him, fork in hand.

"I didn't know what you wanted, so I just guessed. You might notice that I didn't order anything for you that was once alive."

She just sat there, staring.

He'd closed the curtains partway, and muted sunlight drifted in, accentuating his perfect bone structure. Sunlight could be harsh and honest and unflattering. Not so with Daniel. It bathed him in a soft patina, light falling over sun-bleached eyebrows, revealing blond, curling eyelashes. It wasn't a mannequin face like Burton Campbell's. No, Sinclair's had character. You could tell he'd lived.

Her gaze dropped to the blond hair on his forearms, then to his hands. Strong hands, with fingers that were long and sensitive. Unbidden, a memory came to her, the memory of those fingers touching her, slipping inside her as she contracted around them. She put a hand to her mouth, remembering the pressure of his kiss.

She slowly came to realize that he was talking. His lips were moving, but she wasn't listening. She pulled herself away from her erotic daydream, back to his voice, a voice that was low and even.

So much for pretending the previous night had never happened.

But apparently he'd been able to put it from his mind. Apparently it hadn't been a big deal, because he was rambling on about the menu, wondering if she wanted something else.

If she'd been by herself, she would have ordered a milkshake—something with a lot of calories, something she'd never had trouble getting down. But she wasn't by herself, so she just lifted the crescent roll to her mouth.

"This is fine." She took a bite, hoping it really would be fine.

The outside of the roll was flaky. Those flakes separated in her mouth, giving the roll a certain textured hairiness. She quit chewing and swallowed the piece whole, then quickly washed it down with coffee. She did the same with the next bite, and the next. By the time she'd finally finished three bites, Daniel was done. He pushed his plate away, then got to his feet, leaving her to finish her breakfast in private.

In the bathroom, Daniel let out a long breath and raked a lock of tousled hair back from his forehead. Son of a bitch. This was going to be tough, having to spend the rest of the day in close proximity. Every time he looked at her, he got a hard-on. He kept visualizing the way she'd looked as he held her against the wall, her eyes closed, head tipped back, lips parted.

Son of a bitch.

He crossed his arms in front of him, grasped the hem of the Ozarks T-shirt, peeled it over his head, and stuffed it between the towel bar and the wall, getting it out of the way. After that, he shaved, brushed his teeth, and grabbed the T-shirt. For a moment he considered putting it on inside out, but then he shook his head, turned it right side out, and pulled it back on. Cleo Tyler had a cruel sense of humor.

When he stepped from the bathroom, he was relieved to see she'd finished off the entire bowl of oatmeal, another crescent roll, and the glass of orange juice.

She patted her lips with the white cloth napkin. "I can't eat another bite."

And then he got to a subject he'd been pondering for quite some time. "I'll bet they have rubbers in the gift shop."

She grew very still. Was she considering his unspoken suggestion? Checkout time wasn't for several more hours. He wasn't scheduled for duty until tomorrow.

She dropped her napkin on her plate, then put her plate aside. "Yes," she said, seeming preoccupied, as if giving more attention to something else going on in her head than the actual subject matter of their conversation, which was sex. She looked up at him and gave him a smile that almost knocked him down. "I'm sure they do."

She was good, but she wasn't that good. He could see what she was doing. Maybe some other poor joker might have been taken in by her performance, but to him she was as transparent as glass.

He played along. It was sadistic, but he loved watching her get caught in her own trap. "I'll go down and get some," he said. "And we can finish what we started last night."

She got slowly to her feet.

He knew what she was wearing was no more than a costume to her, the black skirt, the tiny top—but knowing that made everything seem a little more dangerous, a little more erotic. Bad and sweet.

She crossed the carpet in her bare feet with their red toenails. She stopped in front of him and looked into his eyes. For the briefest of moments he thought that maybe she wasn't acting, maybe she wasn't working him. In her eyes he saw awareness of him as a man; in her eyes he saw attraction and the memory of something hot, something clearly sexual.

He kissed her.

It was meant to be a teasing thing, but as soon as her lips opened under his, his head began to reel. He could feel himself falling under her spell just like any other blind idiot.

He forced himself to pull away, to hold her at arm's length. Her eyes were half closed, her lips parted, exactly the way they'd been the night before, when he felt her tighten around his fingers. Her lipstick was smeared. He wiped at his own mouth.

"I'll be right back," he said, his voice sounding strained to his ears.

She didn't answer. She only swallowed and nodded.

As soon as Daniel left, Cleo pulled herself together, ignoring her rapidly beating heart. She stuffed her feet into the sandals, then grabbed her purse and swung the strap over her shoulder. On top of the TV were Daniel's car keys. She took them.

At the door she checked the peephole. All clear.

She stepped out the door and pulled in a sharp breath as Daniel materialized in front of her, strong fingers wrapping around her arm.

"I decided you might like to come with me," he said. "You know. To help me pick them out. I thought there might be a particular style you were partial to."

He'd never had any intention of leaving her by herself. He seemed to know her too well. Or was he just adept when it came to the criminal mind? And was that what she was? A criminal?

Yes, taking pay for services not rendered would put her in that category.

Not backing down, she looked him in the eye and said, "I don't have any preference about style. Just make sure you get the right size. I imagine small would be about right."

Did condoms even come in sizes? She didn't know, but it didn't matter. From the look on his face, she'd gotten her point across. People always said that guys were hung up on size. What better way to get him back than an attack on his attributes?

"Small?" he said, quite obviously hoping he'd heard wrong.

She lifted her eyebrows, a silent but reluctant assent. *Yes. 'Fraid so.*

Worry and insecurity seeped into his eyes. She had to bite the inside of her mouth to keep from smiling. They both knew she'd held him in her hands, and there had been nothing small about him. She couldn't believe how easily he was convinced otherwise.

"Does that bother you?" she asked, careful to keep her features neutral.

"No." He shrugged. "No."

He was almost as good at this as she was. It was as if they were standing in the hallway of the hotel, speaking their lines, playing parts.

"Don't worry. I've heard size doesn't really matter to women."

His expression said, *Yeah, right.*

"In fact—" This was dangerous water. Did she

want to go there? She'd told herself to forget about last night, and here she was, throwing it in his face. But the fact that she *could* turn it around, that she *could* throw it back in his face, was oh so satisfying.

"Last night I really didn't need . . . well, *it* at all." She pretended to give the subject some deep thought. "In fact, I probably didn't even need *you*."

There, she thought, watching him with supreme satisfaction. *It's erased*. He'd been so smug, thinking he'd really taken her somewhere, thinking she'd been totally under his control, wanting him to go down on her anytime, anywhere. Let him think that she had never wanted him or needed him.

The insecurity in his face dissolved and was quickly replaced by anger. She watched as a muscle twitched in his cheek. Keeping a grip on her arm, he stuck his card in the reader on the door behind her, waited for the green light, then opened the door, shoving her back inside.

At first she thought she'd gone too far, goaded him past his limit. Was he going to attack her? Force himself on her? Instead he shoved her away as if she sickened him. And that was what she'd been trying to do, wasn't it? To sicken him? To make sure there wasn't a replay of the previous night? She never wanted to find herself at his mercy again.

Never again.

Sex with Jordan hadn't been anything like that. It had never been that weak-in-the-knees, losing-control kind of thing. Together they had been more like two puppies snuggling in the sunlight. It hadn't been dark. It hadn't been mysterious. There had never been a need so great that it overshadowed common sense.

Daniel Sinclair was like the very town he came from. He looked harmless on the surface, but underneath there was something going on, something she didn't want any part of.

"Give me your purse."

When she didn't comply, he jerked it from her shoulder, opened it, unzipped the side pocket, and helped himself to her money, stuffing the roll into the front pocket of his Levi's.

This could still work, Cleo tried to reassure herself. She would do what she'd planned to do at the beginning: stay in Egypt awhile, make a satisfactory effort to try to find the key, then be on her way.

He shoved the purse back at her, saying, "Let's get the hell out of here." He cast a quick glance around the room, looking for anything they may have left. "What am I thinking?" he said with a rough laugh. "You probably already picked up everything that wasn't nailed down."

He surprised her by swinging around and grabbing her, cupping her chin in his palm, making her look directly at him, which she did with unflinching eyes.

"You think this is over," he said. "But it's not."

And then they left, taking the elevator to the lobby. Cleo hung back, playing the part of the respectful, dutiful wife, as Daniel paid for room service and the phone call. The person behind the counter kept looking at the front of Daniel's shirt, his eyes moving back and forth from the shirt to Daniel's face, as if trying to get the connection and failing. That was the beauty of it.

Cleo stood there watching, her arms straight in front of her, both hands gripping the handles of her purse, lightly swinging her hips back and forth.

About halfway to Egypt, Daniel slowed the car and pulled onto the shoulder of the interstate. Cleo, who'd been half dozing, came awake. Why were they stopping?

He got out, slammed the door, quickly rounded the car, and opened the passenger door. "Scoot over." When she didn't move, he gave her a light shove. "You drive."

"Maybe I don't want to. Maybe I don't like to drive. Maybe I only drove yesterday because you seemed a little out of it."

"For chrissake, don't start this again. Just scoot over and drive."

She would have put up more of a fight, but semis were blasting by, shaking the car, stirring up tornadoes of dirt and debris. She moved across to the other seat while he quickly took her place on the passenger side. She adjusted the seat and mirror, waited for an opening, then pulled the patrol car onto the highway.

"Should I really be driving this?" she asked. "I'm

not a police officer." It was probably a little late to mention that her driver's license had expired.

"Like you're really concerned with breaking the law."

"I just don't know why you wanted me to drive."

He was leaning with his elbow against the door, his hand to his forehead. He lifted his hand away and started using it for emphasis. "Because I have a fucking headache," he shouted. "Because you've given me a fucking migraine! Does that answer your question?"

She shot him a quick glance. "Want a couple of aspirin?" She hated to see anyone in pain, even Daniel Sinclair.

"What I want"—he was still talking with his hands, gesturing wildly—"is to get back to Egypt and dump you off at the police station. That's what I want." He tilted his seat so he was reclining. "Don't forget to take Sixty west," he said. Out of the corner of her eye, she saw him cross his arms over his chest. "We don't want to end up in Arkansas."

Cleo actually enjoyed being behind the wheel. She noticed she was passing a lot of people, and she checked the speedometer. Eighty-five. Whoops. She slowed to seventy-five, but a few minutes later the red needle had crept up to eighty-five again.

Two hours later she hit the outskirts of Egypt, where she pulled into The Palms, stopping in front of room number six. She put the car in park and cut the engine. Beside her, Daniel stirred.

"What are we doing at the motel?" His voice was thick and groggy.

"I want to change clothes before going to the police station."

He must have been too sleepy to argue. "Go ahead. I'll swing by the house and check on Beau. Then I'll be back to get you."

He had her money. He knew she wasn't going anywhere.

"Listen," she said, twisting in the seat, her left arm draped over the steering wheel, "let's just forget what happened at the hotel. Okay?" It had been hard for her to bring herself to ask him for anything. But what she was offering was a truce. He had to see that. And anybody with a shred of human decency would take her offer.

He stared at her with spoon-bending concentration. "Not in a million years."

11

There was no sign of Beau.

Daniel strode through the quiet house, shouting his brother's name.

He unlocked the patio door and checked outside. Premonition came to greet him, tail wagging. Daniel gave the dog a distracted rub on the head. "Where's Beau?" he asked.

Premonition sat on Daniel's foot, tail thumping the ground.

Daniel went back in the house, rechecking the kitchen in case Beau had left a note. The counter was empty.

Daniel hurried to the bedroom, peeled off the ridiculous T-shirt, and slipped into a wrinkled but tackiness-free cotton print shirt. He buttoned the buttons, tucked in the tails, then hurried out to his car.

Before picking up Cleo, Daniel took a swing down Main Street so he could check out Beau's usual haunts, slowing when he got to the Tastee Delight. No sign of Beau. The two picnic tables sitting in the shade of the awning were empty. He pulled up to the curb. Leaving the car and air conditioner running, he got out and went to the order window, tapping impatiently on the counter with his knuckles.

Someone appeared behind the glass. A man. About Daniel's height, wearing a blue and white Tastee Delight cap and a blue Tastee Delight shirt.

Beau.

"What the hell are you doing in there?" Daniel asked in disbelief.

Beau just grinned, proud as a new mama. "I work here."

"Since when?"

"Since today. I said this would be a neat place to work, and Matilda said I could start today."

"Matilda?"

"The manager."

"Is Matilda in there?"

"Yeah. You wanna talk to her?"

Damn right he did. "Yeah. Yeah, I do."

A moment later a woman with a serious face and a brown ponytail that fell to her waist appeared from somewhere in the back.

"This is my brother, Daniel," Beau told her.

"Hi." The word came out more as a question than a greeting.

"Can I talk to you a minute?"

"Sure." She glanced at Beau, obviously realizing that Daniel's impatience and irritation had to do with his brother. "Why don't you finish mopping?" she suggested to Beau.

As soon as Beau trotted off, Daniel leaned close to the screen. "What the hell's going on here?" he asked in a loud whisper.

Frown lines appeared between her brows. "What do you mean?"

"Hiring Beau."

"Beau's been coming here every day for the past two months. He knows every single item on the menu. He's clean. Is he *ever* clean. And he follows directions. He's meticulous. Everybody likes him. And he's enjoying himself. What is it you don't understand, Mr. Sinclair? Are you insinuating that I'm taking advantage of Beau? I'm paying him minimum wage, just like I pay every other new employee. After he's been here a month, that will go up, the way it does for everyone else."

"It's just—" Daniel scratched his head. He'd never thought about Beau having a job, making a living.

"I think you underestimate your brother," the woman said.

She was right. What was his problem? He should be glad that Beau had a job. Here he'd moved back to Egypt to take care of Beau, but Beau seemed to be getting along fine without him. Deep down, did he want Beau to be dependent on him? Was that was this was all about?

•   •   •

The motel room was every bit as bad as Cleo remembered, except that now it smelled like stale french fries, and her chopped-off hair was lying in a pile on the bathroom floor.

She threw away the stale fries, but for some reason she couldn't make herself throw away the hair. She scooped it off the floor and put it on top of the TV.

It was weird being back in the motel room, seeing the belongings she'd thought she would never see again. It was almost as if she'd left a part of herself behind and had come back to get it.

Not wanting to remain in the room any longer than she had to, she quickly changed clothes. She put on a white V-necked cotton tee and a pair of faded jeans that were ragged at the bottom and alarmingly loose around the waist. She was dropping weight.

While slipping into her sandals, she twisted her hair into a bun, then jabbed a wooden hair pick through it to hold it in place. She hoped Jo wouldn't be able to tell that she'd whacked off her hair.

After that, she gathered up a few tools of her trade and put them in a small bag.

When she'd first become interested in psychic phenomena, she tried all the aids. Although she taught herself to read runes and the tarot, she'd never felt anything other than a fraud. In fact, she'd come away from the lessons relieved and convinced that she had no power. That was until the child disappeared. But she hadn't used cards or stones to bring about the answer, to bring about the nightmare.

She pushed that thought out of her mind, replacing it with another: *If Mr. Daniel Sinclair wants a show, then I'll give him one.*

Daniel hadn't yet returned to pick her up. She took the opportunity to go to the gas station two blocks away in hopes of finding something she could eat. She ended up buying a loaf of white bread and a bottle of clear soda pop with the change she was able to scrounge from the bottom of her purse. In the motel she opened the pop. Then, sitting on the bed, she took out a slice of bread, carefully removed the crust, and slowly force-fed herself.

She was half done when she heard the sound of a car pulling up, followed by a knock at the door. She quickly put the half-eaten piece of bread back in the bread bag, sealed it with a twist tie, then hid the bread under some clothes in her suitcase. She picked up the bottle of pop, grabbed her bag of supplies, and headed out the door into the blazing sun, where Daniel was waiting, arms crossed at his chest, feet crossed at his booted ankles, one hip against the hood of his car, scowling.

He pushed away from the car and took his place behind the wheel while Cleo slid in the passenger side.

She could feel his muddled anger. His bad vibes were filling the car, invading her space.

Silently he pulled out of the weedy parking lot onto the two-lane highway.

"Was everything okay with Beau?" she asked.

"Fine," was his terse reply.

She sensed that he was preoccupied. "And Premonition?" she ventured, wanting her inquiry to sound casual, hoping to hide her anxiety.

"Fine, too," he said with distraction. "They're both fine." *So don't ask any more questions* were his unspoken words.

His preoccupation and moodiness didn't improve when they reached the police station.

"Shit," he muttered under his breath. "It looks like Jo's invited half the town to witness the sideshow."

It seemed he'd finally acknowledged her presence. "Are you calling me a sideshow?" she asked, her anger toward him building by the second. "I resent that."

"Let's not start this crap again."

"*You* started it. I'm just speaking up for myself."

His answer was a groan of misery, a sound that seemed to ask, *What did I ever do to deserve this?*

Because of the additional cars, they had to park halfway down the next block. Daniel cut the engine, then rubbed his forehead with his thumb and forefinger.

No wonder he had a headache, Cleo thought. He had enough tension in him to power an energy plant.

When they stepped inside the building's cool darkness, Cleo was relieved to find that there weren't as many people inside as she'd feared.

Jo immediately greeted her. "I want you to meet my good friends." She introduced Cleo to two women who could have been twins, they looked so much alike with their gray hair, pink tops, and tan orthopedic shoes. And Cleo couldn't help but notice that they had the same tightly permed hairdo as Jo.

Burton Campbell was there, along with Harvey Jamison. The former was all pleasant smiles, the latter scowling as much as Daniel. Parker was hovering nervously behind his desk.

"Daniel told us you went to St. Louis to pick up some supplies," Jo said. "We've been holding our breath, just waiting for you to get here. What is it you have in mind, dear?"

Daniel had lied about her bungled escape attempt? Why? Certainly not for her. He must have done it for Jo.

"Mr. Sinclair probably explained that I wasn't getting any kind of feelings or readings," she said, playing along with Daniel's explanation of her disappearance, "so I felt I needed some items to help move this along." She pulled out a small white candle. That was followed by incense, which she handed to Daniel. "Would you light one of these for me?" she asked, smiling sweetly. She'd gotten the incense at a special shop in Portland. It was some of the strongest she'd ever smelled.

He shot her a dark look, grabbed the sticks, and wandered away, presumably to find some matches.

"What did you get in St. Louis?" Jo asked.

"Candles," Cleo said, thinking quickly.

"We could have found candles here in town," Jo

said. "You didn't need to go all the way to St. Louis."

"These are special candles. They've, uh, been anointed with powerful herbs so that they'll hold energy. And they were blessed by the light of the full moon."

From somewhere behind her Daniel let out a snort. At the very same time the sweet smell of frankincense drifted over her shoulder.

"Imagine that," Jo said, her voice full of awe.

"I'm glad you've assembled a group of people." Cleo looked around. "Four women and four men. It will give us the balance we need." One thing she could really do if the need arose was bullshit.

"Count me out," Daniel said. "I'm just the wheels. I'm just here to haul Miss Clara Voiyant around."

"You have to stay," Jo said. "Cleo said we need four men."

"You know how I feel about this stuff."

"So what if you don't believe in it?" Jo said. "I don't think that's a requirement." She looked at Cleo for help. "Is it?"

Cleo smiled, while inside she was seething about the sarcastic Clara Voiyant business. "No. We just need his presence." There was no way she was letting him leave, not after hauling her back here.

"That's all you're getting," he said. "A body."

Cleo drifted close to him and whispered, "I never wanted your mind anyway."

Before he could answer, before she could even see his reaction, she swung back to the group as they waited patiently and solemnly for instructions.

"Pull all of the shades," she told them. "We want it to be as dark in here as possible." While they scrambled to darken the room, Cleo lit the candle and put it on the floor in the center of the room.

Jo's friends clapped their hands and giggled in excitement while the men shuffled their feet, looking nervous, all except for Dr. Campbell, who just kept smiling like some idiot salesman.

"Now we'll sit cross-legged around the candle and hold hands."

"Ooh, a séance," Jo said.

"For chrissake," Daniel muttered.

"A séance?" Dr. Campbell asked, his smile wavering.

"Oh, for cryin' out loud," Harvey said, echoing Daniel's sentiments.

There wasn't a peep out of Parker.

"Not really a séance, but kind of like one," Cleo explained, ad-libbing as she went. "It's the same principle. I will be kind of like the lightning rod. We use our combined concentration to set up an energy field that I hope will bring me a vision.

"Okay: man, woman, man, woman. We want to alternate." They joined hands and made a circle around the candle, with Daniel somehow ending up on her left, Harvey on her right. They spread out, dropped hands, then tried to sit down on the floor.

"I don't believe I've sat cross-legged since I was a child," one of the twins said.

"Sitting cross-legged channels the energy better,

but if you can't do it, that's okay," Cleo said, taking pity on the women. "We have enough people that it shouldn't·matter. In fact, it might be a good idea to not have such a strongly knit circle."

That let the twins off the hook, and they both decided it might be a little more ladylike to sit with their knees together, legs bent to one side. "My mother always said ladies don't sit with their legs crossed. It's vulgar. Oh." She put a hand to her mouth. "I didn't mean that anybody here is vulgar. It's just that it wasn't appropriate when I was growing up."

"All right, now everybody join hands and concentrate on the key," Cleo instructed. "Stare at the candle flame and visualize the key in your mind." She looked around the circle. Everyone was staring at the candle flame—everyone except Daniel. He was staring at her. She gave his hand an impatient squeeze and nodded toward the center of the circle. "*Everyone* stare at the candle."

His eyebrows drew together and he pursed his lips, adequately conveying his contempt for the entire project. But he turned his face toward the flickering flame.

Cleo let her voice become low and hypnotic. "Just watch the flame and think about the key. Just think about the key. Visualize the key in your mind. When you think you're ready, let your eyes fall closed. Slowly, slowly . . . Now, with your eyes closed, you should still be able to see the flame. And within that flame, the key."

Cleo hadn't tried to hypnotize herself in years, not since she'd lived in Madison, Wisconsin, after Jordan died. Today actual hypnosis was the furthest thing from her mind. She only intended to use the basic technique to give everyone a thrill. A ceremony that involved candles and sitting cross-legged on the floor seemed the very thing Daniel would despise, so it was the very thing she was using to get back at him.

But instead of being the one in control of the situation, the candle flame took over. It pulled her in, sucked her in, swallowed her. It wasn't like the time in Madison. She didn't feel transported. Instead she felt heavy, incredibly heavy . . . sleepy . . . so sleepy . . .

Her eyelids drifted shut, her breathing became even and rhythmic. And suddenly she was asleep. Asleep while she was awake.

Walking down a road.

Barefoot. There were her red toenails. And the bump on her middle toe, a souvenir of the time she'd broken it playing softball with no shoes.

A barn.

A big red barn.

With a rusty weathervane at the top.

Weathervanes were cool. But for some reason she didn't like this one.

The weathervane was metal, in the shape of a pig. And it creaked, turning this way and that even though she could feel no breeze against her skin or hear any rustling of dead weeds along the side of the road.

Suddenly the dream changed.

Suddenly she was inside the barn.

Part of the roof had been ripped away, leaving a gaping, jagged hole. She looked up. Through the hole she saw dark, roiling clouds.

Wake up, she told herself just the way she did when she was having the pumpkin dream. *Open your eyes. All you have to do is open your eyes and it will be over. All you have to do is open your eyes and you'll be safe.*

But she couldn't open her eyes.

A hand pressed against the back of her head, making her look at something on the ground.

And then suddenly a shovel was in her hand. She knew she was supposed to dig in the spot right in front of her bare feet with red nail polish.

She dug.

She didn't want to, but she had no choice.

The shovel hit something solid.

She leaned over and peered into the dark pit.

At the bottom of the hole was a pumpkin.

A broken, smashed pumpkin.

No. Oh, God, no.

She screamed and flung herself away, smacking the back of her head on something hard. And then everything turned black.

12

Cleo regained consciousness in slow stages. First there was a gradually increasing awareness of her surroundings. Then came the far-off drone of voices, a drone that slowly became more distinct until she could finally distinguish one person from another.

There was Jo's voice, breathless and worried, coming from nearby, as if she stood directly over Cleo.

"Are you all right, dear?"

"Give her some air. She's just fainted." Dr. Campbell.

And the twins, shocked and puzzled. "Is she supposed to do that?"

Another voice she couldn't quite place. Parker? "I don't know if we should have stopped holding hands. It might not be a good idea to break the circle."

"For chrissake," another voice broke in.

Daniel.

"Can't you see she's just putting on a damn show? What the hell's the matter with you people?" His voice shook with frustration and anger. "The woman's an accomplished actress. A con artist."

"How can you say that?" Jo again. "Look how pale her skin is."

"Her skin is always pale. And it's so damn dark in here. Somebody blow out that candle."

He moved away, the soles of his hiking boots ringing against the wooden floor, making it shudder beneath her cheek. Awareness of the hard surface upon which she lay finally gave her a sense of where she was.

Egypt, Missouri. The police station.

With Daniel Sinclair raving like a lunatic, making her head hurt even more.

She smelled smoke, the kind of smoke a candle makes when it's blown out. That sensory stimulation was followed by one of sound, of window blinds being angrily pulled open. Through closed eyelids, Cleo perceived the room changing, becoming bigger, brighter. She felt a breeze on her face. She moaned and slowly opened her eyes.

Jo was leaning over her, fanning Cleo with a magazine. "How are you feeling?" Jo asked. "Better?"

Cleo nodded. With Jo's help, she managed to sit up. Wrong move. Her stomach churned. An acid taste gathered in the back of her throat.

"Bathroom," she managed to whisper.

Immediately grasping the urgency of the situation, Jo shoved a wastebasket in Cleo's face. Cleo wasn't going to throw up in front of an audience if she could help it. That wasn't going to be part of the show.

She shoved herself to her feet and grabbed the metal wastebasket from Jo. Then, with the wastebasket clutched to her chest, she bolted down a long hallway, Jo keeping one arm around her waist, a hand to her elbow, steering her in the direction of the bathroom.

As soon as Cleo spotted the toilet, she slipped out of Jo's grasp, slammed the door in the woman's face, and dropped to her knees. She threw up, hitting her target. When she was done relieving herself of a partially digested slice of white bread and a bottle of soda, she flushed the toilet. Then she pushed herself away to sit with her back against the wall, her forehead against her knees, her arms wrapped around her legs.

What happened out there?

There was something wrong with her. Really, really wrong with her.

I'm crazy.

No.

Outside the closed door, she heard voices—an argument. It seemed Daniel Sinclair wanted to open the door; Jo was trying to keep him from achieving that goal.

Without looking up, Cleo heard the door open, then close. She heard the sound of a metal lock sliding into place.

"Well," Daniel said from somewhere up above her. "It seems like we're always ending up in bathrooms together."

What's wrong with me?

"What was all that about out there? Was it to get back at me?"

There was a knock on the door. The doorknob rattled. "Open this door right now, Daniel Sinclair." It was Jo's voice, muffled by the door.

I'm scared.

"You can quit the act. There's nobody here but you and me."

I'm so damn scared.

"Did you hear me?" Strong hands wrapped around her arms, pulling them away from her face.

Dazed, unable to make any sense out of what he was saying, she lifted her head. Through a watery blur she saw him, saw his furrowed brow, saw his startling blue eyes, his mouth, which had felt so wonderful pressed to hers.

He's mad at me. It was what she wanted, wasn't it? *He hates me.* Why should she care?

As she watched, she saw his anger dissolve, replaced by puzzlement, doubt.

She lifted a trembling hand to her face. Her cheek was wet. Tears. Tears were pouring down her face, running into her mouth. She'd told him a lot of lies. She felt bad about that. Now, for some reason, she wanted to tell him the truth. She wanted him to be her friend.

She pressed her fingers to her lips, trying to get her mouth to stop trembling, but she couldn't. Shock waves came from deep inside, shuddering out to her extremities. She told him the truth in a hushed whisper, in a rush of trembling. "I don't know what's happening to me."

He had only one thing to say to that. "Shit." But once apparently wasn't enough. He said it again. "Oh, shit."

Daniel felt as though somebody had slammed a fist into his gut. While he struggled to pull himself back together and figure out what was going on, he continued to stare at Cleo.

Her face was wet, her lips swollen and trembling. He'd never seen a person's face so wet from tears. Was it all a part of her act? No, nobody could look that lost, that miserable. But just in case, he reached out, wiped a finger across her cheek, then stuck his wet finger in his mouth.

Salt. The tears—they were real.

"Why'd you do that?"

"What?"

"Wipe your finger on my face, then stick your finger in your mouth."

He tried to think of something brilliant, but a good excuse eluded him.

Meanwhile, a transformation was taking place before his eyes. The misery vanished from her face, to be replaced by anger. "You ass." She placed both hands on his shoulders and shoved, her strength taking him by surprise. He tumbled backward and hit his head on the porcelain sink. "Ow!"

His cry of pain didn't bring her any remorse—that was quite apparent from the look on her face. She slapped his leg. "You were checking to see if my tears were real."

"Is everything okay in there?" The door rattled. "I thought I heard someone fall. Are you all right, Cleo? Daniel isn't trying to manhandle you, is he?"

At the moment Daniel was wedged half under the sink, the drainpipe poking his spine, one arm raised in case Cleo decided to smack him again.

"Everything's fine," Cleo said loudly, keeping her eyes on Daniel. Her hair was slipping from its moorings, a wooden stick—a chopstick kind of thing, only shorter and with a point at one end—and was creeping down her neck.

"Your hair," he said, waving a couple of fingers in the direction of the slide, hoping to distract her so he could get to his feet and get the hell out of there.

"What about my hair?" She leaned close. Jabbing a finger into his leg with every syllable, she said, "Other than the fact that I cut it for no reason."

He pointed again. "It's doing weird shit."

Gravity won. The stick jumped ship and clattered to the tiled floor. At the same time, her hair uncoiled to hang on either side of her face in all its ragged, uneven glory.

"There's a lady in town," he said, remembering how beautiful her long hair had been, thinking it was none of his business, "who used to cut my mother's hair—"

"Shut up!" She shoved at his knee, but she didn't slap him. Instead she reached up and twisted her hair back into place, picked up the stick, and shoved it through the bundle she'd made on the back of her head. And it stayed. The whole business stayed.

Amazing.

Without moving out from under the sink, he reached up, feeling along the cold porcelain until his fingers came in contact with the paper towels he knew were there. He grabbed a couple and handed them to her. He had the feeling she would have thrown them down if she hadn't needed them so much. She wiped her face and blew her nose. *Then* she bundled up the paper towels and tossed them in his face. So that's how you do that.

She got to her feet, reached to unlock the door, swung it open, stepped over him, and left the room.

He scrambled to his feet and followed.

Cleo's appearance was greeted by excitement and questions. Everybody wanted to know what had happened, and especially if she'd learned anything about the missing key. While she and Daniel had been ensconced in the bathroom, someone had blown out the incense and picked up the candle.

"What happened?" Jo asked. "Did you see anything?"

Cleo wanted to forget about what had happened, but she could see nobody was going to let her. And why not use the nightmare—because she was convinced that was what it was—to send them scurrying in quest of the key? A barn—there had to be lots of barns around. She rather liked the thought of Daniel driving around the county, digging around in dark, cobwebby barns in this smothering heat.

Now that it was all over, now that she was thinking more clearly, she figured out why she'd blacked out. It was easy. Hardly a morsel of food had passed her lips since her arrival in Egypt. And what she'd seen was just a continuation of her old nightmare. Once she got out of Egypt, once she got out of that awful motel, things would return to normal.

Everyone was waiting for an answer to Jo's question. Aware of Daniel just behind her, she said, "Yes, I did see something."

Jo let out a gasp. The twins clapped their hands and kind of bounced a little. Harvey let out a snort. Parker said nothing, and Dr. Campbell took her by the elbow. "Sit down and tell us about it." He led her to a cozy spot in the corner of the room, where she took a seat on a soft, fabric-covered chair, the séance group gathering around her, all but Daniel, who perched a hip on the corner of Parker's desk, his arms crossed over his chest.

"I saw a road," Cleo began. "A gravel road."

"Yes?" Jo asked.

Cleo knew she could have made up anything, but she went ahead and stuck to the dream, hoping to convey its eerie mood, thus lending credibility to her story. "Then the road turned to dirt." She concentrated, trying to remember. "Dirt with grass growing in the middle, and weeds on either side." In her mind, Cleo pictured the road. She remembered her red toenails. And something she hadn't seen in the dream: dry dust from the road sifting over them, covering her bare feet in a fine powder. She looked up. Through the tangle of weeds was the peak of a barn.

"A barn," she said. "I saw a barn."

Behind her, Daniel let out a low curse. Jo waved her hand at him, irritated by his interruption.

"A red barn. It was old. I don't think it was being used. There was a feeling of abandonment to it."

Her heart was racing. She didn't want to go any closer.

"On top of the barn was a weathervane." She remembered the way it creaked, turning slowly in one direction, then another. "It had a pig on it."

She remembered going inside, remembered the shovel, remembered digging, remembered the horror that had gripped her.

"Is that everything?" Jo asked.

Fifteen seconds ticked by before Cleo answered. "Yes. That's everything." The rest was too personal. The rest had nothing to do with them. It was her own nightmare, the nightmare she carried in her soul. It had nothing to do with them.

"Well, that gives us a place to start," Jo said, for the first time sounding not quite as enthused. "I must admit I was hoping for something a little more precise. Are you sure you didn't see anything *inside* the barn?" she asked hopefully.

Cleo shook her head.

"This has gone far enough," Daniel said. "Can't

you see she's scamming you? She's going to send us off on a wild-goose chase so that she can skip town. A barn? Come on. There are hundreds of abandoned barns around here. And the weathervane. Half of them have pigs on them. Because half the farmers around here used to raise hogs." He made a pleading motion with one hand. "Come on, Jo. Open your eyes."

Dr. Campbell cleared his throat, then offered his opinion. "I have to agree, Jo. It's all a little vague."

"I thought you were all for this," Daniel said.

"I was, but that was before. We don't want people laughing at us. We don't want to end up on the national news with the entire country laughing at us."

Jo was quiet, her brow furrowed in thought. She turned back to Cleo. "You wouldn't skip town, would you?" It was apparent that her confidence in Cleo was slipping fast. Her question was more of a plea. She was begging Cleo to say no. "You wouldn't run out like that—would you?"

Cleo swallowed, her gaze going from Jo to Daniel. She could see in his eyes that if she didn't tell Jo, he would. "Actually," she said, not looking at anyone, drawing small nervous circles on the arm of the green paisley-print chair, "I already skipped town once." Her voice dropped. "Daniel came after me and brought me back."

"Oh."

With that one short word, Jo managed to convey just how crushed she was.

Cleo felt horrible. How could she have done such a thing to such an open, trusting person?

"Was anything that happened here real?" Jo asked.

"The barn. I did see a barn. I swear."

"Well," Jo said, still obviously trying to take in the extent of Cleo's deception, "I guess that's something."

Cleo couldn't stay there any longer. She pushed herself out of the chair. Without looking to the left or right, she aimed herself in the direction of the door. People fell away, letting her through. Without stopping to get her belongings, she headed for the door, shoving it open, stepping out into the bright sun, the smothering heat. She hurried down the steps, then turned left on the sidewalk, knowing Beau and Daniel lived over there somewhere. She would leave. How, she wasn't sure. She had approximately thirty-five cents to her name, give or take a few pennies. She didn't like to hitchhike—it was dangerous and degrading—but she would do it.

She'd gone perhaps two blocks when she heard a car pull up beside her. She didn't look to see who it was. Instead she kept walking, her eyes focused straight ahead. The car slowed, keeping pace with her.

Daniel. She felt sure it was Daniel.

He honked.

The ass!

She kept walking.

The car stopped. She heard a door slam, then Daniel was running to catch up with her—something he did very easily. He jumped in front of her and grabbed her by both arms, walking backward as she continued to walk forward.

"Hold up," he said, a little out of breath.

"Don't worry. I'm not going to put up a tent and open a palm-reading shop on Main Street. She had to get Premonition. She *needed* Premonition. How could she have ever thought of leaving him? She must have been delusional, temporarily insane. "I'm going to your house to get my dog, and then I'm leaving."

"That's what I wanted to talk to you about. Jo doesn't want you to leave."

She stopped.

He stopped.

"She wants you to stay. She wants you to try it again."

"That's ridiculous." She put an arm up and shoved her way past him to continue walking. He fell into step beside her.

He pulled out his billfold, extracted two twenty-dollar bills, and handed them to her. "Tomorrow. She wants to try it again tomorrow. In the meantime—" He held the money in front of her. "Take it." He shook it, but she still refused. "You have to eat."

Truer words were never spoken. She snatched the money and stuffed it into the front pocket of her jeans.

"I want to get my dog." She'd left him behind once. She couldn't do it a second time.

The sun was so bright that whenever they stepped under the shade of a tree, they were plunged into cool darkness.

"Let me give you a ride back to the motel, then I'll pick you up later to get your dog."

"What's wrong with now?"

"Beau's not home. He should be there when you get the dog. I don't want him to come home and find him gone."

She could understand that. What she didn't understand was why Jo wanted her to stay after everything that had happened. She suddenly realized they were still walking away from Daniel's car. She stopped. He stopped. "I don't get it," she said, looking up at him. "Why does she want me to come back?"

"That's the way Jo is. She believes in giving people second chances."

"Unlike you."

"That's right. Unlike me."

13

Cleo sat on the edge of the bed, staring at the stained wall with its greasy handprints. She tried to make sense out of her feelings, but like so many things in her life, it was too hard, too complex. She found herself thinking back to a time she didn't like to remember, to a past that hadn't been photo-album perfect. . . .

People said they were the ideal family. A mother, a father, two children—a boy and a girl. They went to church as a family. They went to Bible school and the county fair as a family. They were *involved*. But it was all a carefully constructed front.

Cleo's father, Ben Tyler, had been born into wealth, coming from an impressive lineage of town founders, state politicians, and businessmen. But unlike his outgoing father and grandfather, Ben Tyler had possessed a crippling shyness, making him a perfect target for Cleo's mother, Ruth Dixon.

The Dixons were the most undesirable of the

undesirables in the tightly knit community of Norfolk, Indiana. None of the Dixon men worked. They were too busy lying and cheating and drinking.

Marrying Ben Tyler and his old money gave Ruth the respect and the community status she craved. And while she worked to continually upgrade herself, Ben dissolved into the background to become the shadow Cleo always thought of as her father.

Ruth's standing in the community became an obsession, a driving force behind everything the woman did and thought. So when Cleo came home from college that first Christmas with a boyfriend who wasn't from that shining inner circle, who wasn't even from the community of Norfolk *at all*, things got ugly. Her mother turned on her and on poor unsuspecting Jordan. Jordan, who made Cleo laugh, who was the best thing that had ever happened to her.

Ruth pulled her daughter aside and told her that Jordan wouldn't do at all.

The longer Cleo lived, the more she came to realize that everybody had an agenda, some more self-serving than others. At the moment when Ruth had taken Cleo aside to tell her that Jordan wouldn't do, a fog lifted and Cleo finally understood her mother— and was horrified by what she saw. Ruth Tyler's agenda had always been for her children to make her look good to her friends and the people in the community. Her children existed for the purpose of upgrading her social standing. And of course, dating someone from beyond the community did nothing toward that end, because in a small town outsiders didn't get you any points.

"That's too bad," Cleo had answered when her mother told her Jordan wouldn't do. "Because we're moving in together."

"B-But—" Ruth stammered, indignant, disbelieving. "I forbid it. And you have to do what I tell you. I'm your mother. I've done everything for you. Everything!"

It was true. As children, Cleo and her brother had been embarrassingly pampered. Later, Cleo's shrink had explained that the spoiling was her mother's way of keeping her children dependent on her, making them feel incapable of taking care of themselves. While Ruth had loved and doted on the children Cleo and Adrian had been, the adults they became were beyond her grasp. Ruth Tyler seemed to resent the grown-ups who had taken her children's place.

"It's Jordan or me," Ruth had announced, confident of her rank.

For Cleo, the choice was easy.

Cleo walked out of her parents' home that day and didn't return until a year and a half later, when her father slipped out of the world as quietly as he'd lived in it. After the funeral, Ruth tried to talk Cleo into moving back home, going through the usual guilt manipulations, but they no longer worked.

The funeral would have been easier to bear if only Adrian had been there. He would have come if Cleo had begged him, but the last thing she wanted was to make him do something out of guilt. He'd had enough of that in his life. They both had.

"I'm not going, Cleo," Adrian had quietly told her when she'd called with the news of their father's death. "She'll think I'm going for her. You know, I used to resent the way Dad wouldn't stand up to her, but now I realize he couldn't. He wasn't that kind of person. He wasn't a steamroller." The conversation drifted back to the funeral. "No, it's just between me and Dad. And that's the way I want to keep it."

Cleo cried right there on the telephone. But it wasn't because she missed her father. How could you miss somebody you'd never even known? No, she cried because she hadn't known him.

"I'm sorry," Adrian told her.

"Make a lot of noise," she said. What she meant but couldn't say was, *Don't waste your life.* "You just be sure to make a lot of noise."

If Adrian didn't understand her, that was okay. She could say things like that to him. She could say anything.

There might have been some harsh words spoken the day of the funeral; Cleo couldn't remember. But when Cleo left, she wondered if she would ever see her hometown again.

She hoped not.

Six months later, however, she had the accident that left her with a broken arm and cracked pelvis. She had nowhere else to go when she left the hospital but home.

The thing that was the most difficult to take was her mother's obvious pleasure at the turn of events. She was *glad* Jordan had died. She kept going on and on about how nice it was to have Cleo to herself, and how things never would have worked out for Cleo and Jordan. "In two years you would have had a toddler, with maybe another child on the way, and he'd be long gone," she told Cleo one morning as they sat across from each other eating breakfast in the very kitchen where Cleo had played at her mother's feet as a small child.

Cleo's toast stuck in her throat. She looked at her mother, thinking she couldn't have heard right. But she had.

"It was destiny," Ruth said. "Destiny stepping in and taking charge."

"Mother, I *loved* Jordan. And I'll probably never be able to have those children you're talking about." She'd been two months pregnant at the time of the accident. "I had a miscarriage, remember?" The bleeding wouldn't stop, and when the doctors were finished with her, she'd been told that it was doubtful she'd be able to have any more children.

"The miscarriage was a blessing, since you weren't even married," Ruth said. "It was all for the best. There are other men out there. And children . . . well." She gave Cleo a penetrating look. "Children are a heartache."

For the first time since returning home, Cleo felt anger breaking through the blessed numbness.

Seeing it, Ruth continued. "Of course, if you're so set on having children, you could adopt. But it takes a long time to get a white baby. That's what I've heard, anyway. And you'd have to have a white baby. But then there's also that nice Grant Cummings, who owns the lumberyard. His wife left him with three kids to take care of. Still, I always imagined you married to a doctor. . . ."

I have to get out of here.

It was the first clear thought Cleo had had since the accident. And when it came, she couldn't let it go. She recognized it as truth, as a very important truth. If she was ever to find Cleo again, she had to leave.

Noticing that her daughter wasn't eating, Ruth reached across the table, spooned a glob of strawberry preserves on her toast, and began spreading it for her. "Here you go. You always liked my strawberry preserves."

"Mother, I'm full. I don't want any more."

Ruth wouldn't listen. Had she ever listened?

She just kept spreading the preserves as if Cleo had never spoken. When she finished with the second piece, she put down the knife and pushed the plate closer the Cleo.

"There you go."

"I can't eat it."

"Why?"

"I told you, I'm full. Don't you ever listen?"

"Don't you like my strawberry preserves? I made them just for you. When you were little . . ." Her face

lit up, giving Cleo a brief glimpse of the love she had
showered upon Cleo as a child. "I remember how you
were always in the garden, eating strawberries. You
used to pull that little wagon with a stuffed animal in
it, and you'd go out and pick strawberries. And then
you'd bring them back in, and we would wash them,
and sit here at this table and have them with cream.
Do you remember?"

"Yes," Cleo said with a sigh. They'd had this conversation a thousand times. The problem was, Cleo
was no longer that little girl whose mother was her
entire world. And then she spoke the words she knew
would set her mother off. "I'm leaving tomorrow,"
Cleo stated, not a trace of emotion in her voice or in
her heart. It was just something she knew she had to
do. "I'm going back to Madison."

Ruth shook her head. "What you need to do is
move out of that apartment and come back home. You
can't take care of yourself when you're well—how are
you going to take care of yourself with your injuries?"

"I'm twenty years old."

"You can't take care of yourself."

"I'm leaving tomorrow."

"I won't allow it."

Cleo pressed her lips together. There was no use
arguing. She would simply leave.

And she did.

She called a cab to take her to the bus station. All
the while, Ruth screamed at her, following her around
the house as Cleo gathered up her things, following

her out the door to the end of the walk where she went to wait for the cab. But never helping in any way. No, Ruth Tyler would never help her daughter leave.

The cab pulled up and the driver put Cleo's suitcase in the trunk, casting nervous glances at both women as he skirted the car's fender. And then Cleo was sitting in the backseat. Through the closed window, she saw her mother standing on the sidewalk, her face a mask of rage.

And Cleo thought, *That person is my mother. That selfish, horrible person is my mother.*

Yes, people said they were the perfect family.

Back in Madison, Wisconsin, at the second-floor apartment she'd shared with Jordan, Cleo opened the door to a pile of mail on the floor, most of it addressed to Jordan. Not far away was a piece of dried toast with a bite taken out. On the night of the accident, before they left to see *The Rocky Horror Picture Show*, Cleo had laughingly fed him the piece of toast as if it were wedding cake. He'd taken a bite, then grabbed her and lifted her off her feet, the toast dropping to the floor unnoticed.

One day shortly after her return to Madison, Jordan's parents came by to pick up his belongings. They packed, often grabbing things that weren't Jordan's while Cleo numbly and silently watched. They asked her how school was going, and she said it was okay, even though she'd dropped out. She wondered if she should tell them about the baby, but decided not to. It was too hard to put it all together, and it would just make things more unbearable for them.

Cleo got to the point where she left the apartment only to get her prescription pain pills. One of those times, when she was walking home from the pharmacy, she passed the library, stopped, and went inside.

She walked up and down the aisle, staring blankly at titles, until she came across a book on clairvoyance, *Talking to the Dead*. And another one, *Transcending Time and Space*.

Cleo checked out both books, along with a few others on similar subjects.

She read the books over and over, absorbing the information like a sponge. And when she was done, she went in search of more knowledge. She found everything she could on the subject of speaking to the dead. It was what she needed. It was the reason she'd been drawn to the library, to find the books that would lead her back to Jordan. More than anything, she wanted to talk to him, needed to talk to him. She wanted to tell him she was sorry for the fight they'd had. . . .

After it was over, she could never be completely certain if it had really happened, or if she'd somehow put herself into a sort of dream state and imagined the entire thing.

The first step was self-hypnosis.

Night after night she practiced faithfully, carefully following the instructions. She would sit on the floor in the living room of the one-bedroom apartment, light a large white candle, and stare at the flickering flame, going through the hypnotic steps. It got to the point where she could put herself into a trance almost instantly. But that was all she could do. Until one night . . .

As she felt herself slipping away, she repeated Jordan's name over and over, her lips moving silently. In her mind's eye she pictured his face, willing him to come to her.

And then it happened.

There was a huge roaring in her head. The room spun. It seemed as if she were being sucked through a dark tunnel.

Then everything stopped.

Quiet. It was like a movie with no sound, except she was in the movie.

She found herself standing by the side of a road. It was dark. It was raining. Behind her was a narrow bridge. In front of her, in the distance, stood a two-story house with lighted Halloween decorations. In the distance, past the house, a car was moving toward her, the headlight beams cutting through the rain.

Cleo stood there, rooted to the spot where the road curved sharply into a bridge. As she watched, the car came closer. She tried to step back, but she couldn't lift her feet. Her eyes wouldn't close. Suddenly the car was almost upon her. Its headlights reflected off her white shirt. She saw the driver's face, saw his look of surprise and heard his cry of alarm. In his haste to miss her, he jerked the wheel. The car skidded, the rear end coming around. There was a crash, a grinding and squeaking of metal, the sound of shattering glass. The driver's side had taken most of the impact, hitting the cement footing straight on.

The silence rang in her ears.

Cleo tried to move. This time she was able to take a step. Then another, until she was somehow beside the car, looking in.

There were two people inside.

Jordan and Cleo.

Cleo came to on the hard wooden floor of her apartment. Her head hurt, her eyes hurt, her entire body hurt. She blinked, and blinked again, struggling to bring the candle into focus. It had gone out. All that was left was a puddle of wax with a square piece of metal in the center that had held the wick.

An acid taste was collecting in the back of her throat, a familiar sensation she couldn't place, a portent of something . . . but what? The answer hit like lightning.

She was going to throw up.

She lurched to her feet. With the floor tilting like the deck of a ship, she staggered to the bathroom, making it just in time. Afterward she got a drink, half crawled from the room, and dragged herself into bed. She didn't wake up until the next day.

Remembering what had happened when she was in the trance was nothing like trying to remember a dream. A dream was always vivid right after you woke up, but then quickly faded until it became almost impossible to recall. This was different. Very different. It was like remembering something she'd done the day before. Something she'd *really done*.

My God, she thought. *What if I made it happen? What if I killed Jordan and our baby?* Had he seen her standing there and swerved to avoid her?

Cleo put a trembling hand to her mouth, letting out a sound that was half cry, half sob. She thought back to the night of the crash, to a scene she'd replayed in her head again and again. They were in the car on their way home. They were arguing about cleaning the apartment. Jordan didn't do his share. In fact, he never did anything. They were both working and going to school, so it was only right that they share the household chores. Jordan always said he would help, but when his turn came, he never seemed to have the time, and Cleo always ended up doing his work, too.

At one point in the argument Jordan had glanced over at her, then back at the road. It was the briefest of seconds. But when he looked back up, he let out a cry, as if something beyond the car had startled him. Cleo thought she saw a flash of white; then the cement wall was directly in front of them.

Minutes later Jordan had taken his final breath.

With the last of her money, Cleo bought a supply of candles and tried the trance again.

Nothing happened.

She tried again and again. For two weeks.

Nothing.

Not a damn thing.

During that time the phone rang and rang and rang, until she jerked the cord out of the wall, effectively silencing it. During that time she forgot to shower, and forgot to wash her hair, and forgot to eat.

And then one day there was so much knocking on the door that it scared her. It was angry knocking. Furious knocking.

She didn't answer it. She didn't dare go to the door.

The knocking stopped. Footsteps moved back down the stairs. A short time later she heard a key turning in the lock. The door opened, then caught, stopped by the safety chain. Through that three-inch opening, someone shouted. A man's voice. A familiar voice.

"Adrian?" She got to her feet but didn't move toward the door. "Adrian, is that you?"

"Cleo, unlock the door!"

"What are you doing here?" He lived in Seattle. Seattle was a long way from Madison, Wisconsin.

"I've been trying to call you. Open up!"

It took her a while—she was so weak—but she finally got the damn chain unfastened. Normally Adrian would have hugged her, especially since they hadn't seen each other in almost a year. It seemed as if he started to, but then stopped. She saw the shock go through him.

"Christ," he mumbled.

Cleo put a hand to her hair. It was matted and tangled. She looked down. She was wearing a long-sleeved top that had once been white but was now smudged with smoke from the candle. It was stretched out, as if she'd been wearing it a long time. Her jeans were hanging on her hips, her bare, bony toes poking out under the frayed hem.

He came in and quietly closed the door, as if he thought the sound of the latch might set her off. Adrian wasn't a big person, not much bigger than Cleo herself, but when he walked into that room there was something huge about him, something almost bigger than life.

She was so proud of him.

She was so glad he was her brother.

They had been through a war together, the battle of growing up, of finding themselves, of making sense of the senseless. They'd been through a massacre and survived.

Adrian grasped her gently by both arms. "I came to get you," he said, speaking slowly.

She nodded, wondering what the hell he was talking about and where he was taking her.

"You're going to come back to Seattle with me."

"Seattle?"

"Yes."

"I can't." She couldn't leave this room. It was the place where she'd made contact. It was part of the equation.

He looked around at the mess, the candle wax on the floor, at Cleo. "What have you been doing?"

She smiled a little, remembering. "Transcending time and space." Adrian would understand. Adrian would be proud of her.

She didn't know how it happened, but suddenly she was sitting at the kitchen counter with a bowl of soup in front of her. It was cream-colored, with flecks of something in it.

"Eat," Adrian commanded.

She stared at it. And stared some more. *What were those things?*

While she stared into the bowl, she felt him lift her hand, felt him wrap her fingers around the cold metal of a spoon.

"Eat," he repeated. "Or I'll force-feed you."

And he would.

So she ate, trying to avoid the dark things. She was doing pretty well, until she got about halfway done and the concentration of dark things began to overpower the liquid. She accidentally got a dark thing.

It had a strong taste.

A mushy texture.

Mushy . . . mushroom. She was eating mushroom soup.

The spoon clattered to the floor as she ran for the bathroom to throw up.

That was the beginning of Cleo's eating problems.

Adrian helped her pack up her stuff. Actually, Adrian did most of it. Cleo just sat staring at nothing.

She didn't know why he was going to all this trouble. "I can't leave," Cleo told him.

"You can't stay."

He was her older brother. He knew about such things. She nodded, realizing he was right. At least for the moment.

While they packed, he discovered that she would drink milkshakes if they didn't have any pieces of anything in them. So he plied her with shakes until she got diarrhea and had to stay in the bathroom half a day.

Two days after his arrival, all of her belongings were packed and put in storage, and they were on a flight to Seattle.

She woke up the next morning to find herself face-to-face with a small child who stood staring at her, a wet finger dangling from her pouty mouth.

"Are you Macy?" Cleo asked haltingly, her voice broken from sleep and the weakness that was so much a part of her now.

"That's my bed." Macy dragged the wet finger from her mouth and poked at the mattress with its Winnie the Pooh sheets. "My bed." Then she patted the woven pink blanket that was flung carelessly over her pajama-clad shoulder. "My bankie."

"Don't worry. I won't take your bankie."

With the sober seriousness of the Pope, Macy dragged the blanket from her shoulder and tucked the bulk of its pink softness under Cleo's cheek.

Cleo could only blink back tears and try to smile.

• • •

Adrian didn't believe in waiting. That morning he got Cleo in to see his shrink.

"She's good," he told Cleo as he drove her to the shrink's office. "I no longer feel guilty about things I have no control over."

"You mean you're now able to forgive yourself for not living up to Mother's agenda?"

"Nothing to forgive."

"But are you able to forgive her for having that agenda?"

"I said my shrink was good. I didn't say she worked miracles."

Cleo told the shrink about how she could transport herself through time and space.

"Grief," said Dr. Mary Porter, "can do strange things to a person's head. Remember that at the time you were on painkillers, you were sleep-deprived, and you were most likely suffering from post-traumatic stress."

They discussed many things, but often the conversation would swing back to "dreams" Cleo had had as a child. There was one dream in particular that, no matter how many years passed, remained solidly ingrained in her memory.

"I'm little, and I'm alone in the woods," she told Dr. Porter. "But I'm not scared. I'm skipping and singing jump-rope songs. I'm wearing a red velvet dress with black patent-leather shoes. I can feel the breeze on my skin, I can smell the heavy vegetation. And suddenly I come upon three people, two men and a woman. They're just standing there in the middle of the woods. An intrusion on an otherwise happy moment. One of the men turns around and yells at me, and his face is pretty and ugly at the same time. And then I see he has a gun in his hand."

As a child, Cleo would come out of the daydream with her body covered in sweat. It always seemed so real. So vivid.

"What do you think that was all about?" Cleo asked Dr. Porter. Even though she hadn't had the dream in years, she could still remember it the way someone else might remember a wedding or a graduation.

"No one really understands the intricacies of the human mind," Dr. Porter told her. "But personally, I think dreams, daydreams included, are a way for us to subconsciously heal ourselves. A way for us to make things right. There may have been something going on in your childhood, something you may not even remember now, but whatever it was, your subconscious wanted to fix it, make it better. And since you quit having the dream, whatever it was that was bothering you must have gone away."

It seemed like a good enough answer to Cleo.

With continued counseling, along with drug

therapy, Dr. Porter helped Cleo get past her eating disorder and her grief, but Cleo could never convince Dr. Porter that that January she'd transported herself back in time. And Dr. Porter could never fully convince Cleo that it had not happened.

14

It was officially his day off, so after dropping Cleo at the motel, Daniel swung by the gas station to pick up a six-pack of beer and some cigarettes. He'd quit smoking three years ago, but his nerves were frazzled. He ordered the cigarettes from the clerk, then, at the last minute, took a detour down a nearby aisle, picked up a package of condoms, and tossed them on the counter along with the beer and cigarettes. He stared at the clerk, daring him to say something about his purchases. There was nothing Daniel hated more than having a checkout clerk talk about the stuff you were buying. It was none of his damn business.

Admirably poker-faced, the clerk rang up the purchases, bagged everything, and gave Daniel his change.

Daniel grabbed the stiff paper bag and left, figuring everybody in town would know that the town cop was not only drinking on duty, he was getting laid and enjoying a good smoke afterward as well.

Outside, he almost mowed down a woman with two little kids. He sidestepped, mumbling an apology, then looked directly into the woman's face.

Julia Bell.

Shit.

That was the bad thing about a small town. Your past was always jumping up, smacking you in the face. "Julia?" he asked, even though he knew it was his old girlfriend. He'd kept reluctant tabs on her. Years ago, his mother had written to let him know Julia had gotten married. And written again when she was pregnant with her first child. After his mother's funeral, he spotted Julia's name in the guest book and knew she'd been there even though he hadn't seen her.

She was heavier than she'd been when he'd known her, but not overweight. And she'd lost the sparkle she used to have, but she had something else, something that was maybe better: contentment. Daniel knew that was what Julia had wanted out of life. Contentment. Security.

Back then, sharing a can of cold spaghetti hadn't cut it, hadn't been the adventure for Julia that it had been for him.

"Hi, Daniel." She smiled up at him in a calm, happy-to-see-an-old-classmate sort of way, while his heart thundered in his chest.

"Are these kids yours?" he asked, even though he knew they were. Two girls. He'd caught their names in the county paper a few times. School stuff.

"Sara's five and Jessie's six."

"Are you still teaching school?"

"Second grade. I love it. I was sorry when I heard about your mother," she said. A look that was part pity, part understanding crossed her features. "And I know how badly you always wanted to get out of this town. I think it's great what you're doing for Beau."

She would understand. And it was a weird feeling knowing that she was possibly the only person on earth who would, because thinking back to when they'd been together was like remembering two completely different people.

One of the girls made a little squealing sound. He looked over to see the older one making faces at the younger. The younger one swung a fist and Julia had to intervene. "Don't hit your sister."

"She's making faces."

"Are you making faces, Sara?"

Sara shook her head. As soon as Julia turned back to Jessie, Sara stuck out her tongue at her sister, then whipped it back in, her face impassive.

"It was nice seeing you," Julia said, distracted now with the battle taking place. "I'd better get going."

"Yeah, nice seeing you."

He stood there a moment, the cold beer chilling his arm and chest. *I could have been part of a life like that,* he thought. *If only I hadn't always been reaching for something that wasn't there.*

•   •   •

At home Daniel took a beer bottle from the six-pack, put the cardboard container in the refrigerator, grabbed a book of matches, and went outside to have a smoke.

Premonition greeted him, happy to have the company even if it was only Daniel. Daniel swung his leg over the lounge chair and sat down, adjusting his hips and legs until he was comfortable. He put the open beer beside him on the cement patio, then pulled the cigarette pack from his shirt pocket. He opened the cigarettes and tapped one out. At first he just held it, enjoying the smooth feel of the paper and the smell of tobacco. He finally stuck the cigarette in his mouth, fished the matches from his pocket, and lit the cigarette, pulling the sweet smoke deep into his lungs.

And thought about the past.

There had been a spread of several years in his childhood when he'd wanted to become a priest. It didn't matter that he wasn't even Catholic. He'd been taken with the majesty of high mass and the mysterious, old-world feel of the Catholic Church before it decided to go so hip. But then, several years later, he found out priests couldn't have sex, so that was the end of that.

He'd met Julia Bell when he returned from his year in Scotland. While he was gone, her parents had moved to Egypt from St. Louis, looking for a safe place to raise Julia and her two younger brothers. She had a smile that could knock a guy sideways.

He told her of his dreams to see the world. He talked to her about Scotland and his family crest and how he wanted to go back there someday, maybe live there. He told her that he wanted to go as far north as Siberia, as far south as Tasmania. And even though she didn't know a lot about the places he spoke of, she begged to hear his stories, begged to hear his dreams.

"Let's go to Europe when school's over," he said a few months before they graduated from high school. "We can stay in hostels. You've got to see Scotland."

Ever since getting back from Scotland, he'd been working his butt off, saving every penny he made so that he could return.

Julia wasn't as excited about it as he thought she would be. That was something he should have taken as a warning but didn't.

"It's so far away," she said.

"Don't you want to see different places?"

"Sure, but how about someplace closer? Someplace in the United States. Like California, maybe."

That's what they did. Not only did they go to see California, they moved there.

She waited tables. He got a job working on a deep-sea fishing boat where rich people spent the day going for that trophy catch. And while he didn't go along with the idea of pulling such beautiful creatures from the sparkling blue water so that they could die in the blinding sun and later end up on someone's wall, he loved the sense of freedom. At twenty years old, he could ignore the bad and embrace the good, and it was good feeling the salt spray against his skin. It was good having a rolling deck under his bare feet while sea birds cried and circled overhead, begging for the chopped-up fish they used as bait.

His body got hard, his skin turned a deep golden brown, his hair was bleached white by the sun, until he looked like someone born to water and sky.

When he and Julia weren't working, they made love and talked about going to college. Julia would marvel at the hardness of his body and how he'd adapted so well. He looked pure California, while Julia, with her dark hair and light skin, continued to exude the wholesome Midwest.

"Do you ever wonder what we're doing here?" she asked him one night.

Her question took him by surprise. They were just getting started. They were just beginning the adventure. "No," he said.

"Not at all?"

"No."

She grew very still and very quiet.

And then she began to cry. She was homesick, she told him. She wanted to go back to Missouri.

"I can't go back there," he said. "Not now. Maybe never. What's in Egypt?"

"My family. My friends. I miss my mom, my dad. Even my brothers. I don't know what I'm doing here."

"*I'm* here," he said, hurt to discover that his company wasn't enough, hurt to discover that while he'd been thinking they were having the greatest time of their young lives, she'd been miserable.

Maybe he didn't love her enough. Because he couldn't make himself leave, not after getting a taste of the world. He couldn't make himself go back to Egypt.

They had to sell his stereo in order to buy her a bus ticket home. After she left, Daniel could no longer afford the tiny apartment they'd rented together. His boss let him move his few belongings into the cramped sleeping quarters of one of his boats, and that became Daniel's home. The room was stuffy and claustrophobic, so most of the time he slept on the deck, with the moon overhead and the water gently lapping under his ear.

That kind of nomadic life was okay for a kid just out of high school, but Daniel began to feel sickened by the constant carnage. He began to look to the future, and what he saw was a Coast Guard cutter.

Three years after joining the Coast Guard, he gave up his sea legs and took a position with the San Diego police. He somehow ended up in a couple of hostage situations, and before he knew it, his life of freedom had turned into one of high stress and fearsome responsibility. So he'd started drinking and smoking—and became damn good at both.

The front door slammed, bringing Daniel back to the present, to the patio, the cigarette, his unfinished beer, and Beau's return from work.

It was weird, Beau having a job. Daniel still wasn't quite sure what to make of it.

"I'm out here," Daniel yelled through the screen door.

As soon as Premonition saw Beau, the dog jumped to his feet and started whining and running around in circles.

Beau kept trying to pet him, but Premonition was so excited to see him that he couldn't hold still. It took about two minutes for them both to calm down. As soon as they did, Beau spotted the cigarette butt in the grass.

His face fell. "You're smoking," he said in disbelief and horror. "Why?"

Daniel silently cursed himself. He should have tossed the butt in the flowers where Beau wouldn't find it.

"It was a rough day. I needed a cigarette. Just one."

"No, no, no." Beau grabbed the open pack and squeezed them in his fist.

Daniel jumped to his feet, almost knocking over the beer bottle. He tried to wrestle the pack from Beau, but Beau took off across the yard, Premonition at his heels. Daniel was right behind him. He tackled him, both men flying to the ground. "Damn it, Beau," Daniel said, trying to pry Beau's hand open to get the cigarettes.

"You're not getting them, you're not getting them," Beau yelled. "I turn my back on you a minute, and this is what happens."

Daniel laughed, recognizing the famous line as one of their mother's.

The dog was right on top of them, thinking it was a great game.

"Premonition!" Beau yelled, getting the dog's attention. "Here!" He gave the cigarette pack a heave. The dog went after it, catching it before it hit the ground.

Daniel got to his feet, with Beau following. "Ha, ha," Beau said, delighted. "Now they're full of dog slobber." Then he saw the grass stain on the front of his shirt and immediately went into a panic. "My shirt. It's dirty. I have to wear it tomorrow. Look what you did." He was close to tears.

"It's okay. We'll wash it. We'll use some of that presoak stuff on it, like you've seen on TV. It'll get out a grass stain," Daniel said with a confidence he didn't feel. Would it? He hoped so. Otherwise Beau would be up all night worrying about the shirt. "We'll do it right now. Come on. Get the shirt off."

They had to go to the store to find something for grass stains. By the time they got home, it was getting dark. Inside, the message light on the answering machine was on.

It was Cleo, wondering why he hadn't come to pick her up so she could get her dog.

"She's getting Premonition?" Beau asked, fresh panic setting in on top of an already fragile state of mind.

Daniel rubbed the gooey stain stick across the front of Beau's shirt, wondering how in the hell it would get rid of the stain, wishing he didn't have to tell Beau about Premonition. "Yeah, I was going to tell you, but then I forgot, what with all the shirt business."

He brought the two sides of the shirt together, trying to grind in the stain remover.

Beau and Premonition followed him to the laundry room, where Daniel stepped over piles of dirty clothes, tossed the shirt in the washer, poured in some liquid soap, and turned the machine on, dropping the lid with a bang.

This was exactly what he'd feared would happen, that Beau would become attached to the dog. It had just happened a little faster than Daniel had expected. He turned to Beau, all set to explain that Beau couldn't keep the dog, but then his words tangled in his throat.

Beau was crying.

At that very moment, someone pounded on the front door.

15

Cleo knocked on the door again, then stepped back and tucked the plastic straw in the corner of her mouth, sucking the last bit of Tastee Delight vanilla shake from the bottom of the cup.

The door finally opened. Daniel just stood there looking at her through the screen.

"Remember me?" she asked. "You were supposed to give me a ride so I could get my dog."

He scratched his head. "Yeah," he admitted with a distracted air. "I've been a little busy."

"I walked, if you're worried about how I got here. I can see you are." In truth, she hadn't been able to stay in the motel room one more second.

Since he wasn't going to ask, she had to. "Can I come in?"

He pushed the screen door open. "Sure." He didn't sound sure at all.

She stepped inside the cool, welcoming room. "Where's Premonition?"

In the distance, beyond the kitchen, she could hear the sound of a washing machine. It was a homey sound. A comforting sound.

Daniel crossed his arms high across his chest. "Listen . . . about your dog."

The empty paper cup she was holding fell from nerveless fingers, hitting the floor with a hollow sound. "Oh, my God. Something's happened. He's been hit by a car!"

"No, no," Daniel quickly assured her. "He's fine. It's just that, well, Beau's become attached to him. Really attached, and I was wondering if you'd sell him to us. After all, you were going to leave him here, anyway. So what would it matter? This way you can actually get something out of it."

Sell her dog?

Sell Premonition?

Earlier she'd planned to leave him with Beau, but that was because she'd thought it would be best for everyone. Selling him had never been part of the equation.

The cup forgotten, she strode past Daniel, intent on stepping into the backyard and getting her dog. But when she reached the screen door, she stopped.

In the semidarkness just beyond the illuminated circle cast by the porch light, Beau knelt on the ground, his arms around Premonition. And he was crying. There he was, a man who was getting gray at the temples, hugging her dog, sobbing his eyes out.

She should never have come to this place.

Everything was wrong. It had been wrong from the beginning.

"I'll sell the dog."

The words were out of her mouth before she'd even assessed them. Why had she said that? She would *give* Premonition to Beau, but she would never, *never* sell him.

Without appearing to give Cleo a second thought, Daniel cut in front of her, slid open the screen door, and stepped outside. "Beau!" he shouted, moving toward his brother at a half run. "Good news. You can keep the dog."

Beau looked up and said something Cleo couldn't hear.

Daniel nodded.

Beau's smile, when it came, was brilliant. Dazzling. He jumped to his feet, laughing, Premonition dancing around him, letting out a couple of excited barks.

Tightness gripped Cleo's throat, letting her know that grief was coming on.

Moving with a jerky awkwardness, she turned and walked across the living room to the front door. Blindly she groped for the handle, found it, and tumbled out onto the porch, almost falling to her knees. Recalling the way Daniel had come after her before, she hurried down the steps. Instead of taking the sidewalk, she ran across the street, disappearing into the darkness between two houses.

She kept running. Past houses casting warm light,

past barking dogs, through backyards and front yards, until her side ached and her lungs were raw. She stopped, her breathing harsh in her ears, hands braced on her knees. Then, with a palm pressed to her side, she walked.

She couldn't go back to the motel room. Not yet.

She kept walking until she passed an old cemetery. The iron gate was open. She took that as an invitation and was soon wandering among the moss-covered tombstones. Gradually her lungs began to feel more normal. She collapsed in an open area, the grass cool under her cheek, the ground beneath her smelling like a mysterious concoction of things old and new.

In the peacefulness of the cemetery, she drifted off to sleep. . . .

Daniel Sinclair was lying on the grass beside her. He pulled her into his arms, pressing his mouth to hers. Somehow their clothes disappeared, and his body was touching hers, hot skin to hot skin. As she looked into his eyes, he filled her, a confident smile on his face, a man in total control. *Let go*, he told her, his lips not moving, only his hard body. *Just let go*.

She felt herself letting go, falling away, while he continued to smile at her, cool as could be.

She woke up with a start, the slanted, erotic mood of the dream still upon her. It took her a moment to realize she was still in the cemetery. She groaned, her body stiff, her clothes and skin covered with dew. How long had she been there? She pushed herself to a half-sitting position. It had to be late. There were no lights on in the nearby houses. There was not a single sound of a vehicle anywhere.

Off in the distance, sounding miles and miles away, a dog barked.

She got stiffly to her feet and began moving in the direction of the motel. By the time she reached the highway that led to The Palms, she still hadn't seen any sign of life. It seemed as if she were the only person alive on the planet. Rather than walk next to the highway, she clung to the ditch. At one point a lone semi moved in her direction, the headlights cutting through fog she hadn't realized was there until that moment. She jumped behind a tree, waited for it to pass, then continued on to the motel.

There was no welcoming beacon lighting the way. The neon sign that announced the name of the motel had long ago ceased to work, and, like everything else about the place, no one had bothered to fix it.

Gravel crunched under her feet as she approached her room. Suddenly she spotted a dark form uncurling itself from in front of her door. Then a voice came to her out of the darkness.

"Get lost?" The voice and shape belonged to Daniel Sinclair.

She was too tired to deal with him now. "What do you want, Sinclair?"

"To tell you that Jo wants you to come in for another reading tomorrow."

He could have called to tell her that.

"And to find out what you want for your dog. How about a hundred bucks?"

She couldn't talk about Premonition. If she did, she'd start crying. And she wouldn't cry in front of Daniel Sinclair. "I don't want anything," she said, her head bowed over her open purse, acting extremely interested in finding her key. Her fingers came in contact with the slice of plastic, but she continued the pretense of a search.

"Oh, come on. I know better than that. You always want something."

She pulled out the key, and stuck it in the lock, turned the key, and pushed open the door.

She flipped on the wall switch, revealing the room in all its squalid glory. Nothing looked out of place, and yet she had the feeling someone had been there.

She stepped inside, tossing her purse down on the bed. Daniel was right behind her, closing the door with a solid click, sliding the chain lock. He tossed something beside her purse. A packet of rubbers.

"I want you, Cleo Tyler."

Just like that. She had to admire his directness. And yet she knew the words were a confession, something that came with great reluctance, something he wasn't proud of.

"I want you bad."

Remnants of her dream still lingered in her mind. The next day she was going to leave, money or no money. She'd had it with this town. She'd had it with

Daniel Sinclair. But there was something so enticing, so decadent, about making love with someone you hated. There would be no worry over whether she measured up, because what difference did it make? She didn't care what he thought. She *knew* what he thought. That she was trash. That she was devious. That she existed only for herself.

Let him think it.

She hated him.

She picked up the packet he'd dropped on the bed. She waved it a little, as though she were shaking down a packet of sugar. "I hope you brought more than one."

He reached into the front pocket of his jeans and tossed two more on the bed. "I've had a hard-on ever since I had my fingers inside you."

She swallowed, recalling the way his body had felt pressed to hers. Her hands hovered over her top. Should she just strip? He solved that problem by reaching for her jeans. He unbuttoned and unzipped them. They were so loose, they dropped to the floor. "Wait," she whispered, slipping out of her sandals, then kicking free of the pants. "The light."

Instead of turning off the light, he said, "I've waited too long." He unzipped his own pants, freed his erection, grabbed a packet, opened it, and slipped on a condom, all in a flurry and whirling and heart-racing breath. With one hand he tugged at the front of her underwear, practically ripping it from her. She fell to the bed, her feet still on the floor. He followed her down. Then, without removing any of his clothing, without kissing her or touching her, he entered her, his arms braced on either side of her head.

If it hadn't been for the night in the other hotel, she might have given him the benefit of the doubt. But Cleo knew he knew how to bring a woman pleasure. He just wasn't bothering.

She hated him. Oh, God, she hated him.

She stared at him, at his face, her anger shimmering like an aura around her. He was thrusting his hips against her, his eyes closed, his breath hard and fast, a lock of hair hanging over his forehead.

"Pig," she said, calmly, clearly.

He hesitated.

"I hate you," she added, as he drove into her one final time before collapsing on top of her.

"Was that supposed to be like a vaccination?" she asked while he was still inside her, his chest rising and falling, his breathing ragged. He was all hot and sweaty, while she felt cold everywhere except where their bodies touched. "An unpleasant job you had to do in order to get me out of your system?"

She shoved at his shoulders, pushing him off her. She scrambled from the bed, grabbed her pants, and put them on, quickly zipping them up, not bothering with the top button. She heard the strike of a match, then smelled cigarette smoke.

She swung around and grabbed the cigarette from his mouth. It was bent and smashed, as if he'd found it under a sofa cushion somewhere. Thinking about it made her feel ill. Thinking about what she'd just done made her feel even more ill.

Before he had a chance to get the cigarette back, she ran to the bathroom and tossed it in the toilet. It hit the water with a sizzle, the paper quickly becoming transparent, the brown tobacco seeping out, turning the water a yellow-brown.

She reached for the lever to flush the toilet. She had to get rid of the slimy cigarette. Her stomach heaved. She squeezed her eyes shut, but that wasn't any better. With her eyes closed, she could see the cigarette butt as if it were still there.

In the bedroom, Daniel ran shaking fingers through his sweat-soaked hair. What the hell was the matter with him? What had he pulled a stunt like that for? He'd wanted to get back at her for her stinging insults to his manhood and sexual prowess. He hadn't wanted her to think he was softening toward her. And she was right, he'd wanted to get her out of his system.

What an ass he was. Sure, she had come there with the intent of taking the town of Egypt for a ride, but that didn't justify his treating her like that. No woman should be treated like that.

She'd been in the bathroom quite a while. Probably waiting for him to leave. Instead of leaving, he got to his feet, knocked softly on the bathroom door, then pushed it open.

She was standing with her back against the wall,

her eyes closed. In the weird light cast by the small fluorescent bulb, her face looked colorless except for the blue beneath her eyes and on her lips. She looked small and fragile, making him feel even more disgusted with himself. He started to reach for her, but his hand stopped a few inches from her arm. She'd probably prefer that he didn't touch her. He dropped his arm to his side. "Listen," he began. How had this happened? What a hell of a day it had been. Or two days—it would be morning soon. "I'm sorry."

"Go." The word came on an exhalation of air, as if she hardly had the energy to get it out.

He frowned. How many days had she been in Egypt? Three? Four? It looked as if she'd lost weight in the short time she'd been there. He thought back to that first day, when she'd eaten with them. She'd thrown up.

Yeah, but she ate breakfast at the hotel, he told himself.

But had she really? Had he seen her eat anything? No.

His stomach plunged. Was there something wrong with her?

He reached for her again, and this time he touched her, his fingers wrapping lightly around her arm. "You've got to get some sleep."

Surprisingly, she didn't argue. Like a zombie, she let him lead her from the bathroom to the bed. Once there, she sat down, then rolled away, her face to the wall, her back to him, her knees drawn close.

He pulled the top sheet up over her, then looked around for a bedspread. There wasn't one. He spotted an orange corner sticking out from under the bed. He pulled it out and was ready to spread in over her when she said quite clearly, "Nothing orange. I don't want anything orange."

He looked at the spread clutched in his hands. You couldn't get much more orange than that. He dropped the spread and kicked it back under the bed. He turned on the lamp next to her, turned off the overhead light, and sat down on the edge of the bed, his elbows on his knees.

It wasn't long before he heard her steady breathing. He should go home, he *would* go home, but he couldn't make himself leave. He opened the drawer under the phone, expecting to see the usual Gideon Bible. Something rolled to the front. A brown pill bottle. He picked it up and read the label. *Cleo Tyler. Take one four times daily for anxiety.*

The address was Seattle. He didn't know she'd lived in Seattle. But then, he didn't really know anything about Cleo Tyler except for the fact that she hated him. And had every right to.

16

Cleo came awake in stages, awareness gradually filtering into her brain. The room was dark, but she sensed that it was morning, possibly late morning. The air conditioner was clanking away, blowing its musty breath around the room. She remembered that Daniel had been there before she'd fallen asleep, but he must have left sometime later.

She checked the bedside clock. 9:30 A.M. She let her head drop back on the pillow. Had Daniel said something about Jo wanting her to come in for another reading? She couldn't go through that again. And she didn't want to see Daniel again. Ever.

She got up and showered, trying to keep her bare feet away from the edges of the shower and the shower drain. There was no telling what was lurking there. Afterward, she didn't feel a whole lot cleaner, the odor of the motel room having seeped into her pores. It was hard to say how long it would take to get the stink out of her system once she left, which would be soon.

She dug through her suitcase, trying to find something clean to wear, finally coming up with another long, crinkly skirt that was a lavish mixture of deep blue, purple, and black, with some crescent moons thrown in. She didn't feel like wearing a skirt, but everything else was dirty. She put it on, then pulled out the black top she'd worn the first day. She sniffed it. All she could smell was motel room. She slipped it over her wet hair, then crouched down on the floor and began tossing things into her suitcase.

A knock on the door made her jump and catch her breath. She pushed herself to her feet and tiptoed across the room. Through a crack in the louvered windows, she peered out. Daniel stood there in front of her door, holding something in his hand—a cardboard carryout tray, with paper cups and a white bag with the top rolled down. Behind him, the sky was dark and threatening.

She stepped away and pressed her back to the wall.

He knocked again. "Open up, Cleo."

Why had she slept so late? Why hadn't she set the alarm so that she could have gotten out of town before anyone was up?

But she'd been so tired. She *was* so tired.

She heard the sound of a key slipping into the lock.

He had a key to her room! The bastard had a key to her room!

She was poised to dive under the bed when suddenly she remembered the orange bedspread. All she could do was stand there, her back to the wall, as the door swung open, sending a rectangle of gray light onto the smashed shag carpet.

He kicked the door shut behind him and put the tray down on the foot of the bed before he spotted Cleo standing in the corner, fingers pressed to her mouth.

"I thought you might want something to eat before we go to the police station." He settled himself on the bed, gently so as not to tip anything over. "I was going to get orange juice, but then I thought—" His words broke off. His gaze dropped to the floor, where a corner of the orange bedspread stuck out from under the gray mattress. "I got coffee," he went on. "Muffins. Didn't have much to choose from at the Quick Stop."

"Milk?" she asked, moving out of the darkness, taking a couple of hesitant steps toward the bed. "Did you get any milk?" Something white would be nice. Something white and pure and clean.

"Yeah. As a matter of fact, I did." He reached into the bag and pulled out a small carton of milk.

She suddenly felt very close to tears. He'd brought her milk.

He held the carton out to her, his arm stretched as far as it could stretch. Without moving any closer, she reached out and with trembling fingers took it from him, the cruelty of the previous night almost obliterated by his gift.

He'd brought her milk.

She struggled with the carton. It didn't open smoothly, and now the place where she would have to put her mouth was a jagged, rough tear. She knew how it would feel against her bottom lip. Like stringy, soggy, saturated paper.

"Here."

From somewhere, maybe the sack, he produced a fresh paper cup. He took the milk from her, poured it in the cup, added a straw, and handed it back to her.

She accepted it, put the straw in her mouth, and began to drink. She could feel the liquid filling her mouth and running down her throat to settle, cold and comforting, in her stomach. "I love milk," she told him.

"No kidding."

She tipped the cup and sucked hard on the straw, getting every last drop.

"Want a muffin?" he asked.

She looked up to see him holding a muffin, the top a smooth golden brown.

"What kind is it?" she asked suspiciously.

"I don't know. It was the only one they had left." He peeled the paper from one side and broke it open. Plain. Plain and white.

Before he could come up with a diagnosis, she grabbed it from him, broke off a piece, and popped it in her mouth. It melted on her tongue. "I love plain things," she said, breaking off another piece, biting into it.

"Coffee?" he asked.

She shook her head. "You drink it." The cup was white, which was good, but it was made of Styrofoam, which was bad. Small pieces of Styrofoam could break off and float on the oily surface of the coffee.

He removed the lid and lifted the Styrofoam cup to his mouth. She couldn't watch. She turned on the pretense of looking out the window, but nothing could be seen through the nearly opaque glass louvers. She finished the last bite of muffin, stuffed the wrapper in the paper cup, and dropped it in the trash can, beside the open condom packet.

She stood staring down at the condom packet, wishing she hadn't seen it, wishing the past night had never happened. And she'd been doing a pretty good job pretending it hadn't happened until that moment.

"We've got to get going," Daniel said from behind her. She heard the bed shift and knew he'd gotten to his feet. "I told Jo I'd have you at the police station by ten."

Cleo's heart began to beat faster. She couldn't put herself through that again.

"I have to brush my teeth."

She pushed past Daniel to shut herself in the pitch black of the bathroom. She groped for the chain, found it, and pulled, the fluorescent light flickering, then finally stabilizing. He eyes were huge, with blue shadows under them. Those purple lips. Her wild hair.

This time there would be no trance, she swore to herself. She would fake it. Nobody would ever know. She would pretend. And this time she would describe in more detail everything she'd seen before.

She'd forgotten to comb her hair after her shower, and it had begun to dry just the way it had fallen after she'd removed the towel from her head, except that several strands had taken on a life of their own and were curling wildly. She tried to get a brush through it. That just made it bushier and thicker. She pulled it back and held it in place with a huge gold clip, the only clip she'd ever found that was big enough to go around the thickness of her hair. After that, she brushed her teeth, put on some red lipstick to cover the purple, turned off the light, and stepped out to join Daniel, who was waiting, one shoulder against the door.

Neither of them had mentioned the previous night, but that was all Daniel could think about. He wanted to bring it up, but she seemed so calm and collected that he decided it might be best to simply not mention it. Not now, anyway.

He waited while she slipped her beautiful feet into her sandals, waited while she gathered her purse.

When he'd unlocked the door and stepped into the stuffy room, she'd taken his breath away. She'd emerged from the darkness with her shiny, freshly scrubbed face devoid of makeup, her hair wet and coiling on each side of her face, and for a moment he'd forgotten how to breathe. She'd looked young. Vulnerable.

Now she looked exotic. She looked like someone so beyond his reach. Nevertheless, he had reached her, he thought; he'd touched her. But not really. He didn't know her. He didn't know her at all. And he had the feeling that was the way she wanted it.

He wished he'd kissed her last night. Kissed her deep and hard, the way he had that first time. Last night. He'd wanted her to see what it felt like to be treated with such insignificance, but Christ, he'd gone too far.

On the way to the police station he attempted to apologize. "Look," he began. "About last night—"

"I don't want to talk about it."

"I'm sorry. That's all."

She didn't answer. *And why should she?* he thought. *Why should she waste her breath on me?*

He wouldn't have to ask if it had been good for her. He knew the answer to that. Why had he wanted to hurt her? And why had he been so dead set on denying her pleasure? It had backfired, because by denying her pleasure, he'd denied his own.

Daniel parked next to Burt the Flirt's sport utility vehicle. Campbell was a good outlet for the frustration and anger Daniel was feeling toward himself. Didn't the guy ever work? he wondered. Didn't he have teeth to drill?

It looked as if it was going to be pretty much a repeat of the last performance, with all the same cast members. The shades were drawn, the candle was lit. They made a circle, everyone sitting in the same order except for Daniel and Dr. Campbell. Daniel traded places with the dentist so he could sit directly across from Cleo.

Just as she had the day before, she spoke in a low, husky voice, a voice that was soothing and melodic, a voice that could almost put a guy in a trance.

"Watch the flickering flame," she whispered. "Watch the flame."

A minute later she told them to close their eyes, to visualize the flame in their mind's eye. Daniel closed his eyes and kind of tipped his head back, enough so he could watch Cleo through the haze of his lashes.

And what he saw was that she didn't close her eyes at all. And she didn't even look at the flame. Instead, her eyes went from one person to the next, as if assuring herself that they were with the program and that nobody was cheating.

When she got to him, he let his lids fall closed, an almost imperceptible movement. A short while later he lifted them slightly, enough to see Cleo.

"The key," she said. "Everyone focus on the key." A pause. Then, "You must now replace the flame with the key. Concentrate. Focus."

As he watched, a little secret smile hovered at the corner of her mouth, a look of satisfaction.

He had to admit that for a moment in the bathroom yesterday, he'd wondered if maybe she hadn't been faking, but watching her now, there was no denying that she was a fraud through and through.

As he watched, she suddenly gasped and stiffened, the way he guessed one was supposed to do when being possessed by some spirit, some unknown force.

Her chest was thrown out, her head back, her long, lovely throat exposed to the light and shadow of the flickering flame. It took Daniel back to another time when she'd thrown back her head in just such a way and had let out just such a gasp.

And then the spirit must have left her. She suddenly went limp and melted on the floor. The only difference was that this time she didn't fall as hard.

Everyone gathered around her, except for Daniel. He got to his feet and simply observed.

The twins fanned her face, Harvey stared in fascination, Jo made a lot of clucking sounds, and Burt the Flirt told everybody to get back and give her some air.

Finally the master thespian sighed and allowed herself to be pulled to a sitting position.

"What did you see?" Jo asked. "Anything different this time?"

Cleo stared blankly ahead, as if looking into a world nobody else in the room could see. "Yes," she said, reaching blindly for Jo's hand, finding it, hanging on tightly. "I saw the barn again."

"The barn?" Jo said, sounding a little disgusted.

"Yes, but so much more. This time—" Cleo's words broke off. She pulled her gaze back from the mysterious place she'd gone, focusing on Jo. "This time," she whispered, "I went inside."

All three women let out a titillated gasp. "What did you see?" they asked in unison.

"At first it was hard to see anything," Cleo said. "It was so dark and creepy."

Creepy? You could have used a more descriptive word than that, Daniel thought. *You're getting sloppy, Cleo.*

Almost as if she'd read his mind, she shuddered for effect, then said, "It smelled like rotten things. Rotten wood. Rotten hay. Rotten ground. Rotten animals. There was this feeling of *decay* about it. It's a bad place. I know it's a bad place. But I made myself go forward, made myself take another step, and another." She got that trancelike look on her face again. "I stepped forward, and I could see my red toenails in my sandals. And it was weird, because I was wearing a slip. A black slip. I could see the lace edge of it against my leg." She kind of gave herself a shake, as if she realized she was getting sidetracked. "Someone handed me a shovel and told me to dig. So I started digging. And I kept digging until—" Her words came to an abrupt halt.

"Yes? Yes?" Everyone asked.

"What was in the hole?" Jo asked. "What did you find?"

Cleo ran her tongue across her lips, then looked directly at Jo. "The key."

17

After the séance, Cleo pleaded a headache and exhaustion. "This kind of thing always leaves me feeling like a limp rag," she said, smiling weakly. From the corner of her eye, she could see Daniel staring at her, his expression unreadable.

"Can I give you a lift back to your motel?" Dr. Campbell asked.

Cleo jumped at the offer—anything to get out of riding with Daniel. She was pretty sure he'd been watching her throughout the reading and knew she'd faked the whole thing. The last thing she wanted was another interrogation.

"That would be great," Cleo said, gathering up the incense and candles.

She'd briefly thought about trying to cut a deal with Jo, maybe settling for a thousand dollars if she let her leave now, but Cleo no longer wanted anything from the town of Egypt except to leave it.

Outside, Dr. Campbell opened the passenger door

for her. *Wow*, Cleo thought, sliding into the plush, almost decadent seat. Sport utility vehicles were certainly getting luxurious.

Campbell took his place behind the wheel. After a few deft maneuvers they were heading in the direction of The Palms.

"You were amazing back there," he said, keeping his hands in the ten-and-two-o'clock position.

"I can't take the credit," Cleo said. It was so much easier talking to Campbell than to Daniel. She could make small talk. Not very well, but she could do it. "It just comes to me."

"It doesn't matter how it happens. It's still amazing. I'd like to hear more about it," he said, pulling up in front of her motel room. "Would you like to get something to eat tonight? So we can talk?"

He didn't want to talk about her "gift." Why was it guys had to pretend? Of course, no matter how he'd suggested a possible evening together, her answer would have been the same. "I'd really like to," she said, "but I have plans." That should let him out of a tight spot without damaging his ego.

To her relief, he didn't argue. "Maybe another time."

"Yeah," she said, knowing she would be long gone in a matter of hours. "Maybe another time." She grabbed her purse and stepped from the vehicle. "Thanks for the ride."

He nodded and gave her a friendly smile.

Inside the motel room, Cleo finished packing her

clothes. In the process, she came across a couple of Premonition's squeaky toys, worm medication, the special shampoo that kept his skin from getting itchy and flaky, and his vaccination papers. The harness she would keep. Maybe she'd get another dog some-day.

She packed everything else, everything except her hair, which she tossed in the wastebasket near the bed. Now all she had to do was wait until dark. When the town was asleep, she would leave.

She tried to watch TV, but the reception was so bad that she gave up. She turned on the clock radio. All it did was emit a loud screech. She shut it off, toss-ing the remote control on top of the television.

With nothing else to do, she lay down and tried to sleep. She would need to get some rest if she was going to spend the night hitchhiking.

A short time later she fell asleep and immediately began to dream.

Laughter. Somebody was laughing. It was coming from directly behind her, almost as if it came from somewhere deep inside the wall behind her head.

Wake up, she told herself. *Wake up*.

She woke up.

The motel room was cast in shadow, the way it had been that morning, so dark that it could have been night.

Laughter.

Still coming from the wall behind her head. Coming from the next room.

She sat up, her bare feet rubbing against the clammy shag rug. The orange shag rug.

The laughter was still there, just behind the wall. Shrill laughter. A woman's drunken laughter. Between the bursts of laughter, Cleo could hear the rumble of a man's deep voice.

She stood up and moved closer to the wall, thinking to press her ear to it. In order to brace herself, she put out her hand. It sank, disappearing into the wall as if it had been dipped in murky water.

I'm not awake, she realized. *This is still the dream.*

She should have known, because it had the creepy, slanted mood of the old dream, the pumpkin dream. There was a feeling of expectation, of knowing something bad was going to happen, something bad that she could do nothing about.

She stuck her arm deeper into the wall, all the way to her shoulder. Then, even though she wanted to wake up, even though she didn't want to do what she was doing, she followed her arm through the wall . . . until she was in another room exactly like the one she'd left, except that the new room was a mirror image. The bed was on the east wall instead of the west, the mirror across from her. In this room, the orange bedspread was still on the bed. The orange curtains still covered the window.

At first she thought she was alone, but then she realized she wasn't. Suddenly there was a man in the center of the room. Where had he come from? His back was to her. He was bent over, intent upon some task. As she watched, he pulled up the corners of the orange bedspread and began wrapping something, bundling something, rolling something.

What is he doing?

Finished, he picked up the bundle. It must have been heavy, because he almost collapsed with the weight of it. He let out a grunt and tried to shift the weight. Instead, the bundle slipped from his fingers and slumped to the floor at his feet. He mumbled and cursed, stepping over the bedspread and grabbing it by one end. Walking backward, he began to drag it toward the door, leaving a dark stain on the rug.

Cleo followed the stain, followed the man out the door to where an open car trunk was waiting. He looked up at Cleo.

And now she could see it was Harvey.

"Aren't you going to help me hide the key?" he asked, looking directly at her, not surprised or alarmed that she could see everything he was doing. "Grab that end."

She didn't want to touch the orange fabric, but she reached down, gripping it tightly with her fingers.

They lifted. The bundle hardly weighed anything. Why had he needed her help at all?

"Get in," he said, motioning for her to get inside the trunk along with the bundle.

She shook her head.

"Go on. I'll give you a ride."

She did need a ride. That was right. "Out of town?" she asked.

"Anywhere."

"You have the key, don't you?"

"I *am* the key."

"I don't understand."

"You're not supposed to. This is a dream."

She looked at him more closely and realized it wasn't Harvey standing there, but Dr. Campbell. It had been Campbell all along.

"I hope you're flossing," he told her.

"I am."

"Don't lie to me," he said in a calm voice.

"I'm sorry. I didn't know you could read my mind."

"Get in the trunk."

"I can't."

"Get in! You have to get in."

She turned and tried to run. She *was* running, but her feet were mired in something thick and deep. The rug. The orange shag rug. She couldn't get anywhere, couldn't make any progress. She knew he was right behind her, right behind her, right behind her—

She felt a hand on her arm.

She screamed and turned.

Cleo came awake, her heart racing, her clothes damp with sweat. The scream woke her up. The sound of it was still ringing in her ears. Had she really screamed aloud? If so, had anyone heard her?

She sat up, her heart pounding, the creepy sensation of the dream still heavy in her.

That it was dark, truly dark, was the first thing she

noticed as she waited for her heart to stop pounding. She groped for the bedside lamp, found it, and clicked it on. She checked the clock. Almost 9:00 P.M. It only seemed as if she'd been asleep a few minutes, when in fact she'd slept several hours. Her body had that heavy, gritty feeling that came with a long sleep that had taken place at the wrong time of day. On the foot of the bed were Premonition's things. It was still too early to leave town, but she had to get out of the motel for a few hours.

She cleaned up, put on a dry top—unfortunately, one that she'd worn before—grabbed the stuff from the end of the bed, and headed out into the night.

18

The cuckoo clock chimed the half-hour.

Wearing nothing but a pair of cargo shorts that hit at the knee, Daniel sat slouched in one corner of the couch, his bare feet on the coffee table, the remote control resting on his thigh. His hair, still wet from the shower, dripped on his shoulders, the water trickling down his chest.

He looked up at the hand-carved clock, a clock that had come to America on a ship along with his Scottish ancestors. The bird disappeared and the wooden door clicked shut behind it. Only nine-thirty. The evening was creeping.

The clock was another obsession of Beau's. Daniel preferred not to wind the bird part of it at all. Who needed a cuckoo chirping and clicking twelve times in the middle of the night? But Beau, being the obsessive-compulsive person he was, cranked both pinecone weights to the top every morning before breakfast, giving the bird a full twenty-four hours to chirp away. A couple of times Daniel had tried to talk him into winding only the clock, but Beau insisted that both be wound.

It was Saturday night. The Tastee Delight stayed open until ten-thirty on Saturdays. The house seemed so damn empty with Beau gone. Beau hadn't even left the dog to keep Daniel company. Instead he'd taken Premonition with him, explaining that he wanted Matilda to meet him.

"She has a fenced yard behind the store," Beau had said. "Where Premonition can stay until I get off work."

Daniel knew it was good for Beau to have a job. Good for him to be somewhere where he could see a lot of people. Beau thrived on contact with others.

Here all along Daniel had been thinking of Beau as a burden, albeit a welcome one. But in reality, he wasn't a burden at all. Taking care of his brother had given Daniel's life a purpose, a direction. Now, with Beau increasingly more independent, Daniel was beginning to wonder where he fit into the picture.

Preoccupied, Daniel picked up the remote and flicked through the channels, not seeing anything that could serve as a distraction.

Suddenly a knock sounded at the door, even though he'd heard no footsteps. He turned off the TV, dropped the remote on the couch, and answered the door, flipping on the porch light at the same time.

Cleo.

He ran a tongue across dry lips.

Through the screen, she said, "I brought some of Premonition's things by." She lifted a small white-paper bag that looked suspiciously like the very bag he'd delivered breakfast in that morning. "Toys. Shampoo. He has to have a special shampoo, other-wise he gets a rash."

Daniel pushed open the screen door, and she stepped inside, a sudden gust of wind almost sucking the light door from his hand. The air smelled like rain. "Couldn't it have waited until tomorrow?" he asked.

"I was out for some fresh air anyway. That motel room—" She swallowed and made a nervous gesture with one hand. "It can get smothering at times."

She seemed a little keyed up. A little distracted and nervous.

Without waiting for an invitation—and in all honesty, she might not have gotten one—she dropped the sack on the coffee table, then sank into the floral-patterned couch with a sigh, leaning back her head and closing her eyes.

"This room is just so heavenly," she said without opening her eyes.

He latched the hook on the screen door so that the wind wouldn't blow it open, then closed the solid wooden door, silencing the sound of the wind.

He and Beau didn't hang out in the living room much, but their mother had. She used to sit in the very spot where Cleo was now reclining. He could still picture her curled up in the corner with her reading glasses slipping down her nose, poking a needle through the hoop she always carried. Counter cross-stitch was what she called it, because that was what Beau called it. She could never convince him otherwise, so she'd just joined his camp. When it came to Beau and his stubborn streak, that was usually the best way to go.

Daniel had never thought about the room being heavenly. But now, as he looked at it with fresh eyes, he could see that it was definitely a woman's place, from the African violets Beau so patiently cared for, to the doilies scattered here and there.

Cleo was so quiet and so still that he wondered if she'd fallen asleep. What did she want? What was she after? With Cleo, he got the feeling that things didn't just happen by chance. Everything she did, everything she said, seemed to be part of a greater plan. So what was she up to now?

Her hair was tied back, but some of it had escaped to curl wildly about her face, the red of her hair contrasting with the porcelain paleness of her skin, which in turn set off the color of her full lips. Her eyelashes, pale and devoid of mascara, rested childlike against her cheeks, casting shadows.

While he stared at her, she opened her eyes. Her lids were kind of puffy, more sleepy-looking than usual, and he wondered if she'd been asleep before taking her walk.

"Where's Beau?" she asked, glancing around.

"Working. Till midnight."

"Oh."

Was she thinking what he was thinking? Was that the reason she'd come?

"What's going through your mind?" she asked. "You've got a strange look on your face."

"I was thinking of the saying 'Third time's the charm.' You familiar with that?"

She gave him a lazy smile, lifted her arms above her head, and stretched. "How about this one? 'Three on a match.' We know where that comes from."

"Yeah," he said. "Three soldiers light cigarettes with the same match." A smile tugged at one corner of his mouth. "And the last guy gets blown away."

She got to her feet and smoothed her skirt, as if preparing to leave. He didn't want her to leave.

"That was quite a show you put on today," he said.

She tipped her head to one side and looked boldly into his eyes, trying to find the truth in there somewhere. "You liked it?"

"You had those people eating out of your hand."

"But not you."

"No. Never me."

She took three steps closer, bringing her away from the couch and the coffee table. "You knew I was faking?"

"Yeah."

"But you didn't say anything."

"I've warned them already. I've warned them and warned them, but they won't listen."

She came closer, so she was directly in front of

him. He could see the starlike pattern in her eyes—
green shot with black. "You're not saying words they
want to hear," she whispered. Her hands were at her
sides, her head tilted back so that she could retain eye
contact. Scarcely inches separated them.

What did she want? After last night, he wouldn't
have thought she'd want to breathe the same air as
him, let alone stand so close. "Why did you come
here, Cleo?" *Cleopatra, with your red toenails and red
lips.*

Cleo frowned. "I think," she began, sliding a sandaled foot between his bare feet, hooking a thumb in
the belt loop of his low-slung shorts, just above his
hipbone, in a way that seemed way too familiar. He
liked it. "I'm not entirely sure, but I think I came to
see you."

He smiled then, a smile that felt as though it blossomed from deep inside him, a smile that was suddenly
reflected in Cleo's face. "I was hoping you'd say that,"
he said.

He felt the weight of her pressing against him. He
would never say it in words, but he had to do something to make up for last night. A thought came to
him. A great thought. So great he marveled at his own
brilliance. He took her by the shoulders and set her
away from him. Her smile immediately faded.

"I have an idea," he said. "Wait here." He turned
and hurried down the hallway, opened the storage
closet, flicked on the light, and began digging.

Cleo stood in the living room, her arms crossed at

her chest, watching as Daniel disappeared into a huge walk-in closet. She could hear things being slid across the floor, as if he was shifting boxes around.

Should she leave? This was her opportunity.

Why did you come here, Cleo? she asked herself.

She thought she'd come to get away from the motel room, and to bring Premonition's things, but had she really come to see Daniel one last time before she left? Was she becoming so accustomed to subterfuge that she could no longer see into her own heart, her own soul? Cleopatra, queen of denial.

Daniel must have found what he was looking for, because he emerged from the closet, a box in his hands, and then disappeared immediately into another room that must have been the bathroom, because a few seconds later she heard the sound of running water. Then he was back out with the same box. "Wait right there," he said before diving into the last room off the long, narrow hallway, shutting the door behind him.

This was too weird. She couldn't imagine what he was up to, but whatever it was, it had certainly put a damper on her libido. He wasn't planning on doing something kinky, was he? Maybe the box contained collars and whips and chains and stuff like that.

Daniel?

No, not Daniel.

While waiting, she began to wander around the living room, lifting framed pictures and putting them down, easily picking out Daniel and Beau.

Their mother had been beautiful, with a sweet, angelic face, a kind face. She looked like a real mother. There was a picture of a man who she thought might have been their father, but the photo was of poor quality, and very old.

She heard a door slam. Then Daniel reappeared in the living room. "Come on." He motioned for her.

She moved down the hall with trepidation.

"You first," he said, indicating the closed door.

She hesitated.

"Go on."

She put her hand to the knob, turned it, and pushed open the door.

He'd given her the darkness she'd asked for the night before. And in that darkness, he'd lit perhaps a half dozen candles. From the far side of the room came a steady whooshing sound she couldn't identify. Drifting out the door, swirling around her ankles, was fog.

She stared at the place her feet should have been—she couldn't see her toes.

"A fog machine," he explained, applying gentle pressure to her shoulders. She moved forward, the gradual movement stirring up the fog, making it swirl. He shut the door behind them. "I came across it at a garage sale back when Beau was putting together a magician's act. He never did get the hang of any magic tricks, but he sure could wow 'em with the special effects."

Somewhere under his thick layer of hostility and

resentment beat a tender heart, she realized.

Fog.

First for Beau, then for her. Nobody had ever given her fog.

She laughed through the hands she had pressed to her open mouth. And then, for some inexplicable reason, she began to cry. Silently. Quiet tears that were suddenly on her cheeks. With her back to him, she quickly wiped them away so that he wouldn't see.

He wrapped his arms around her, pressing a flat hand to her lower belly. She felt his breath against her ear, his lips against her neck.

Fog. Imagine that.

She turned in his arms, loving the solid warmth of him, loving the smoothness of his satiny skin under her palms.

His lips found hers. The kiss was just what she'd remembered. Explosive. Electric. A surprise. A wonderful, wonderful surprise.

It was mouths, and tongues, and hot, whispered words.

At one point he laughed, a low sound, full of wonder and delight, that filled her head, that melded perfectly with the tone of their coming together.

This time there was no anger. No resentment. No holding back.

It was all sweet, open, aching vulnerability, a hoping, a wanting, a dreaming in a dark room with no walls, in a dark room with no color, with magic swirling about their feet.

He tugged her top over her head, dropping it into oblivion. He reached behind her and unfastened her bra, slipping it down her arms, dropping it with the blouse. She toed off her sandals.

Her hands were in his damp hair.

His mouth was on her breast.

She unbuttoned his shorts. He wasn't wearing underwear. She slid the zipper down, releasing him, cupping him.

He let out a sigh. His shorts slid down his hips. He stepped free and kicked them away. She ran her hands across the flat planes of his hips, up his back, his shoulders, his chest. He was all smooth skin and hard, hot muscle.

She felt his fingers on the waistband of her skirt, searching.

"It's elastic," she said on a breath, with a smile. She slid it down her hips, along with her underwear, stepping free.

She was weak. She was shaking. She couldn't stand any longer. She sank into the fog, sliding along his body. He followed her down until they were knee to knee, chest to chest. Under her knees was something soft—a rug or a blanket. She felt his fingers against her bottom and against her neck. He lifted her to him, the strength and heat of his erection pressing against her belly, taking her breath away. She could hear his labored breathing, could feel his trembling muscles.

He pressed her down until she was lying on her

back, the fog swirling around them, enveloping them. She felt his hands on her knees, felt the callused tips run up her leg, her inner thigh. And then his mouth, his clever, sensual mouth, touched, kissed, licked the pulsing heat of her, his tongue curling, dipping, so strong, so able. A shudder went through her. Then another. Her entire body spasmed, then spasmed again and again. She might have cried his name; she wasn't sure. All of a sudden the warmth of his body was gone and she was lying there, enveloped by the fog, needing to be held, still teetering on the edge.

And then he was back, all hot and sweating. He slid inside her, stretching her, moving against her, thrusting, sweaty skin slapping, sticking, sliding, hot and panting breath in her ear, pumping harder, faster, the breathing quicker, quicker.

Her head went back. Her body stiffened. She felt herself spasm around him.

She couldn't stop. Her body just kept shuddering and shuddering.

"Can't stop." It was a cry of half ecstasy, half fear.

"It's okay," he whispered breathlessly. "Let go. Just let go."

She dug her fingers into his thighs. "Faster. Harder."

The momentum increased.

The fog swirled.

Lightning crashed—whether it was outside or in her mind, she never knew. She met him one last time, then went limp, a sensation of complete and utter euphoria spreading to her toes and fingertips.

19

For about five minutes Daniel couldn't move. But after a while he became concerned because Cleo wasn't moving, either.

"Cleo?" He lifted a hand to touch her temple. Her riot of hair was damp with sweat. His fingers followed a strand to the end, to where a silver chain lay against her collarbone, stuck to her damp flesh.

"Hmmm?" she asked vaguely.

"You okay?"

"You could say that."

He smiled. He didn't want to let her go, didn't want to break the mood, but he had to deal with the rubber. But before he did, he kissed her long and deep and tender, in case this was it. In case it was their last kiss. In case she jumped to her feet and darted away, which would be very like Cleo.

And then he slipped away from her, her body imprinted upon his where cool air met hot flesh. He could feel everywhere they had melded.

He took care of business, then turned off the fog machine, the absence of the rhythmic drone plunging the room into an ear-ringing silence. Then he dropped backward on the bed, one hand tucked behind his head, the other resting on his rising and falling chest. Would she join him? Or would she leave?

She joined him.

The bed dipped as she settled herself beside him, curling up next to him, her breast pressed against his rib cage, one leg draped across his knees, her foot tucked under his ankle. He brought his arm from behind his head and wrapped it around her shoulders, pulling her closer. She didn't seem to mind. In fact, she let out a deep breath and snuggled closer.

He wanted to know more about her, yet he knew she probably wouldn't allow him to get in her head. It surprised him to find that he knew her as well as he did, well enough to know she wouldn't reveal anything about herself that might leave her vulnerable and exposed. But he asked a question anyway. "You ever been married?" He stroked her arm, trying to imagine her in a deep relationship, unable to do so.

"No," she said. Then, "You?"

"No."

"I guess we have something in common." The words were spoken in a lighthearted manner, but there was something underneath—pain, maybe—that he didn't want to dwell on.

His fingers came into contact with the chain around her neck. He followed it around until he came to a small, simple ring. "Does this have any significance?"

She was quiet a moment. "No," she finally said.

He might not know anything about Cleo's life—her past, her plans for the future—but he knew *her* well enough to know she was lying. He was also fairly sure she hadn't been faking her ecstasy moments earlier. He'd felt the heated softness go rigid, felt her contract around him.

Maybe she *could* read minds, because at that very moment she slid over him, on top of him, a knee on either side of his hips. Then she stretched, reaching past him to blow out the candles on the headboard, leaving only one flame burning in the corner of the room. "Where are the rubbers?" she whispered.

He groped the surface of the bedside table, his fingers coming into contact with the packet. He peeled it open, but before he could pull out the latex, she took it from him.

"I don't think I'm ready," he said, hoping he didn't have to go into some lengthy explanation of how it takes a guy a little while to get wound up again. At that very moment he realized he *was* ready.

With her knees clasped against his hips, her bottom resting on his thighs, she wrapped her hand around him. His breath caught while she studied him with her hands. Then she began with the condom, struggling to unroll it.

She couldn't get it on. "I think that small comment was way off."

"Here. I'll do it."

"I want to."

"You're not pushing hard enough. You aren't going to hurt me."

She shoved harder, the latex finally sliding into place. And then, before he could make any move, she came down on him, her hands gripping his waist.

"Don't move," she commanded.

She slid her hands up his ribs, his chest, to his shoulders, following with her body, until they were chest to chest.

"Just stay in me like this."

Stay in me like this, stay in me like this. Her words echoed in his brain.

"Stay this way, stay this way. Don't let go. Don't let go."

Her voice had the rhythmic cadence of a hypnotist's, and for a fleeting moment he wondered if that was what she was trying to do—hypnotize him. But he was already hypnotized.

"How long can you stay like this, without moving?" she whispered, her breath against his ear.

"I don't know. I never tried it."

They just lay together, holding it, holding it.

His head hummed. His heart thudded. His breathing quickened.

And still he held on.

Suddenly she pushed herself upright, her hands braced against his belly. It felt as if she were devouring him, imprinting him on her every sense. She began to trace patterns on his chest, her fingers circling his nipples, the palms of her hands sliding down his ribs, not lightly, but as if she was trying to memorize the very structure of his muscles, his bones.

"Cleo," he gasped. He couldn't lie still anymore.

"Shh. Don't move."

He hung on a little longer, until she began to move for him. She pulled herself completely away, and just when he thought he couldn't take it any longer, that he would throw her on her back and pound and grind his thighs against hers, she came down on him hard. Again and again.

"I can't get enough of you," she gasped.

And at that moment he realized she spoke the truth.

He pushed her to her back, then followed her over. His mouth found hers while he slipped the crook of his arm under her leg, pulling her knee to her chest, thrusting into her again and again, never wanting the moment to end, holding himself back, holding, holding.

And then he felt the tendons in her legs go hard. He felt a quiver run through her as her hot velvet turned to solid muscle, contracting around him.

He tried to hang on, tried to prolong the moment, but he couldn't. She was taking him with her, milking him dry, until he lay a wasted man in her arms, his breathing ragged, his heart pounding in his head.

It was mind-blowing. Nothing like this had ever happened to him—like sex, but more than sex. Something beyond consciousness. Something Zen.

Five minutes later she asked, "Did I hurt you?"

He laughed, and felt the sound reverberate between their tangled bodies. He pressed a firm kiss against her damp brow. "You're incredible. Amazing. Where did you learn something like that?"

He knew it was the wrong thing to say as soon as the words left his mouth. He could feel her withdrawal. It wasn't a physical thing, it was mental, like a door slamming in his face.

He knew she would leave.

Don't go.

His mind was getting ahead of logic, racing blindly into tomorrow, wondering what he could do to make her stay.

"Where did I learn something like that?" she asked airily, their bodies unable to get any closer, their minds unable to get any farther apart. "From one of my many lovers."

He made a sound of frustration deep in his throat. He rolled away from her to sit on the edge of the bed, tossing the used rubber into the wastebasket. Then he lay back down beside her. Close, but not touching.

"You haven't had many lovers," he said, sensing that she was lying again, hoping she was lying again.

"No?"

"No."

"You don't know anything about me. Except that I'm a con artist. Isn't that what you called me? And if I'm a con artist, then it would stand to reason that I've slept with a lot of men."

"Come on, Cleo. Don't start this."

"Are you actually trying to give me some redeeming qualities, qualities that two hours ago I didn't have? Wow. Sex certainly changes everything. It can make saints out of sinners, and sinners out of saints." Her anger was building, pulsating in the small room. "Two hours ago I was the lowest lowlife in Egypt, Missouri. But now that you've had sex with me, well, I must not be the lowlife you thought I was."

Was that what he'd done? Was that what had really happened here?

She rolled out of bed and began putting on her clothes. Her panties. Her bra. Her skirt. Her top.

He slid across the bed, snatched his shorts off the floor, and quickly put them on. She jammed her feet into her sandals, lifting one foot at a time, hooking the back strap over her heel.

"What about you?" he said, buttoning and zipping his shorts. "You've done nothing but lie since you got here—even *before* you got here, with that blind stunt. You and your phony séances and all that spooky barn crap." He brought up his hands to cup her face.

The chain around her neck caught the light, shimmering against her skin. He linked his fingers around it, lifting the ring to her face. "What about this? You lied about this not a half hour ago."

She shoved at his chest and pulled back at the same time. The necklace snapped. The ring went flying.

Daniel heard it hit the wall and fall with a ping to the wooden floor.

She didn't take her eyes from his. "Do you want the truth?" she said, jabbing at his chest, at maybe the very spot her lips had recently kissed. "I'll give you the truth. That necklace? It belonged to my fiancé. But he's not alive anymore. You wanna know why? Because I killed him. Oh, not on purpose, but it was my fault."

She was crying now, but he doubted she knew it. "That was four years ago, and I hadn't had sex with anyone until *you*." The last word was spat from her mouth, as if it were something vile.

She was telling the truth. Sweet Jesus, she was telling the truth.

He wanted to hold her. He tried to pull her into his arms, but she pushed him away. "You've touched me enough," she said. "Don't touch me anymore."

He put up both hands. "Okay, okay."

She jerked open the bedroom door. Harsh light from the hallway hit him in the face, casting her in shadow. But enough light fell over the contours of her cheek for him to see the wetness there, for him to see that her lips were swollen from his overzealous kisses.

How had this happened? How had things gotten so out of control? They'd just made love. That was all. And yet it had triggered an avalanche of emotions. He hadn't known that to touch her physically had meant to touch her mentally, pushing an already delicate psyche close to the edge. Guilt could wear a person down, could eat at a person's soul until there was nothing left but fear and bitterness.

"Wait." He started to grab a shirt from a nearby chair, but then he caught a flicker of a shiny object on the floor near the foot of the bed. The ring. He picked it up, surprised at its lightness.

He opened his hand. Lying in his palm was a fake gold ring. It was the kind of ring kids bought from gum machines, the kind whose size could be adjusted simply by squeezing.

Doubts crept in.

Had the past five minutes been nothing but an act, too? Had he finally fallen for her subterfuge, the way everyone else in town had?

Forgetting the shirt, he turned to go after Cleo, but his foot touched something cold. The broken necklace. He snatched it up and ran down the hall toward the living room.

Empty.

He ran outside, heavy, icy raindrops hitting him in the face, the sidewalk cold and wet under his bare feet.

He stopped and stared down the dark, lonely road. He wouldn't go after her. She would just elude him, the way she'd eluded him from the beginning. Maybe she did know something none of the rest of them knew. Maybe she could make herself disappear and appear at will.

"Cleo!" he shouted into the darkness. "Don't you want your ring?"

There was no answer. Only the black emptiness and the lonely patter of raindrops on the leaves above his head.

He was looking at the ring again when he heard footsteps coming from the opposite direction. He swung around, expecting to see Cleo emerging from the darkness. Instead Beau appeared, Premonition at his heels, a smile on his face, the blue Tastee Delight cap turned backward. "Daniel!" he said, his voice holding joy at seeing his brother, as if Daniel's presence were some remarkable treat. "What are you doing out here?"

Daniel curled his fingers around the ring. "Waiting for you," he told Beau. "Waiting for you."

Seeing Cleo's dog—because he could only think of it as Cleo's dog now—brought a fresh wave of misery to Daniel. Had he taken one of the only things she cared about?

Beau was much too wired to sleep, and Daniel too confused. Instead of going in the house, they sat down in the wicker chairs on the front porch, Premonition at Beau's feet, and listened to the rain.

Beau told him about all the hamburgers he'd prepared, and all the shakes he'd made, and how Matilda had let him clean out the shake machine after they closed.

Then he hit Daniel with something Daniel had never expected.

"If I had kids, would they be like me?"

Daniel's heart just kind of stopped. He wiped

a hand across his forehead, thinking fast. "Good-looking?"

Beau didn't waver. "You know what I mean."

Yeah, Daniel did know what he meant.

The great security that came with growing up in a small town meant that everybody had accepted Beau. Everybody liked him. Even though Beau knew he wasn't like other people, Daniel had been thankful that it had never seemed to bother him. Oh, there had been the time in second grade, when Beau had been held back while his friends and classmates moved on. That had been tough. There had been a lot of tears shed that year.

In third grade it almost happened again. Instead, by some silent agreement, Beau moved on to the next grade with his new friends. He stayed with that class through middle school and high school, earning a diploma just like everybody else. That never would have been possible in a big city.

"Will they be different, like me?" Beau asked.

Daniel knew that when Beau had a question, he wouldn't let it go until he got a satisfactory answer, an answer he felt was fair. He would settle for nothing less than the truth. "When you were born, your oxygen was cut off for a little while. That changed something in your brain, so you have to work harder to learn things. But what happened to you wasn't genetic. It isn't something you have to worry about passing to your kids."

That seemed to satisfy Beau.

But then a little later, when Daniel was lying in bed unable to sleep, his mind jumping from Cleo to Beau and back, a thought suddenly came to Daniel.

Was Beau thinking about getting married?

20

Rain pounded the dark street, cooling the hot asphalt, running down Cleo's face, plastering her hair to her head.

She didn't care.

She liked it. Liked the feel of the cold rain on her hot skin, liked the way it absolved her of Daniel's touch, erasing the imprint of his lips, his hands, his body. Why had she gone there?

You wanted him. You know you wanted him.

Yes.

As a child, she'd always had urges to jump off high places. She'd wanted to experience the sensation of flight. But even at a young age she'd understood that there was risk involved. She understood that she could break a leg, or both legs. Or even worse, get killed. You don't jump off a high place just because you want to.

Down the block, a car turned in her direction, twin headlight beams cutting through the rain. Cleo quickly stepped behind a tree, hiding until the car had passed. When it was gone, she returned to the edge of the road and continued walking in the direction of the motel.

She wasn't cold. Her feet were slipping and squishing in her sandals, and her broomstick skirt was heavy with the weight of the water. It slapped against her legs, clinging to her skin. But she wasn't cold.

At the motel she dug the key from her purse and stuck it in the lock but didn't turn it. Why had she come back? Why didn't she just keep walking? Walking until she was out of Egypt, out of Missouri.

You can't walk away from your dreams. You can't walk away from your fears.

There had been a brief moment back there at Daniel's when she'd forgotten who she was, when she'd forgotten the bad things, forgotten the dreams that haunted her and the guilt that stalked her. There had been a moment in Daniel's arms when she'd felt alive.

For someone who moved through her days trying not to feel, it had been a little like a rebirth, like being born all over again. But like so many things in life that were good, the feeling had lasted only long enough to leave her with an emptiness in her soul, a black, bottomless void that scared her and hurt her.

She had pushed him away. She was aware of that. But it was the only way she knew to get by.

She turned the key. She shoved open the door. She stepped inside, closing the door behind her, her skirt dripping on the carpet. She reached for the wall switch. She turned it on—and jumped, her heart exploding.

"Oh, my God," she said, a hand to her chest, to her thundering heart.

Dr. Campbell was lying on the bed, one hand behind his head, his feet crossed at the ankles.

It was the first time she'd seen him in anything other than an expensive suit. Instead, he wore a crisply pressed white shirt tucked neatly into a pair of belted dark jeans. On his feet were loafers and a pair of patterned socks. The soles of his shoes were barely scuffed—they had to be brand-new. Everything he was wearing looked brand-new.

"You scared me to death," she said.

He smiled his Dale Carnegie smile, a smile that never reached his eyes. "That makes us even."

"Excuse me?" Her mind was muddled. She struggled to pull herself together. What was he talking about?

In one lithe motion, he swung his feet to the floor and sat up. "*You've* been scaring *me*."

She tried to make sense of his words and failed. The *plop-plop* sound of water dripping from her skirt to the carpet laid down a steady beat, a foundation of confusion, of dreaded anticipation.

He got to his feet. "Don't you know?"

She shook her head.

He mirrored the motion with a head shake of his own. "I tried to talk Jo out of hiring a psychic, but she wouldn't listen."

"I thought you were backing her up. You seemed so interested."

"When I realized there would be no talking her out of it, I gave her my support. That's how you make it in the world. I expected you to spout a bunch of shit, then take your money and leave."

He was mad because she hadn't gone out with him. "It's nothing personal," she explained. "You're just not my type."

He waved her words away. "Then you started talking about barns and digging a hole. What did you see in that hole?" he asked. "It was something that scared you, wasn't it?"

"Nothing. I didn't see anything." She wouldn't tell him about the pumpkin. She wouldn't tell anybody about the smashed, broken pumpkin.

"You saw something. I know you saw something."

A thought, an image, flashed in her brain. It was like one of her dreams, but not a dream, because she was wide awake. A man. Holding something in his hand. A shiny knife, with blood dripping from it.

Drip, drip, drip. Blood hitting the carpet, falling on her feet.

Drip, drip, drip.

The man in front of her had done something bad, something very bad, something he didn't want her or anyone else to know about.

She was distantly surprised to find that life suddenly seemed precious, that it was something she didn't want to give up on, not just yet anyway. "I don't know anything," she said, watching him with the intentness of a cat. When the moment came, she would fling open the door and run, all in one swift motion.

She watched him. Watched his empty eyes, in a face that was perfect angles, a face that should have been handsome but wasn't. She watched him. Watched the lids droop to cover his eyes, cover his pupils.

She spun. She grabbed the doorknob.

It was like running in quicksand. In the way of all nightmares, her body became sluggish and heavy, and no matter how her mind screamed at her to run, her legs were no match for the quicksand.

She opened the door, one, two, three inches. A hand above her head shoved it shut. Campbell's body slammed into hers, smashing her against the door. Lights flickered in front of her eyes. She blinked, trying to see.

The knife.

He had a knife.

The knife came down on her. But then the knife changed, turning into something else. A hypodermic needle. She opened her mouth to scream. At the same time she felt something sharp as he plunged the needle into her neck.

The scream died in her throat. The only sound she could emit was a choking gasp, the pain having robbed her of air.

It was fate, she thought, understanding the futility

of everything. This room—it had warned her from the beginning, constantly foreshadowing this very moment.

She gulped at the stagnant motel air but couldn't seem to pull in an adequate supply. She began sinking. Down, down, to the orange carpet. Down, down, until she was lying in a puddle on the floor, her face against the abrasive, stinking orange that she so hated, so feared.

Dr. Campbell loomed over her, smiling his dead smile. "Go nighty-night." He had something in his hands. The orange bedspread. He brought it down over her head. She tried to scream, tried to struggle, but she couldn't move. She felt detached from her legs, her arms, her body.

I can't breathe.

That was her last thought as the darkness swallowed her.

"She's gone." Jo's voice barked from the cell phone Daniel held to his ear.

Daniel turned left on Main Street, cruising at patrol speed. "Who?" he asked, even though he knew damn well who.

"Cleo! I went to the motel to pick her up this morning, and she's gone. Her suitcase. Everything."

Daniel felt sick. Guilty. Responsible. But it wasn't his fault, he told himself. She was an adult. He couldn't feel responsible for everything and everybody, couldn't blame himself for every bad thing that happened.

"This is where you're supposed to tell me you were right all along."

"I'm not going to do that."

"Good. Then while you're on patrol, why don't you swing by The Palms and pick up the bill? I was so upset this morning that I forgot to get it."

"Sure thing."

Daniel pushed the power button, put down the phone, and hung a right, heading in the direction of The Palms.

Before getting the bill from Willie, he decided to check out room six.

Empty, just as Jo had said. Cleo's suitcase plus all of her clothes were gone. He checked the bathroom. Except for a bar of soap in the shower, it was empty, too. He checked the drawer next to the bed. The pill bottle was gone.

He got down on his knees to look under the bed, expecting to find the bedspread where he'd stuffed it two nights before. Instead there was nothing but a pair of orange curtains. He got to his feet and made another perusal of the room. No bedspread. Ordinarily he'd just think she'd taken it. The problem with that idea was that she'd *hated* it. She hadn't wanted the bedspread anywhere close to her. You don't swipe something you hate.

In the harsh light streaming through the louvered windows that probably hadn't been washed since Millie and Babe owned the place, the room looked even tackier. The stains on the carpet showed up even more. And the walls were smeared with handprints, grease left by a million previous occupants. He'd been against Cleo's coming, but Christ, why hadn't somebody found her a decent place to stay? A room at somebody's house or something.

He checked the room out thoroughly, not really knowing what he was looking for. Every time he passed the door, wet carpet squished under his feet. He spotted something on the door. He leaned closer.

Blood. It looked like dried blood.

It could have been there for years. For all he knew, this could be the room where the prostitute had been murdered.

He felt something hard under the sole of his boot. He backed up, then dug around in the matted carpet. Caught under the orange fibers was a small clear plastic cap, the kind used to cover the needle of a syringe.

It could have been there for years, too.

He left the room, closing the door behind him. At the lobby desk he found Willie. "I need a list of any phone calls made from room six," he said.

"I don't know if I can do that," Willie said. "Invasion of privacy and all that."

"Cut the crap," Daniel said wearily. "Just get me the numbers."

Willie went to the handprint-smeared computer and clicked a few keys. The printer hummed, then began to print out. Willie tore off the paper and handed it to Daniel.

"Don't clean room six," Daniel told him. Then he thought he'd better clarify that. "And don't rent it to anybody."

"That's a waste of a perfectly good room," Willie griped.

"The police department will pay for it."

He couldn't refuse payment on a room nobody was using.

Back in the squad car, Daniel looked at the list of numbers. It wasn't exactly a list. There were only two phone numbers on the paper: his and a number with an area code he thought might be Washington state. He picked up his cell phone and punched in the number.

An answering machine. A man's voice.

"*You have reached the home of Adrian, Mavis, Macy, and Carmen Tyler. Please leave a message.*"

Daniel hung up. A brother? Almost had to be.

What a strange feeling, to have made love to a woman he knew absolutely nothing about.

He started the car and headed for the police station.

21

Cleo was in a place where nothing mattered.

A dark place.

A place that smelled of decay.

A place where sharp things poked and scratched the side of her face.

Drugs were singing softly but insistently in her veins. If she had cared to lift her head, she couldn't have done it.

Tired. She was so tired.

But it was a good kind of tired, the kind of tired that was the door to oblivion, to a numbness that was deeper than the deepest sleep. That numbness welcomed her. It wrapped its arms around her, pulling her under.

The next time Cleo surfaced, she was slightly more aware of her surroundings. This time she knew that the material scratching her face was straw or hay. This time she felt the stiffness of her body, the dryness of her mouth, the thickness of her tongue.

Drugged.

She'd been drugged.

Open your eyes.

She forced her eyes open. Her lids were so heavy, so incredibly heavy.

Darkness.

She let her eyes fall closed. Too heavy. She groaned and uncurled her body from a fetal position, rolling to her back, her arm dropping limply at her side.

She tried to pull her thoughts together, tried to figure out what was going on, what had happened to her. She remembered a face, a name.

Campbell.

Why? Why is he doing this?

She had to get up. She had to get away.

But she couldn't move. She was being sucked under again, pulled down, swallowed.

Daniel took the steps in front of the police station two at a time, so preoccupied with Cleo's disappearance that he didn't see Burton Campbell until he almost smacked into him.

"Heard your psychic skipped town," Campbell said.

"Maybe," Daniel said curtly. The last thing he wanted was to chitchat with Campbell.

"What do you mean, maybe?"

"I'm not convinced she left of her own free will."

Campbell's eyebrows lifted in surprise. "Yeah?" He turned his eager Boy Scout curiosity on Daniel. "You saying somebody made her leave?"

"I don't know."

"Who would do that? And why? I'll bet she just skipped town. She was a flake. A con artist. You said so yourself."

"I don't seem to recall you backing me up on it."

Campbell shrugged. "It seemed harmless enough."

"I gotta go. I've got some calls to make."

"If you need any help, let me know."

Daniel had checked out the phone number he'd gotten from Willie and found out it was a Seattle prefix. Now, in his office, he tried the number again. And this time Adrian Tyler answered.

"This is Daniel Sinclair," he began. "I'm a police officer in Egypt, Missouri."

"Cleo," the man said immediately, almost as if he'd been expecting Daniel's call. "Something's happened to Cleo."

"Nothing's happened," Daniel said quickly, hoping to reassure him. "Are you her brother?"

"Yeah." The panic was still heavy in the man's voice. "What's going on? Is Cleo all right?"

"It looks like your sister left town before fulfilling her obligations, but I'm just making sure that's all there is to it. Have you heard from her?"

"Not for several days. What do you mean, left

town? You're talking about my sister as if she's running some kind of scam. Tell me what you know, tell me what's going on."

Daniel told him about the empty motel room, leaving out the blood and syringe cap, since he didn't know if there was any connection.

"Cleo wouldn't just leave without a good reason. There had to be some reason. Something you're not telling me."

Daniel thought about the night before, about how upset Cleo had been when she left his house. He should have gone after her. "There were some reasons, things I won't go into right now, but I know she wanted to leave. It was no surprise to find her room empty."

"She would have called me. She always leaves a number where she can be reached."

"If you hear from her, call me collect," Daniel told him. He gave him three different phone numbers, then hung up.

Thirsty.

Cleo was so thirsty.

She tried to swallow, but her throat was too dry.

The drugs were wearing off. Her head hurt. Her body ached from lying in one position for so long. Her skin hurt.

She opened he eyes again.

Darkness. Total darkness. Yet she had the feeling

it wasn't night. She rolled to her stomach, then pushed at the straw-covered surface until she was on her hands and knees. She waited a few moments to catch her breath, the pain in her head more intense now that she'd shifted positions.

Ignoring it, she got her feet under her. She wasn't wearing shoes. Where were her sandals?

Steadying herself with her hands, she slowly straightened, stirring up the straw beneath her, along with the smell of age and must and mold and dead things.

Blindly she reached in front of her. Touching nothing, she shuffled around, slowly turning, her arms outstretched. She took one slow, cautious step, then another, and another, her fingers finally coming in contact with rough, weathered wood. She felt along a wall, her hands moving over boards and seams. She turned, feeling along the next wall. And the next. And the next. No door. But there had to be a door!

She must have missed it. That had to be what had happened. Somehow she'd missed it.

She felt the walls again, this time going higher and lower, her panic increasing with each step, with each turn of the corner as she counted the walls, hitting four, going around again, then again.

A loft. Or an attic, she thought. That was why there was no door, at least no door on the wall. She dropped to her knees, digging through the straw, sweeping it away until her palms came into contact with something damp, something cold. Dirt. Cold, damp earth.

No.

The vision she'd had that day in the police station—it had come true. *She* was what she'd seen when she looked in the hole. She'd seen herself, her pathetic, broken self.

She threw her weight against the wall, hoping to hear the weathered wood splinter under the impact. There wasn't the slightest give.

Underground.

Sweet God in heaven, she was underground.

With both fists she pounded on the wall. She screamed until she was hoarse, but nobody came. Nobody heard.

Her legs folded under her and she collapsed in the straw. Nobody would hear. Because nobody was coming. Nobody was looking for her. Daniel would be glad she was gone. He would think, *Good riddance.* Jo would be hurt that she'd left, but Cleo's disappearance wouldn't surprise her. The only person on the entire planet who would miss her was Adrian. And he wouldn't begin to suspect anything for a week or two. By then she could be dead.

Cleo came awake with a start.

Hollow footsteps, moving closer, closer, stopping just above her head.

She opened her mouth to cry for help, but stopped herself before the words could escape.

From somewhere up above, she heard scraping, like the sound of wood being dragged across wood. Suddenly a door above her head creaked open. Dim light seeped in. With eyes open a slit, she watched from under her arm as a ladder was lowered.

"Cleo?"

Campbell.

Her heart beat frantically in her chest. Her breathing was a roar in her ears.

She watched as he climbed down the ladder. He wore the same shiny shoes he'd worn at the motel, the same dark jeans. He bounced a little when his feet hit the straw, and made a rustling sound as he approached.

She closed her eyes. She thought about her self-hypnosis, willing her breathing to steady.

"Cleo?" The voice was near, just a few inches from her face. He shook her arm. He slapped her face.

She moaned but didn't open her eyes.

Let him do something stupid, she told herself. *Let him make a mistake*.

"I brought you some clothes."

She heard the crackle of a paper bag.

"And something to drink."

He was fast. She knew he was fast. But she had desperation on her side.

She heard the hiss of a plastic twist cap. The next thing she knew, something cold and wet splashed in her face.

She inhaled, sucking liquid into her lungs. She choked, her body racked with spasms, coughing until her chest felt raw. When she could finally breathe again, she fell back against the straw, staring at him through watery eyes.

"What . . . do you want?" she asked.

"I want you to shut up." Somehow he managed to retain his pleasant voice, speaking as if they were discussing dental care. It made the situation all the creepier, all the scarier.

"You think I know something about you, but I don't. I don't know anything. Why don't you let me go? I'll leave. I'll go far from here."

"And not tell anybody about me?"

"I don't *know* anything about you!"

He reached out and stroked his fingers down the side of her face. "Don't lie. You know everything about me."

Her instincts had been right from the beginning. Never trust a guy with a good haircut, expensive shoes, and a perfect set of teeth.

He sat down in the straw and leaned back on one elbow, crossing his ankles. "Here," he said, reaching into the paper bag beside him. "I brought something for you." He pulled out a black nylon slip and tossed it at her.

She grabbed it as it slid down her face, fingering the slick fabric. "This isn't mine."

"Did I say it was? Put it on."

She dropped it. "Maybe later."

He picked up the slip and angrily shoved it at her. "Put it on. Now. While I watch."

"No." She threw it back at him.

"What?" he asked in disbelief.

"I said no."

He laughed in the friendliest, most amused way, the sound making the hairs on her arms stand up. "You want to know what's funny?" he asked, still chuckling. "Nobody's looking for you. Did I tell you that? *Nobody*. In fact, everybody's glad you're gone. Guess who I saw just a few hours ago? Ol' Sheriff Sinclair. You know what he told me? He said, and these were his exact words, 'I'm glad the bitch is gone.' That's what he said. 'I'm glad the bitch is gone.' So I guess what I'm getting at is that it's just you and me. And you'd better be nice to me, you'd better do what I say, because I'm the one in control here. Now put on the slip."

She had to humor him. It would be her only chance to catch him off guard.

She picked up the slip, then got shakily to her feet. She moved away from him to stand in the darkest corner of the room. With her back to him, she removed her top.

"Bra too," he said.

She took off the bra, then slid the black slip over her head, pulling it over her skirt. She reached under the hem of the slip to remove the skirt, sliding it down her hips and stepping free. The lace hem hit her at midthigh.

She suddenly realized it was the slip from her vision.

She slowly turned around, arms at her sides.

"Nice," he said, nodding.

He looked at his watch, frowning for the first time. "I have an appointment in forty-five minutes."

"Then I guess you'd better be on your way," she said. When he was on the ladder, she would grab his ankle and knock him off balance. He would fall. She would get away.

But he didn't move toward the ladder. He moved toward her.

She moved to the left.

He followed.

She could overpower him, she tried to tell herself.

He pulled something from the pocket of his jacket. A syringe.

He snapped off the cap and began moving closer.

She grabbed his arm with both hands, feeling the muscles bunch under the fabric of his shirt.

He was too strong for her. The needle came around and plunged into her arm.

She screamed. While she still had strength, she swung at him, slapping him in the side of the face. He grabbed her by both wrists, twisting her arms, shoving her to her knees.

The room tilted. Warmth seeped into her limbs and she slumped to the ground.

But she didn't black out.

She could feel his hands moving over her, stroking her legs, her thighs, moving higher.

She tried to push him away, but she couldn't move. She couldn't lift her arms.

He unzipped his pants, then tugged at her panties, while she tried to remove herself, tried to fly away.

Fly away, fly away.

She braced herself for the pain of his forced penetration.

Waiting, waiting.

It didn't happen.

Instead he hit her. Hard, against the side of the face, the blow bringing her around. And then he was shoving himself away from her as if she had some disease, as if she were some sickening, rotten thing.

Open your eyes, she told herself. *You have to open your eyes.*

Her eyelids were so heavy, so incredibly heavy. She finally managed to open them a crack, enough to see Campbell standing over her, zipping up his pants. *He must not have been able to perform,* she realized with overwhelming relief.

"Sinclair was right," he said. "You *are* a bitch."

22

Inside room six of The Palms, the air conditioner had conked out. It had to be ninety degrees in there, the heat intensifying the smell of ancient body odor. Daniel was searching the room again, looking for any clues he might have missed the first time through.

He dumped out the wastebasket on the bed, mentally cataloging the items. A couple of smashed paper cups, a straw, the magazine she'd asked to borrow that first day.

The used rubber.

He cringed at the memory of that night, trying to block it from his mind. He had to stay focused.

He flipped through the magazine. It was full of holes where pictures or articles had been cut out.

Why?

He held the wastebasket to the edge of the bed and scooped all the trash back inside, the magazine hitting the bottom with a metallic thud.

On the wall was a dime-store landscape, the frame

warped, the colors faded. With both hands he lifted it from the wall, disgusted to find that it covered a hole. A fucking peephole. He hung the picture back on the wall, not bothering to straighten it.

He ripped the sheets from the bed, then pulled off the stained mattress, leaning it against the wall.

Lying on the box spring was a yellowed piece of stationery with *The Palms* in faded green print across the top. Glued to the paper were pictures cut from a magazine.

He picked it up.

Pictures of barns. It looked as though she'd cut out every barn picture she could find, gluing them down, overlapping them.

Why the hell had she cut out pictures of barns? To convince any remaining skeptics of her validity? Or was there more to it than that?

He rubbed the back of his neck. Damn, it was hot, suffocating.

He laughed, but it was a sound devoid of humor.

He was probably the biggest sucker of them all. He'd accused Jo of being scammed, but he was the one who in the end had refused to believe that she'd walked out on them. One mind-blowing night in her arms, and he was suddenly one of her followers, her damn slave.

He tossed down the paper and left the motel room. He had to get out of there.

The air outside, even though it was close to ninety and just as humid, felt cooler than the staleness of the motel room. He stood there a moment, filling his lungs with the fresh air, when he heard the ring of his cell phone. He reached through the open window of the car and grabbed the phone.

"Yeah?" he barked into the receiver, figuring it was Jo wanting him to pick up a twelve-pack of Coke for her.

"Daniel Sinclair?"

Hot. It was so damn hot.

He moved away from the car to stand next to the motel room door, seeking out shade, even if there was only a couple of feet of it. "Speaking."

"It's Adrian Tyler."

Daniel slumped against the wall, his eyes closed, his head back. *Thank God.* "You've heard from Cleo." It was a statement, not a question.

"No."

Daniel straightened and opened his eyes.

"I want to know what's going on," Tyler said.

"No news."

"Maybe I'd better come down there," Tyler said, sounding pissed, sounding as if he'd spent the past several hours stewing around, letting things grow out of proportion. "You hillbillies are probably sitting on your asses, scratching your armpits and chewing a wad of tobacco while the trail gets cold."

The man was as charming as his sister. "Calm down," Daniel said. On one hand, he was irritated by Tyler's insults; on the other, he understood the guy's frustration.

"I want to know everything," Tyler said again. "Where was she staying? Someplace that wasn't safe? I'll bet you put her in some dump, didn't you? Some crack house." Tyler paused, then groaned. Daniel could imagine him grabbing a handful of his own hair. "She was walking on the edge as it was," Tyler said, his tone becoming more pleading than angry. "Don't you know how fragile she is? Couldn't you see that? Or didn't you give a damn?" His voice wavered and broke.

"What do you mean, your sister is fragile?" Daniel asked.

"She has some problems. I don't mean she's crazy. It's nothing like that. I'll bet she pretty much told you she was a fraud, am I right?"

"Yeah, but she didn't have to tell me. I knew it before she got here. I'd heard about that deal in California, about how she stepped in and took credit for finding that little girl."

"That deal in California," Tyler said. "You wanna know about that deal in California? Cleo didn't want anybody to know about her involvement. The cops were happy to take credit, but then the press stepped in and sensationalized the whole thing. She sees things, Sinclair. She's been lying to me about it, but I'm her brother and I can see through her, no matter how good the act."

"If she's psychic, why pretend she isn't? How does that make sense?"

"It's something to do with a car wreck she was in. I can't tell you any more. I've told you too much already. Cleo's a private person. She wouldn't want anybody to know the stuff I told you. And the only reason I told you was because I want you to find her."

"I'm not even sure she's missing."

"Something's happened," Tyler said with conviction. "She knows how I worry, and she never goes anywhere without giving me a telephone number where she can be reached. I know her. And I know this isn't like her. Not like her at all."

Daniel didn't know what to think. Maybe the whole damn family was nuts. But he couldn't deny that he'd had an uncomfortable feeling about this from the beginning.

With the cell phone to his ear, Daniel went back into the motel room and picked up the paper Cleo had left behind. "I'm in her motel room right now," Daniel said. "I found a collage she made, a bunch of pictures cut from a magazine. What's that all about?"

At first the man was silent. Then he began to speak—a little reluctantly, Daniel thought.

"Her therapist used to have her do stuff like that." His voice sounded sad. Tired. "Whenever she was having a problem handling something, she'd cut pictures out of magazines. That's all I know."

"What about orange? Why doesn't she like the color orange?"

Another silence, as if Tyler was wondering how much he should tell a stranger about his sister. "It has something to do with the car wreck and her boyfriend getting killed. Listen, man. Even though I'm her brother, Cleo never spilled her guts to me. I can't fill in all the blanks for you. I just know you need to get off your butt and do something."

There was more to know about Cleo. A lot more, but Daniel didn't think he was going to get anything else out of the brother, at least not now.

He stared at the collage in his hand. He thought back to the day of the séance, or whatever the hell it was. She'd spewed all that stuff about a road and a barn. He hadn't believed her . . . until he'd gone into the bathroom, until he'd seen the naked fear in her face. In that encapsulated moment he'd believed her. In that moment he would have believed anything she said. But then she'd gotten mad. She'd pushed him. And he'd come to his senses.

Or had he? Had he really?

Had he seen the real Cleo for one unguarded moment? And when she realized how open and vulnerable she'd left herself, she'd lashed out, distracting him, bringing him back to his original impression of her—of Cleo the con artist, Cleo the fraud.

What if she had seen not the key that day but herself? What if she had been not looking into the past but predicting the future?

"Premonition."

Daniel's thoughts were pulled back to the man on the other end of the line. Premonition? How had Tyler known? Was he a mind reader? Was this sixth sense a family trait? A genetic thing?

"Where's Premonition?" Tyler asked. "Cleo never goes anywhere without him. She loves that dog."

Daniel didn't handle guilt well. At the moment it was eating at his stomach. "My brother's got the dog."

"What? I don't get it."

"She gave him to my brother."

"She never goes anywhere without that dog," Tyler said. "She loves that dog." His voice rose. "That dog is like her kid."

"I don't know." Daniel thought about that first evening, the way she'd watched Beau and Premonition playing, her expression appearing calm. Maybe if they hadn't just met, he would have recognized emotions hidden to a stranger.

"I'll call you if I hear anything," Daniel said, sweat running down his spine.

After hanging up, he continued to stare at the collage in his hand.

23

Groping blindly in the darkness, Cleo found the bottled water Campbell had dropped. She unscrewed the cap and drank thirstily. Before she was finished, an odd warmth began seeping into her arms and legs. She tried to put the cap back on the bottle but couldn't match the threads. On the third try, she managed to make them meet. Before she could screw the lid on tightly, the bottle slipped from her numb fingers, cold liquid splashing on her legs. She wilted against the straw, unable to hold her head up any longer.

Then she slept, a sleep fraught with dreams.

She was back in the motel room.

Cleo looked at the reflection in the mirror. Instead of seeing herself, she saw a stranger—someone with blond hair, full breasts overflowing from a tight black slip.

Waiting. She sensed that the woman was waiting for someone.

The door opened. A man walked in.

The woman who was Cleo, but not Cleo, dropped to the bed, her arms outstretched.

The man kissed her. Kissed her so hard it hurt, so hard she tasted blood. She laughed, not wanting him to know she was scared.

Cleo closed her eyes tightly. She didn't want to see any more. He was going to hurt her. She *knew* he was going to hurt her.

He bit her neck. She screamed and tried to pull away from his grip.

She couldn't.

He was going to hurt her. Hurt her.

Kill her.

Don't look.

She had to see who it was, had to know even though she didn't want to know. She opened her eyes. She made herself look directly into the passionless eyes of Dr. Burton Campbell.

The sound of the dental drill rang in Dr. Burton Campbell's ears.

His patient flinched and tried to pull away.

"Almost done, Mrs. Cabot."

He pressed harder, his mind drifting to the woman in the barn. He'd thought it over and decided he was going to have to kill her. He didn't want to. He wasn't some psycho, killing people for the sake of killing them. But he had a reputation to protect, and the only way to be certain nobody would ever find out about the prostitutes was to kill Cleo Tyler. It was that simple.

Beneath the sound of the drill, Mrs. Cabot, a woman in her mid-fifties, a woman with very little tolerance for pain, was making noises in her throat, a kind of panicky hum, the sounds getting louder and more desperate by the second. With an internal sigh Burton pulled the drill away, impatient and irritated at her for making this take twice as long as it should.

"Are you feeling some discomfort?" he asked in a concerned, soothing voice.

She nodded, her brows drawn tightly together, her eyes watering.

"I'm almost done," he said. "Just one more minute and we'll have it."

She shook her head and said something that was too garbled to understand.

"More novocaine?" he asked.

He picked up a syringe from the stainless-steel dental tray. "I'll just deaden that a little more for you," he said, patting her arm, leaning over her. "We don't want anyone to be in pain." He jabbed the needle into the fleshy part of her mouth, just under her tongue, pushing the plunger too fast, novocaine spilling down her throat.

He hadn't meant to kill either of the prostitutes. Both had been an accident. The last one had told him she liked rough, kinky stuff—that was why he'd picked her—but at the first sign of blood she'd freaked. She'd acted like *he* was the lowlife, the pervert. That pissed him off, really pissed him off. He'd shoved her, held her down. She started screaming. Well, what else could he do but make her stop?

With hindsight, he saw that he should have just shot her full of dope, making it look like she overdosed and killed herself. But she was bruised and bloody, and he'd panicked.

Maybe he could have told a slanted version of the truth and gotten off with a couple of years, but his reputation would have been ruined. And his reputation was everything to him.

But the drug thing might work with the Tyler woman. Oh, yeah. Why hadn't he thought of that before? He would load her up with morphine. When she was too drugged to fight him, he'd find a vein in her arm and finish her. She wouldn't know a thing. It would actually be a *pleasant* experience for her.

His daydream moved on. *He* could even be the one to find the body.

He almost laughed out loud at the idea. How perfect. He imagined himself on the front page of the paper, looking distraught and concerned, maybe a glimmer of a tear in his eyes.

He smiled. "How does that feel, Mrs. Cabot?" he asked, poking a metal instrument against the woman's cheek. "Numb yet?" His smile broadened. "You know I don't like to see my patients in pain."

She closed her eyes in relief, nodding, letting him know he could proceed, that everything would be all right. She was in capable hands.

24

Three days dragged by with no sign of Cleo. Every barn within a ten-mile radius of Egypt had been searched. Nothing. Daniel had hardly slept, his body running on adrenaline, caffeine, and worry.

"Did you check the barn at that Radcliff farm?" Beau asked.

Beau was dressed in his Tastee Delight shirt and cap, sitting at the kitchen table, working on a bowl of cereal before heading out. In true Beau fashion, he wasn't worried about Cleo in the least. Not that he didn't care. If something bad happened to her, he would just pretend that she'd left town.

It had to be nice, Daniel thought, being able to hang on to the naïveté of youth no matter how old you got, no matter how many bad things happened. With most people who suffered a great loss or witnessed an unnecessary act of violence, there was no looking back, no returning to the way it had been before. Because now you had proof that bad things happened for no reason. And life didn't always make sense. And you knew it could strike again, would strike again. The death of a friend. The death of a loved one. A murder. A murder committed for no reason other than to watch a person die.

Beau hadn't been tainted by the horrors of life. He didn't know that most things were out of his control. Control wasn't anything he ever thought about. He could sit there eating his cereal. When he took a bite and it slid to his stomach, the food didn't churn and churn until it turned into a heavy stone. At night he slept a deep sleep, because in his own mind his mother was at a nursing home. In his own mind she would be coming back any day now. And Cleo had simply gotten tired of Egypt.

Daniel had gone without sleep for too long. He couldn't stay focused. "The Radcliff place?" he asked. "There's no barn on the Radcliff place. There used to be, but it burned down along with the house."

"There's a barn. A different barn."

"How do you know?"

"I saw it. When I was riding with Percy, delivering mail. He turned wrong, and we ended up at a barn. There was a lot of weeds in the road. Percy got some of them stuck under the car."

"There was a barn?" Daniel asked, leaning both hands on the table, staring at his brother. "Are you sure?"

Beau took another bite of cereal, swallowed, then

continued. "Yeah, a big, broke barn with one of those wind things on top."

"A weathervane?"

"Yeah. Weathervane."

Beau had an eye for detail. If he said there was a weathervane, then there was a weathervane.

"With a pig. It had a pig on it."

Daniel grabbed his truck keys off the table and headed for the door. "Thanks, Beau."

Hands on her. Cold hands. Rolling her over. Rolling her to her back. Something tight on her arm. Tight, like a big rubber band. Slapping. Somebody slapping the inside of her arm, rubbing, slapping, breathing hard.

A poke. A sharp/dull poke. The rubber band fell away. The ground fell away.

Swallowed.

A delicious warmth trailed through her veins. She could feel it moving through her, soothing and beautiful. She smiled. She sighed. She was sucked away.

Daniel pulled down the lane that led to the Radcliff place, his heartbeat picking up speed.

There was the spot where the house used to be; the only thing left was the cement foundation and a brick chimney. To the left, across the lane, was a small hill of soil, littered with the ugly kind of weeds that went along with disturbed earth. A huge milking barn had once stood there. It had caught fire the same night the house burned down. As far as Daniel knew, the Radcliffs still owned the place, but after that night they'd quit farming and moved to the city.

There was a lane of sorts, leading past the place where the barn used to be. The weeds were so tall and overgrown that his two-wheel-drive truck wouldn't clear them. He shut off the engine and got out, slamming the door behind him.

It was quiet. Peaceful.

Birds called from nearby trees. The sun beat down on his head. He walked along the path, noting that someone had been there within the last few days. Weed stalks were broken, leaves crushed.

That didn't mean anything. It was the perfect place for a party. It seemed he spent half the summer breaking up keggers, feeling like a damn hypocrite.

The road turned to loose black dirt that was almost sand. The weeds were fewer now, the earth unable to hold enough moisture to nurture them.

Directly ahead was a barn. A red barn, like most barns in the area. Individuality wasn't a thing cultivated in Egypt.

Huge locoweed, mare's tail, and goldenrod grew around it. On the cupola was the weathervane, just as Beau—*and Cleo*—had said. On the side facing him was a sliding door that ran on a track and was big enough to drive a combine through. Next to it was a regular door, the kind that had been cut from the side of the barn, hinged, reinforced with a diagonal piece of wood running from top to bottom, and rehung where it had been cut.

He lifted the metal latch and pushed, the bottom of the door dragging across a flat stone that had most likely been pulled from a nearby creek bed and set years and years ago. He stepped inside, pushing the door shut behind him, the rough bottom catching and shuddering.

The barn was old, the support beams hand-hewn, the pegs hand-carved. Old barns were a work of art, a piece of Americana that was vastly underappreciated, with more doors and hidden compartments than a magician's box. From the way the barn was constructed, he could see that it had been used for milking at one time, then later turned into a farrowing barn. Inside, it was dark, slanted beams of light creeping in between rough-hewn boards, falling through a jagged rip in the roof. To the left were stalls that had once held cattle and horses; in the center, huge angled beams supported a second floor where hay bales had once tumbled off a conveyer belt to be stacked for winter. To the right was a tack room, just as dark and musty as the rest of the place.

The barn had been built on a hillside, giving it three levels, with the lower level partly underground. Under his feet the wooden floor echoed hollowly, hinting of empty space below. He walked carefully, knowing how unstable the rotting structure could be. The toe of his boot caught on something. He backtracked.

A ring.

A metal ring set into the floor. He kicked away the straw with his booted foot, slid a board aside, looped his fingers through the ring, and pulled, surprised that it opened so easily.

Cleo's words came back to him. *In the barn there was a hole, a black pit.*

Directly under the opening, he could make out a floor strewn with straw. Past the perimeter of light was nothing but a black void.

"Hello!" he yelled into the darkness, the echo of his own voice the only answer. Then he heard a sound, a small, tiny sound. A kitten, he thought.

"Cleo!"

There was the cry again, louder this time, sounding more human.

Hanging against a nearby wall was a ladder made of the same ancient wood as the barn. Daniel grabbed the ladder and lowered one end into the pit until it was embedded in the straw. He scrambled down the ladder, his feet sinking into the straw when he reached the bottom. He blinked and looked around, giving his eyes a chance to adjust to the darkness.

"Cleo?" he whispered, thinking he'd lost his damn mind, searching the bottom of a barn for a woman who was a thousand miles away. "Cleo?"

He heard it again. A low moan. A sound that was most definitely human.

He moved in the direction of the sound, his eyes gradually adjusting to the dimness of the room until he made out a shape huddled against the wall. His mind recognized lighter patterns as a person's bare arms, a person's bare legs.

He moved closer still, close enough to make out the curved cheek of a pale face, the line broken by wildly curling hair. He fell to his knees in the straw. "My God." His voice didn't sound like his own. "*Cleo.*"

He touched her bare arm. Under his palm, her skin felt cold, bloodless.

"Sinclair?"

The question came without movement, with hardly a breath taken to carry the whispered name to his ears.

One of her arms came up, searching, finding his hand, pulling it to her mouth. She kissed his arm, then pressed it to the side of her face and held it there. "Stay with me," she whispered, clinging to him. "Stay with me in this bad place."

She was out of her head.

Or she'd been driven out of her mind. Adrian Tyler's words came back to him. *My sister's very fragile.*

He swallowed hard. "Come on, Cleo. We've got to get out of here."

She continued to hug his hand, cuddle his hand, press her lips to his knuckles, his fingertips, his palm. "Shh," she said, her breath against his wrist. "It'll be okay."

Christ. Oh, Christ. "Cleo—" He slipped his hand from her grasp, then grabbed her by both arms, pulling her to a sitting position, where she swayed unsteadily, chin to her chest, arms hanging limply at her sides, hands curled. She'd lost weight. He could feel the bones beneath the muscles of her arms. He could feel every tendon, every delicate sinew.

He touched a finger to her chin, tipping her face toward his. All he could see was the glow of her pale skin. He couldn't make out any features. "Cleo, I'm going to get you out of here."

She nodded, her head moving sluggishly. "O-kaay. Ten-four, Eleanor."

He stood. Then, with his feet braced, he pulled her to a standing position.

She was boneless; he couldn't keep a grip on any part of her. He finally managed to get her upright, but as soon as he let go of her arm she began to sink. "Stand up," he reminded her.

For a fraction of a second he felt her stiffen. Just as quickly she dissolved again. Before he lost any more ground, Daniel bent his knees, hitched his shoulder under her diaphragm, then straightened, locking his legs once he was upright.

With Cleo draped over his shoulder, he grabbed the ladder with one hand, his other hand gripping Cleo's legs. He climbed one rung at a time, the muscles in his arms and legs straining. When he was two-thirds of the way through the door with his bundle, he shifted her weight, resting her bottom on the wooden floor. Out of the pit, he let her slump to her side, her legs, from the knees down, dangling at the edge of the opening. Two more rungs and he jumped free of the ladder.

His heart stopped.

Her skin, against the black of the nylon slip, was colorless except for the blue veins in her throat, the blue veins in her arms, the cuts, the bruises . . .

He dropped down beside her and lifted her arm, examining the blue and yellow skin where a needle had been inserted. Somebody had been shooting her full of drugs.

"Who did this to you?" he asked, his voice tight, his fingertips passing lightly over the damaged skin.

"The candy man," she said thickly, laughing softly to herself, her eyes slits.

He gave her a gentle shake, trying to get her to focus on his next words, words he didn't want to say but knew he had to. "Did he rape you?"

"Rape?" she asked foggily. She raised a hand to touch the side of her face, to touch a bruised cheekbone, a gesture that made his chest feel tight, that broke his heart. With her hand still hovering limply above her cheek, the vacant look in her eyes became more focused. "Daniel?" she asked in surprise. "'S that you?"

Jesus. Had she been driven over the edge by some madman? Was he never again going to see the bold Cleo who'd gotten off the train that hot summer day?

He lifted her legs out of the way and closed the door. Then he scooped her up in his arms and walked through the dark barn, out into the blinding sunlight.

She let out a gasp and brought up a hand to shield her eyes. "It's so bright," she said. "As bright as heaven."

"Keep your eyes closed," he told her softly but firmly.

He checked to see if she was listening. Her eyes were wide open, "Are you looking at the sun?" he asked, horrified. "Don't look directly at the sun. Close your eyes, Cleo."

She finally either heard him or once more succumbed to the overload of drugs running through her veins. Whatever the reason, her eyes drifted closed and stayed that way until they reached the truck.

"So thirsty," she said as he arranged her in the passenger seat. The skimpy black slip kept creeping up, revealing a pair of white panties. He pulled the slip down as best he could, then reached under the seat, his fingers coming in contact with a plastic water bottle. He unscrewed the cap, then tried to hand it to her.

"Water," he said, putting it in her hand. She tried to lift it to her face, but her arm began to tremble. She would have dropped the bottle if he hadn't caught it. He raised it to her mouth. "Take a drink."

She took a tentative sip. Then another. She put her hand to the bottle, her head resting against the seat, eyes closed, and took several long swallows. She quit drinking before he could tilt the bottle away. Water ran down her throat, soaking the front of her slip. She kept her eyes closed, her head back.

She was so still. Carved from marble, hardly breathing.

He recapped the bottle and was getting ready to close the door when she groaned and pressed a hand to her stomach. He caught her as she dove from the truck.

It took him a second to catch on, but as soon as she gagged, he knew what was coming. With an arm wrapped around her waist, her bottom pressed against his thigh, he held her while she emptied her stomach of the water she'd just swallowed. He could feel the muscles in her stomach contract, rejecting the most basic of elements. When she was finished, he helped her back into the truck, closing the door behind her.

He got back into the truck himself and found a couple of fast-food napkins under the seat. He wet them and wiped her smooth, colorless face. She didn't respond. She just sat there with her eyes closed, her head against the headrest.

Did her breathing seem extremely shallow? He could hardly detect a rise and fall to her chest.

He pulled the seatbelt across her shoulder and lap, hooking it with a firm click. Then he started the truck to quickly turn around and head in the direction of Egypt and the nearest hospital, some ten miles away.

It seemed like a hundred miles, the frantic, heart-pounding ride spent with Cleo drifting in and out of consciousness, Daniel holding the accelerator to the floor while the old truck hovered somewhere between sixty-five and seventy.

By the time he pulled up to the emergency-room door, Cleo had been unresponsive for the last three minutes. He laid on the horn and skidded to a stop. He cut the engine, yanked on the emergency brake, and jumped out. As soon as his feet hit the ground, he ran around the truck and opened the passenger door. Without waiting for an attendant, he scooped her up and carried her through the double automatic doors, falling into an old, familiar role. "Kidnap victim," he explained as two nurses met him in the hallway. "I tried to give her something to drink, but she just threw it up. She's been pumped full of something—I don't know what."

A gurney appeared out of nowhere. He put her down on it. A blood pressure cuff went around her arm. "Do we need to order a rape kit?" asked one of the nurses.

Now that Cleo was in good hands, Daniel's knees began to shake. He could feel his heart beating in his head. "I don't know."

"We'll find out from her soon enough. In the meantime, I'll order one just in case."

They had some trouble finding a vein. "She's dehydrated," the nurse said, rubbing and slapping, finally drawing blood.

The on-call physician showed up, quickly assessing the situation. "Slight miosis and respiratory depression. Naloxone," he ordered. "Slow drip, so she won't get sick."

They wheeled her away, leaving Daniel standing in an empty hall.

He felt dazed. He kept forgetting he was a cop,

that he was supposed to be the one in control. He found a phone and put in a call to Jo, telling her to contact the state police. Then he found a chair and dropped into it.

He was sitting there, staring at the floor, his skin tight, his eyes gritty. He needed to call Cleo's brother. But he didn't know anything yet. As soon as he knew something, he would call. God, he couldn't think straight.

A nurse appeared with a clipboard.

"She'll be okay?" he asked.

"She's getting fluids and naloxone, so she should come around pretty fast. Now for the fun part. I have all these tedious question to ask, just the standard, basic stuff."

He gave them as much information about Cleo as he could, which wasn't much more than her first and last name. He didn't know if she had insurance. "I doubt it," he said. "But the Egypt Police Department will pick up the tab." It wasn't his place to make such a decision, but he was pretty sure he could talk Jo into it, and she could talk the board into it.

"Allergic to any medications?"

He didn't know.

"Next of kin?"

He didn't know that either. "Her brother, I guess."

"Religious preference?"

He didn't know.

"Previous surgeries? Mental illness, depression, anything going on in her life that could affect what's happening now? When we were changing her into a hospital gown, we noticed a scar on her abdomen. Has she had a cesarean delivery?"

Daniel jumped to his feet. "I don't know! Christ, quit asking me this shit. I don't know!"

25

The next morning Daniel stood a few feet from the bed, arms crossed, letting Jo fuss over Cleo.

Cleo was sitting up, a tray of half-eaten food pushed to the side. Her color was better, her face a little more filled out. But she still didn't look good, didn't look healthy. An IV bag hung from a metal frame while a monitor digitally registered her pulse rate.

"We don't want to bother you with this right now, dear," Jo began, taking Cleo's free hand in hers. "But we have to know who did this to you." Jo was dressed in her usual police outfit, from the shiny badge to her shiny black shoes.

Muted sunlight fell across Cleo's face, making the dark circles under her eyes more pronounced. She looked from Jo to Daniel, then back at Jo. Daniel saw the uncertainty in her eyes and wondered at it. What didn't she want to say? What was holding her back?

"Cleo," Jo urged gently, "you must tell us, dear."

Cleo pulled her hand free and leaned against the pillow behind her back. She turned her face to stare out the window. From the second-story room, the only thing that could be seen was an occasional pigeon. She might have looked calm, but the digital readout on the flashing pulse rate monitor jumped from 90 beats per minute to 120.

In a flat, emotionless voice, she said, "Burton Campbell."

Daniel saw Jo stiffen, heard her gasp.

Leaving Cleo to gaze blankly into nothing, Jo spun around, grabbed Daniel by the arm, and pulled him out of the room and down the hall, out of earshot of Cleo.

"Don't you breathe a word of this," she whispered, her eyes intent. "Burton Campbell! If this got out, think how bad it would make the town look."

"What if he did it?"

"That's the most preposterous thing I've ever heard. I've known Burton Campbell for over twenty years. He comes from good family."

"And that makes a difference?" Daniel asked.

"You know as well as I do that Burton Campbell didn't kidnap that woman in there."

"Do I?"

"You want to believe he did it because you never liked him."

"Maybe I always had a feeling about the guy."

"You believe that ridiculous story?"

"Yes."

"Then you're a bigger fool than I am. What reason would he have for doing such a thing?"

"That's what we're going to have to find out."

"This isn't Los Angeles. Don't you think I know how bored you've been here? How you despise small-town life? You're just looking for excitement. Well, this kind of thing doesn't happen in Egypt."

"You want to keep your town on that top-ten list so badly that you can't see a serious crime when it's right in front of you." That was the problem with small towns. Saving face, keeping up appearances, was always the top priority, even if it meant lying and ignoring what was right under everybody's nose.

"There's been a crime all right, but Cleo Tyler committed it," Jo said. "Can't you see this is all orchestrated to make us look bad? Isn't it too convenient the way she told us exactly what was going to happen to her before it happened? That's because *she knew*. She did it to herself."

"Why?"

"To blackmail us."

"So does this mean you won't put a guard on her?"

"Of course I won't put a guard on her!"

"Do you plan to even question Campbell?"

"No! Listen to me, Daniel Sinclair. I stuck up for you when the whole town was on my back about hiring you. I've put up with your nonconformist, radical ways. With your refusing to wear a uniform, refusing to arrest teens for underage drinking. But I'm the chief of police. *I* tell *you* what to do. Understand? And I don't want an investigation launched. It would make us the laughingstock of the county. I don't want people to know I was taken in by a con artist from the big city."

She ran her fingers over her brown tie, making sure it was straight, then turned and marched away.

There had been a time when Daniel had had some influence over Jo. But she'd quit listening to him ever since some pot she'd confiscated had vanished. She'd accused Daniel of smoking it. The truth was that she'd seized one joint from a sixteen-year-old kid, and with the screwed-up law providing for a mandatory minimum sentence, that meant the kid would be put away in a maximum-security prison for seven years. So Daniel had just flushed the evidence.

He wasn't cut out to be a cop. All the damn rules—that was his problem. He could never obey blindly, not when a rule didn't make any sense. But there had been one time when that tendency to disobey rules had caused the death of four people . . .

Daniel walked slowly back to Cleo's room, rapping on the open door before stepping inside. She was exactly as they'd left her, staring out the window at the expanse of sky.

"I knew nobody would believe me," she said in the same monotone she'd used before.

"Did he give you any reason for abducting you?" Daniel asked.

"I guess it's all for the best," she said, her mind apparently still caught up in Jo's reaction. "Now I can just leave. No tedious questions. No statements to make."

"Cleo, I believe you."

She turned to look at him. There was no relief in her flat eyes. "Why? Why now?"

"I just do. Accept that, so we can concentrate on putting together enough evidence to bring him in."

She was silent a moment. Then, "He said I knew something about him. Something he didn't want anybody to know."

"What?"

"I don't know. That's what I told him. I didn't know anything. But he insisted I did, and that it would eventually come out."

"Is there anything else you can think of? Anything at all?"

"He said something about not meaning to hurt somebody."

Daniel approached the bed and checked the IV. It would be empty in a few hours. "The nurse said this is your last bag of fluid. When it's finished, I want you out of here. It might not be safe."

Her skin grew paler, if such a thing was possible. "I can't go back to that motel."

"I want you to come home with me."

She didn't say anything, and at first he wasn't sure if she'd heard him.

"Why?" she asked.

He rushed on to explain. "So I can keep an eye on you. You can use my mother's old room. I won't touch you, if that's what you're worried about."

From behind him came the soft-soled footsteps of a nurse. "Your brother's on the phone," she said to Cleo. "Do you want us to transfer the call to your room, or tell him to call back later?"

"I'll take it," Cleo said, pressing her hands against the mattress, shoving herself higher in the bed. The nurse left, and Daniel picked up the phone from the bedside table and handed it to Cleo.

"Adrian." There was a softness to Cleo's voice Daniel had never heard before.

"I'm fine," she said. There was a pause. "I swear."

Daniel turned and walked slowly from the room, the murmur of her voice carrying into the hallway. Or maybe his ears were just tuned to her frequency.

"No, Adrian. Don't do that. Please. I'm fine. You don't need to come here."

Another pause.

"You must wonder if it's always going to be like this," she said sadly. "Do you wonder if I'll always be a burden to you?"

He must have answered in the negative, because her voice grew soft again, less tense. "I love you."

That was followed by a long silence on her part as she listened. Daniel could imagine her brother asking questions Adrian didn't want to ask.

"Yes," she said. "They know who did it. They'll find him. . . . No, not yet, but they'll arrest him very soon. I'm not in any danger. . . . Yes, people are watching out for me."

Another question.

"No." Her voice dropped. "I wasn't raped. I swear. And even if I had been, well, it wouldn't be the end of the world, would it? Worse things have happened and I've gotten though them, haven't I?" She was using a tone of voice Daniel was becoming familiar with—the bubbly bluff.

Then she told him again that she loved him and said good-bye.

Daniel left with a heaviness in his chest that he didn't understand.

The first thing he did when he got home was call Campbell's house. When no one answered, he called Campbell's office.

"Dr. Campbell is out of town," the receptionist told him.

"Where'd he go?"

"He didn't say."

"Surely he left a number where he can be reached."

"I'm sorry. The only number he left was his associate's, Dr. Miller, in case of an emergency."

"Isn't that unusual?"

"Oh, no. They always take care of each other's emergencies. It works out very well for both of them."

Daniel hung up, then put in a call to the state police.

"Crime scene was picked clean," the head of investigations told him. "Nothing there."

"*Shit.*" Daniel followed that with a few words of

thanks, then hung up. Without wasting any time, he left the station and headed for the hospital, stopping to pick up some clothes for Cleo on the way.

The IV monitor had been beeping for ten minutes when Daniel appeared, a couple of plastic shopping bags in his hands.

"Clothes," he said, dropping the bags on the bed. "No sign of your suitcase yet, so I figured the only stitch of clothing you have to your name is what you were wearing yesterday."

"It wasn't mine."

"What?"

"The black slip. He gave it to me to put on. Right before he tried . . ." Her words trailed off.

"Where is it?"

"I don't know."

The nurse finally showed up to shut off the beeping machine. "We can take that needle out of you now," she announced in the perky way nurses had.

"Do you know what happened to the clothes she had on yesterday?" Daniel asked.

"Her belongings should be in a bag in her closet."

Daniel checked. The slip must not have been there, because Daniel asked, "Are you sure this is where it would be?"

"Positive."

The nurse loosened the tape on the back of Cleo's hand, then gently removed the needle. There were the customary release papers to sign, then the nurse bid Cleo a cheery farewell.

Alone with Daniel, Cleo picked up one of the bags he'd dropped on the bed. It felt weird to think of him going into a store and buying clothes for her. It seemed too personal.

What a strange thought. Here they'd been as intimate as two people could be, yet his buying clothes seemed more familiar than the act of sex. Why? Was it because it would have required more thought on his part? Was it because he would have had to think about her, about her size, maybe even her likes and dislikes?

She hadn't looked at his purchases yet, she told herself. For all she knew, he could have run into a store and grabbed the first thing he saw.

She pulled out a bundle of clothes. No pink polyester pantsuit, thank God. And nothing orange, which would have been even worse. And no Ozarks T-shirt. No, what he'd gotten her was something she might have picked out herself. A skirt of a gauzy material, decorated with a pattern of tiny flowers. A short-sleeved ribbed top with a V neck and satin piping the color of moss. Panties. Plain bikinis of white cotton, with a bra to match. For her feet, sandals not unlike the ones she'd had.

She hadn't cried, not once, during her entire ordeal. She hadn't even begged for her life, or begged not to be raped. But now she felt the pressure of tears against the back of her throat. She felt a stinging in her eyes. She blinked, her fingers curling tightly into the fabric of the top.

"Hey, if you don't like them," he said quickly, "I can return them."

He tried to take them from her, but she wouldn't let go.

"No. It's okay." His little show of panic had gotten her past the danger point. She no longer felt like dissolving into a storm of weeping. "These are fine."

"Right. Okay." He dug into the front pocket of his jeans and pulled out a knife. He opened it, then began slicing the tags from the clothes. When he was finished, he threw the tags away and closed the knife blade against his leg before pocketing it. He started to leave, but she called after him. "Sinclair?" He stopped, his back to her.

"I might need help," she explained.

He turned around. "I'll get a nurse."

"No. We'll have to wait forever. They're so understaffed. Just wait here. Sometimes I get dizzy when I stand up. Just wait on the other side of the curtain."

It seemed so stupid that they were both acting as if they'd never seen each other naked. But at the moment the pretense was fine. She couldn't deal with it any other way. Not just then.

He slid the curtain shut, mumbling something she didn't catch.

Lying in bed, she slipped the panties on under her gown. But when she tried to untie her gown, she couldn't undo the knot. She ended up calling for Daniel's help.

She bent her head, chin to chest, while he fumbled at the back of her neck, finally untying the knot. Then he quickly disappeared behind the screen again.

She let the gown fall to her waist, then went about trying to fasten the bra. Her arms were too weak, her fingers too stiff. Rather than call Daniel back, she gave up on the bra. Instead she slipped on the knit top. That was followed by the skirt, and finally the sandals, which she dropped to the floor, toed into position, and slipped her feet into. They were maybe a half size too small, but it didn't matter because they had an open back. She stuck the bra back in the bag.

"Ready," she said, sitting on the edge of the bed.

Daniel appeared again, his eyes going over her, lingering on her chest, where the fabric clung to her breasts, then moving back to her face. "Okay?" he asked.

"Fine." She grabbed the bag and stood, waiting a moment for a spell of light-headedness to fade.

I'm so weak, she realized with dismay as they walked to Daniel's truck. It was parked near the front door of the hospital, but her legs were shaking by the time she was inside, Daniel closing the door behind her.

He was acting as if nothing had happened between them. And maybe that was good. She was in no shape to try to analyze the situation, if there was really a situation to analyze.

She didn't know how to have any kind of relationship with anyone anymore. She didn't want to know how. At least that was what she told herself. It had been easy to be with Daniel that night, because she'd thought she would never see him again. That knowledge had given her a freedom, a lack of inhibition, that she normally wouldn't have had.

And yet to have him not say *anything*, to not even acknowledge that it had happened, was bugging her.

He put the truck in gear and pulled away from the curb. "There are no leads on Campbell—"

"It's just my word against his, and who's going to believe me?" she finished for him.

"What do you think about going back to the barn with me? Maybe you could do that trance thing and pick up something."

"Does that mean you no longer think I'm a fraud?"

"You may have faked it that last time, but earlier, the other time . . . I'm thinking it was real."

She thought about what she'd seen that day, about the hole in the ground. She had assumed it was a premonition, that she was the one in the hole, but maybe not. Maybe there was more to it than that.

"Go to the barn," she said.

"Now? I didn't mean now. I meant when you're feeling stronger. Don't you think I saw how you were shaking?"

"I won't be able to get the rest I need until Campbell is in jail. Go to the barn. Maybe there's something there. Something that was missed."

● ● ●

It was early evening when Daniel pulled the truck to a stop in the same weed-filled lane he'd carried Cleo through the day before.

She could barely remember it. All she could recall was a hazy sensation of relief, of feeling safe, the sun shining down on them with a brilliance that was blinding, the drugs Campbell had pumped into her running warm and slow through her veins.

Now the sun was low in the sky, big and orange. *My favorite color,* she thought mockingly. The sun scattered its light over everything, washing the sky, the air, in a hazy glow.

"We don't have to do this now," Daniel said, as if sensing her trepidation.

"I want to. I need to." She got out of the truck by herself, her legs actually feeling a little stronger than they had a half hour ago.

She walked slowly in the direction of the barn, her feet, with their red toenails, moving over the packed dirt of the lane, like her vision, yet unlike. In her vision she'd worn the black slip. In her vision she'd been barefoot. In her vision she'd been alone.

The shadow of the barn moved over her, blocking out the sunlight, bringing with it a damp chill even though the evening was warm. Without the brightness of the sun, everything was suddenly colorless, awash in drab grays.

Then she noticed that Daniel was holding the barn door open, waiting for her.

She couldn't move.

She couldn't make herself take another step.

"Maybe this is far enough," she said, closing her eyes, picturing what the barn looked like inside. Yes, there were the stalls to the left. And up above, the jagged hole in the ceiling, light spilling through it.

She imagined herself taking slow steps forward. Once again she wore the black slip. Once again her feet were bare, the wood beneath them rough. Just like before, she was drawn to an area of the barn where the floor was dirt, not wood.

How strange, she thought, *to have a dirt floor.* But the dirt was significant. There was a spot, a very certain spot, where if you dug with a shovel, you would find something.

Something secret. Something no one is supposed to see or find.

She opened her eyes and stared at Daniel. He looked tired, as if he hadn't slept in days, and he hadn't shaved in days. His eyes were a little glassy, a little bloodshot. Those eyebrows. Those beautiful, sun-bleached eyebrows. He had the most intriguing face. Looking at him made her feel safe, soft, feminine . . .

If they'd met under other circumstances, would things have been different between them? What if they'd both been taking night classes at a community college somewhere, and during the break they'd had coffee together? Or maybe if they'd both used the same library and went to check out the same book at the same time, and realized that they both were interested in ancient civilizations?

A different life.

Another life.

Far, far away.

"I have to go inside," she told him.

He nodded and opened the door wider.

She recoiled. "The smell," she said, bringing a hand to her nose.

"It just smells like an old barn."

"No, this is different." *Like death.*

She couldn't make herself move.

You have to go, Cleo. You have to go inside and show him the spot. As soon as you do, you can leave.

She removed her hand from her face. She stepped forward, into the darkness, into the smell, the putrid smell of bad things, bad places.

Light poured down from the hole above and cut through the cracks in the walls, looking like laser beams, starting out fine and condensed to broaden and finally fade to nothing.

We shouldn't be here, her sandals whispered, shushing across the floor as she moved toward the spot on the opposite side of the barn that she needed to show to Daniel. She had to walk past the stalls and under the hole in the roof.

"Here," she said, coming to a stop. "You have to dig here. Right here."

Daniel looked at her and nodded. Then he moved away. A minute later she heard him rummaging through things in one corner of the barn, heard the sound of clanking metal, until he came back with a rusty shovel. She stepped back and watched as he jabbed the point of the shovel in the ground.

It was time for her to leave.

But she couldn't move. Instead she remained where she was, watching.

With his foot he pressed the shovel deeper.

He dug, sweat running down the side of his face.

Funny, she'd forgotten that it was hot. Now she noticed that yes, it was hot, but she wasn't even sweating.

She should leave. She needed to leave.

"A pumpkin," she said with conviction. She suddenly knew what he would find. "A pumpkin." A shallow grave. A pumpkin in a shallow grave.

Leave. Turn around and leave this place. This bad, stinking place.

She realized he wasn't digging anymore. Now he was bent over the hole, looking closely at something. "Cleo, you'd better get out of here."

Her thoughts exactly. But she couldn't. Her feet wouldn't move.

"I don't want you to see this."

It was too late. She'd already seen it. In her mind. "A print dress," she said. "Red, with dots—no, white flowers on it."

Suddenly Cleo was aware of a change. Something was different. Something wasn't right. She turned to look behind her.

Burton Campbell stood there with his Dale Carnegie poise, his select-me-for-mayor smile. In his hand was a gun.

26

Daniel heard Cleo's gasp. Keeping a grip on the shovel, he slowly straightened from the hole and its grisly contents and turned to find himself looking down the barrel of a revolver.

"Burton Campbell," he said with no surprise.

A range of possible tactics raced through Daniel's mind one after the other, each quickly discarded. Cleo was too close to Campbell for him to attempt anything. If Daniel could get her to step away without attracting the guy's attention . . .

"I don't know what you've done," Daniel began in what he hoped was a conversational tone. "But anything more can only make things worse."

"Don't use those hostage negotiation tactics on me. You of all people should know they don't work. Didn't you single-handedly cause the death of a mother and her two children?"

Daniel stopped breathing.

"Jo told me all about it," Campbell said. "She tells

me lots of things. You know Jo. There's nothing she likes better than being the first link in the gossip chain."

The deaths had been Daniel's fault, brought about by an error in judgment and his damn inability to follow rules, follow protocol. He hadn't thought the kidnapper—who was no more than a scared kid—would pull the trigger. But Daniel had been mistaken. He'd pushed too hard too fast. There were gunshots from inside. By the time he and his team had rushed the house, no one was left alive, not even the kidnapper.

"You're just some charity case of Jo's," Campbell said. "She hired you out of pity. She told me you'd never get a job anywhere else. Nobody wants a mess like you. How old were those kids?"

"Shut up," Daniel said.

"Just goes to show what a fuck-up you are."

Daniel repositioned his grip on the shovel handle.

"He's baiting you," Cleo said. "Don't listen to him."

"You pretend to be in Egypt because of that retarded brother of yours, but I know you're using that as an excuse. You're afraid. Isn't that right? You're nothing but an alcoholic loser with a pitiful moron for a brother."

A cry of rage ripped from Daniel's throat. With one hand he shoved Cleo out of the way; with the other he swung the shovel.

Campbell lifted his arm to protect himself. The shovel connected with flesh and bone, the blade breaking away, leaving Daniel holding nothing but a piece of rotten wood. He threw down the handle and dove, grabbing Campbell with both hands.

"Daniel! No!" Cleo screamed.

Daniel heard the crack of a gunshot, the sound roaring in his brain. Pain, hot and searing, ripped through his shoulder, the impact throwing him to the ground.

"Daniel!" Cleo screamed again.

Time stuttered, stopped, then started again.

Cleo's mind pulled back—a way of distancing herself from the horror being played out before her.

Campbell raised the gun. Feeling like a bystander, Cleo watched until Campbell's arm was extended straight in front of him, the gun barrel pointing at Daniel.

Without conscious thought, Cleo lunged, throwing her body into Campbell.

Taken by surprise, he was knocked sideways just as the gun exploded. The bullet hit the wall with a *pitht*.

"Cleo! Run!" Daniel shouted.

Daniel was lying on the ground, one hand pressed to his shoulder.

No. I can't leave you here.

"Go!" he yelled, his voice thick with agony.

She hesitated too long.

Campbell shoved himself to his feet, his face flushed, his composure gone. "Both of you, outside!" He waved the gun wildly. When nobody moved, his face turned an even brighter red. "*Now!*" he shrieked, spit flying.

Cleo took a step toward Daniel.

"Stay away from him," Campbell ordered.

Instead, she grabbed Daniel's good arm and helped him to his feet. Once upright, he stood there swaying. Sweat ran down the side of his face, dripping off his hair. Blood, shiny and red, glistened against the dark green plaid of his shirt.

Campbell made them leave through a back door.

From there, he prodded them forward into a densely wooded area that didn't look as if another human had set foot there in years. Brambles cut at Cleo's arms and ripped her skirt. Thick, tangled, twisting vines caught her ankles and pulled her hair.

The vegetation was too thick for them to walk side by side, so Cleo took the lead while Daniel stumbled along behind her. She could hear his labored breathing. She could hear him when he crashed to the ground.

She swung around in time to see him struggling to his feet. Once upright, he looked into her eyes. In them, she saw so many things, but the main one, the one that broke her heart, was regret.

"You have nothing to be sorry for," she told him.

He squeezed his eyes shut. He straightened and his breath caught.

"Hurry up," Campbell commanded.

Cleo turned and continued walking.

Where was he taking them?

To their death. She and Daniel were going to die in a tangle of darkness and vegetation. He was taking them to a place where no one would find them.

From behind, Campbell barked out directions, telling her to go left, then right, until they finally worked their way down an embankment.

Cleo stopped so suddenly that Daniel ran into her.

Directly in front of her was an open well, the top level with the ground, the walls lined with stone, the stones covered with years and years of moss. "Oh, my God," she said.

"I'm going to rush him again," Daniel whispered hurriedly, his lips barely moving. "When I do, I want you to run. Run like hell and don't look back."

"He'll kill you."

"He's going to kill us both anyway. At least this way you'll have a chance."

"I'll rush him," she murmured back. "*You* run."

He gave her a crooked smile that said, *Come on. You know that won't work.*

"I see you found it," Campbell said, catching up. "I came across this the other day when I was looking for a good place to hide a body. It's deep. Toss a pebble down there. It takes forever to hit bottom. Go ahead."

When nobody moved, he repeated his request, only this time it was a command. Cleo found a small pebble near the crumbling well and dropped it in. She never even heard it hit.

Deep.

Thinking of dying in the creepy, musty barn had been bad, but this . . . this was worse. This was the monster in the closet, the monster under the bed.

She didn't see any way out. Daniel's idea of rushing him was maybe the only thing there was, and that didn't seem promising. She was so weak she could hardly stand, let alone outrun a madman. She looked at Daniel, begging him with her eyes not to try it. There had to be another way.

He shook his head infinitesimally. *No other way,* his eyes said.

There has to be, she pleaded silently.

There isn't. The regret was there again. And she knew it had nothing to do with Campbell, nothing to do with what was happening to them now.

It's okay. You didn't mean to hurt me.

"These old farms are notorious for abandoned wells like this," Campbell said. "I should adapt that to my rural renewal plan. They should all be sealed so no one can fall in them, don't you think?" His mood had improved now that everything was under control and going his way. "Both of you move a little closer," he instructed, like someone preparing to take a snapshot rather than perform an execution.

"Don't I get a last cigarette?" Daniel asked.

"That's a little too sentimental. Too much of a cliché. Besides," Campbell added, looking past the canopy of green above his head, "it'll be getting dark soon." He pulled the hammer back on the gun. "Who wants to be first? You?" He pointed the gun at Daniel. "Or you?" The gun shifted slightly until it was aimed at Cleo.

"Me." They spoke in unison.

Campbell laughed. "Isn't that sweet."

He was still laughing when a breeze kicked up from somewhere, somehow penetrating the thick foliage. Campbell tipped his head slightly, thinking he heard something. A sound.

Like a little kid.

There it was. A little kid, chanting one of those dumb verses, over and over.

"Old lady, old lady, turn around. Old lady, old lady, touch the ground."

What the hell?

Campbell turned his head, his eyes scanning the hillside, trying to find where the voice was coming from. There! A flash of red. Someone dashing from one tree to the next.

"Not last night but the night before, twenty-four robbers came knocking at the door. I went downstairs to let them in. They hit me over the head with a rolling pin."

"Hey!" Campbell shouted, his eyes straining for another flash of red, his ears intent upon the high-pitched voice. "Hey, kid! Come out of there!"

At that second Daniel threw himself on Campbell. "Run!" Daniel shouted to Cleo as the momentum of his attack sent both men to the ground. He tried to wrench the gun from Campbell's grip, surprised at the man's strength. They rolled, grunting, evenly matched. *Hold on*, Daniel told himself. He didn't need to win. He just needed to give Cleo a chance to get away.

Campbell was on top. Daniel's surge of strength

was quickly fading. If he was going to gain any advantage, it had to be now.

He hooked his legs under Campbell's and flipped them both so that he was once again on top. Campbell jabbed him in the shoulder. Daniel gasped, almost letting go of the wrist that held the gun. In a last-ditch effort, he pounded Campbell's arm against a stone that marked the perimeter of the well.

The gun clattered. Daniel shoved. They rolled again, leaving the gun behind. The absence of the weapon left Campbell's hand free. He used it to pummel Daniel's wounded shoulder. Pain flashed red and black. Campbell didn't let up, hitting him again and again until Daniel tasted blood, until the ground beneath him slanted, the trees above spun. He was going to black out. Had it been enough time? Enough time for Cleo to get away?

A voice cut through the haze and pain. Cleo's voice.

"Get away from him."

Oh, shit. Why didn't you run? Daniel held his breath, waiting to feel another punch.

It didn't come. The grip on the front of his shirt loosened; then he was released completely. Daniel fell back against the ground, a hand to his shoulder. He blinked through a haze of pain to see Cleo standing with her legs apart and braced, holding the revolver in both hands.

"Get up."

Stupefied, Daniel could only watch as Campbell

shoved himself to his feet. "You won't shoot me," Campbell said.

"You don't know me very well."

She was right, Daniel thought with admiration. She'd waste the guy in a second. Then he had another thought: *I'm in love*.

Campbell wiped at a cut on the side of his face. Daniel was bleeding from his nose, his mouth, and his side—and Campbell had gotten off with a little cut.

"Listen, Cleo," Campbell said. "I wasn't really going to shoot you. You know that, don't you?" He started to move toward her.

"Get back!"

The gun wavered. In fact, it was wobbling all over the place. And then Daniel noticed that her whole body was trembling. "Get back!" she repeated.

Daniel rolled to his knees. Then he went about the extremely unpleasant task of shoving himself to his feet.

Campbell stopped, hands up, palms out. "Why don't we just forget about this?" Instead of walking forward, he began to step slowly backward. "I'll go my way, you go yours. What do you say?"

Cleo's mouth began moving, but no words came out. Daniel followed the direction of her gaze—and saw that Campbell was heading for the well.

"Stop!" Cleo shouted.

Campbell just smiled.

"*Stop!*" she repeated. "*The well!*"

You could see it on his face. The exact moment

she said the word *well* was the exact moment Campbell realized his mistake. There was comprehension, then dismay. Then he just disappeared.

Cleo watched as Daniel staggered unsteadily to the edge of the well. What was he doing? *Oh, God.* She dropped the gun and ran to his side, grabbing him by the arm. Daniel fell to his knees and shouted Campbell's name.

"There's nothing we can do," Cleo said, pulling at his arm, wanting him to get away from the edge. If the stones came lose, he could follow Campbell into that dark grave.

Still on his knees, Daniel called his name again.

Nothing. Not a sound.

Daniel rolled to a sitting position, an elbow on his bent knee, hand to his forehead, hiding his face.

"We have to go," Cleo said. "Before it gets dark."

He lifted his head and stared wearily at her. "It's true, what he said about those people. Those kids and their mother."

"Do you think you're God? Do you think you can control everything around you? Bad things happen. That's the way it is." A harsh truth, perhaps, but the truth all the same. "We have to go."

He sat there a moment longer, just looking at her.

"Come on," she said, helping him to his feet.

They began to walk. She stopped long enough to pick up the gun she'd dropped.

He extended his bloodstained hand and she gave him the weapon. With familiarity, he removed the cartridge, pocketed it, then shoved the gun into the waistband of his jeans.

He might not want her help, but she helped him anyway. She looped one arm around his waist, and together they headed up the steep hillside, back the way they'd come.

His weakness seemed to give her strength. Her legs no longer shook. She moved with purpose. And as they walked, the pressure against her shoulder increased. She heard his labored breathing. She felt him tremble.

At one point he stopped, unable to take another step.

"It's not much farther," she said, hitching her shoulder against him, tightening her grip around his waist, hoping he wouldn't slide to the ground.

"You go," he said, his voice a breathless rasp. "Bring somebody back."

She didn't want to leave him there by himself in the dark. "I might not be able to find you."

"I'll yell."

"Not if you're unconscious. Come on. We're almost there."

They finally made it to level ground. The orange glow had long left the sky. Now, in the twilight, the lane lay before them, the tire ruts cutting through the weeds—twin paths to the truck.

He got inside somehow. "Can you drive a stick?" he asked as she slid behind the wheel, slamming the door behind her.

"You're always underestimating me."

With his eyes closed, he smiled. "Like hell."

She drove as fast as the truck could go, which wasn't all that fast, slowing down at the edge of town, where yards were littered with blue-and-white campaign signs with a handsome face smiling out at her: Reelect Mayor Burton Campbell.

27

It took the police and fire department three days to get Campbell's body out of the well. And when they did, he was pretty much unrecognizable. It was definitely the talk of Egypt and the surrounding area, with everybody referring to the body as "Baby Jessica."

No respect for the dead, Jo thought, shaking her head.

Damn him. Damn the prostitute-murdering bastard. Because of him, Egypt, Missouri, would never again make the list of the top ten small towns in America.

Damn him.

Because of him, mothers would no longer let their children roam freely about town. Because of him, people would lock their doors at night, and lie in that darkness, wondering. . . .

Damn him.

The night before, the weather had turned, bringing with it cooler temperatures. Jo had to rummage through the jackets that hung on pegs near her kitchen door, finally finding a blue wool sweater she'd knitted a few years back. It had a collar and deep pockets that she liked to sink her hands into.

She slipped it on, thinking that it was just the right weight for her trip to the hospital to visit Daniel. She'd been to see him the previous day, and the day before that. Both times he'd told her he was no longer working for the Egypt Police Department. She figured one or two more trips and he'd change his mind.

She buttoned the sweater, then reached into the sweater's deep pockets, her fingers coming into contact with several balls of tissue. Always had to have tissues with you. In one pocket she felt the solid weight of something heavier than tissue. She dug until she could touch it, until she could pull it out.

She stared at the object for a long time.

"Crap."

In her hand was the master key.

Daniel sat up in bed, staring out the hospital window. His shoulder hurt like a son of a bitch, but he wasn't taking any more painkillers. The day before, he'd been so wasted when Cleo had stopped by that he just kind of lay there, staring at her with a goofy-ass grin on his face. But now he'd been waiting all morning and afternoon for her to come back.

At least she was staying at his house. That knowledge gave him a small measure of comfort.

But it wasn't Cleo who came. It was Jo.

"They finally got him out," Jo said, pulling up a chair and sitting a few feet from the bed.

"Yeah, I heard."

"The well was a hundred and fifty feet deep."

"And narrow."

"The body in the barn belonged to a prostitute, just like you figured. And we're pretty certain the prostitute who was killed at The Palms was another one of his victims. But that's not why I'm here. I'm here to try to talk you into staying in the department."

"Did you really tell that asshole that you hired me because you felt sorry for me?"

Her silence was answer enough.

"For chrissake, Jo. Am I *that* pathetic?"

"I felt sorry for you, yes, but I was also looking for a good police officer. You fit the bill."

He shook his head, his thoughts returning to an earlier preoccupation. "Have you seen Cleo?"

"A few hours ago. I paid her the other five thousand dollars. I know she didn't find the key, but she was instrumental in exposing Dr. Campbell."

"You gave her money?" he asked, swinging his legs to the side of the bed, his bare feet hitting the floor.

"What's wrong with that?"

"She'll leave, that's what's *wrong*."

He fought with the hospital gown, finally ripping out several snaps, dropping the gown to the floor, leaving him in nothing but string-tied pajama bottoms. His shoulder and arm were wrapped in gauze, his arm anchored to his side.

"Of course she'll leave," Jo said. "She's done here."

"What do you mean, she's done here? What about the key? She still has to find the damn key."

He opened a closet and pulled out the shirt that Beau had brought the previous day. But then he realized he couldn't put it on. He picked up a pair of jeans and realized he wouldn't be able to get into them by himself, either. "Shit." He threw them down, then tried to stuff his feet into a pair of stretchy blue terry-cloth slippers supplied by the hospital. He gave up and threw the stupid things down with the pants.

"The key?" Jo repeated hesitantly.

"Come on. Drive me home." He headed for the door, with Jo following.

"I've given up on the key," Jo said, almost running to keep up. "I've decided to go ahead and get all new locks."

"That will cost a fortune. Just get Cleo to stay and find it." His heart was beating too fast. How the hell had this happened? He'd planned on Cleo being around for at least a couple more weeks. That would give him time to make things right, to make things up to her. In the last few morphine-laden days, he'd imagined them going out to eat, maybe taking in a movie or two. Making love. Not sex, but love.

"We can't let her go," Daniel said. "Not until she finds the key."

"Daniel . . ."

He kept walking. When he got to the exit door,

he turned. She wasn't coming. He went back to get her.

"Daniel."

She reached into her pocket and pulled out a closed fist. She opened it. There in her hand was a key.

"So?" he said, not understanding.

"It's the key," she whispered. "The master key. I found it in my sweater this morning."

He broke out in a sweat. Black spots floated in front of his eyes. He blinked them away and grabbed Jo by one arm. "Okay. We can fix this." He lowered his voice. "Don't tell her. Don't tell her about the key."

"But Daniel, I don't get it."

"I don't want her to go. What's so hard to get?"

"Oh. I see."

"Good."

"Won't she know about the key, though?"

"She didn't pick up on it before."

"Maybe that's because there was something bigger distracting her."

"We have to try!"

"I don't like the idea of lying to a psychic."

"Come on." He grabbed her, pulling her toward the door. "We've got to stop her."

Cleo slipped two hundred dollars into the envelope and sealed it. She double-checked the address: Quick Fill, Shanghai City, Missouri, attention Chad and Jed. That should be enough. She deposited the envelope in the mailbox, then walked over to the wooden bench to wait for the train.

It was the same train station where Daniel and Beau had picked her up. It hadn't been that long ago in real time, but given everything that had happened in the past several days, it felt like years. She'd arrived that day with a suitcase and her dog. Now she was leaving with nothing but the clothes she was wearing.

It had all seemed so simple. How could something so simple turn into such a mess?

The night before, she and Beau had sat outside near the gazing ball, waiting for the stars. And when they came, they had been so brilliant, so breathtaking.

It seemed as a good a time as any to tell Beau that she would be leaving in the morning.

"When you come back, maybe my mom will be here and you can meet her."

Was that the best way to go through life? she wondered. Hanging on to your illusions? It seemed to work for Beau.

"Have you ever been anyplace other than Egypt?" she'd asked.

"Why would I want to do that?"

Why, indeed.

"They're always there," he said.

"What?"

"The stars. They're always there. You just can't see them."

You just can't see them.

A shout drew her back to the present, to the train station and the cool breeze moving across her skin, a warm sun beating down from above.

She looked up to see a man striding toward her, wearing nothing but green hospital pajama bottoms and a white bandage across his shoulder, under his armpits. Daniel.

She got slowly to her feet. What was he doing here? He should be in the hospital. She'd wanted to tell him good-bye but had felt awkward about it. Then she found out that she really didn't have time, and it had seemed easier to just leave.

Daniel stopped in front of her, slightly out of breath, his forehead creased with pain. A wind kicked up, lifting his hair, revealing the dark roots beneath the blond. "Your dog," he said, breathlessly. "You forgot your dog."

She shook her head. He was bleeding under the bandage. She could see a spot of red seeping through the gauze. "I want Beau to have him. I told you that."

"The key," he said, as if he'd only just remembered it.

"I have the feeling it's never going to be found," Cleo said. "You'd better just go ahead and change the locks."

"The rest of your money. It's at my house."

"Put it toward getting the locks replaced."

He got a funny look on his face. "I don't think we'll need it." He seemed to search his mind for more words, finding them. "You know what people in town are saying about you? That you used your psychic powers to save us both."

"I can't take any credit for Campbell's carelessness."

She didn't want to talk about that. To herself she could finally admit that she had something that went beyond normal. But it was still a subject she wanted absolutely nothing to do with. At least not now. Maybe someday, but not now. "About the hostage case you were involved in," she began. They hadn't talked about it enough. That wasn't the kind of thing you could just ignore, hoping it would go away. Cleo wanted to leave him with something—reassurance— as well as a memory of her that wasn't all bad.

"It's not something I like to think about," he said. "People died. It was my fault."

"We can't always be the ones to fix things. If I had died out there the other day, it wouldn't have been your fault."

Yet he'd been willing to die for her. And he would have died if something hadn't distracted Campbell. "And if you'd died—" She swallowed. She reached out and took his hand. "If you had died, it wouldn't have been my fault. Bad things happen." She turned his hand over. With one finger she unconsciously traced the lines on his palm.

From far off came the sad, lonely cry of a train whistle.

"The ring," Daniel said. "I still have your ring at home."

Her mind spun back to another time, to a sweet, dark-haired boy who had loved her. A sweet, dark-haired boy who had died.

For the first time in years, the guilt she'd felt whenever she thought of Jordan was gone. She would never know if she'd really transcended time and space, but if she had, maybe she'd gone there to try to save him; maybe she'd gone there to try to stop the accident, not cause it. And maybe the only person she'd been able to save was herself.

"Mail the ring to me at my brother's address."

"Who gave it to you? Someone you loved?"

"Yes," she said, remembering, nodding, smiling sadly. "What will you do now?" she asked, turning the conversation away from Jordan and her past. She wanted to look forward, not backward.

"Jo is trying to get me to come back."

"Will you?"

"Maybe. For a while."

"Don't let it become a habit. People get locked into sameness just because it's familiar. I hope you get to go back to Scotland."

There were the people who put down roots so deep no one could tear them out. Then there were the ones like herself and Daniel, the travelers, the wanderers, always seeking, never finding, always moving on.

"There's Beau," Daniel said.

"I'm afraid Campbell may have been right when he said Beau was your excuse. Beau's more independent than you think, maybe more independent than you want him to be."

The train pulled to a stop, wheels scraping and squeaking, steam billowing out from underneath. She was the only person getting on. The conductor wouldn't wait long.

Daniel looked as if he wanted to say something.

With a flash of insight, she recognized his hesitation. *He isn't ready for me to go,* she thought, amazed at the revelation. But she had to leave. She needed some time to put herself back together. And in Egypt, Missouri, that wasn't going to happen. Maybe after Seattle she'd go to San Francisco; she didn't know. She couldn't look that far ahead.

Fog. Daniel had given her fog. She'd never forget that. Never. There was a lot of fog in San Francisco.

"All aboard!"

"Bye," she said, taking a step toward the train.

He grabbed her by the arm, pulled her to him, and kissed her. A long, slow, tender, heartfelt kiss that sent her head spinning, her mind reeling.

"All aboard!"

The kiss was over. He was no longer touching her.

His eyes. She couldn't pull her gaze from his eyes. From the longing, and the pain, and something else— something she thought she had to be imagining, something she told herself was a trick of the light. Love. She thought she saw love.

"Bye."

She turned and hurried up the train steps. She'd

barely stepped inside before the train began moving away. By the time she made it to a seat by the window, Daniel was just a silhouette standing in front of the station, already a part of her past.

Daniel stood and watched the train until it disappeared, hardly noticing the hot sidewalk under his bare feet, hardly noticing the pain in his shoulder.

What had he expected? Nothing in their so-called relationship had merited a handshake, let alone a heartfelt good-bye.

Maybe it wasn't love. Maybe he was jealous because she was leaving, moving on to someplace new and unknown. Maybe he was attracted to her because of what she represented: the world, everything that wasn't this, wasn't here; someone rare, someone unique, someone exotic and strange and wonderful. Someone who wasn't afraid of tomorrow.

No, maybe it wasn't love.

28

Cleo was having the dream again. Not the pump-kin dream. She hadn't had that since leaving Egypt. No, this was a different dream. A warm, lovely dream.

Daniel Sinclair was there. The sky was vast and blue, the grass beneath their feet as green and welcoming as tomorrow. Somewhere in the distance she could hear the sound of the North Atlantic pounding against solid cliffs, and the cry of gulls wheeling overhead.

In the dream Daniel's hair was longer, blowing in the sweet breeze. In the dream he wore a kilt. In the dream she loved him.

In the dream she had a secret, a wonderful secret she'd saved until this moment, this one perfect moment.

He knew she could have no children, but his love for her was strong. "We'll adopt," he'd told her. She'd seen the flicker of sadness in his eyes, though. It had lasted only a moment, but she'd seen it. You know these things about the people you love. You can read what others cannot. That was why she was certain her news would bring him unbridled joy. Because she knew him.

They walked, holding hands, fingers lightly brushing fingers. She swung around to face him, stopping him. She looked up into his eyes. She wanted to see the happiness there when she told him. "I'm going to have a baby."

He didn't disappoint her. First there was a flash of joy, then confusion, then joy again. "How? Are you sure?"

She took his hand and pressed it gently to a stomach that had just the slightest swell. She nodded, smiling up at him through tears she'd sworn she wouldn't shed. "They did an ultrasound to be certain."

He pulled her into his strong, warm, comforting arms. He smelled like the sea, and he smelled like the sun, and he smelled like Daniel.

She took his face in both her hands, pulling him closer. And then his lips touched hers, all warm and soft. "I love you," he said. "I love you so much."

A shrill scream came out of nowhere, pulling Cleo partially out of the dream.

"Mom!"

From somewhere in the distance, somewhere far away from her dream, a child shrieked. "I was watching TV first, and Carmen changed channels! *Mom! Dad!*"

Cleo awoke with a jolt, finding herself sleeping in her niece's bed.

The dream. It had seemed so real. She closed her eyes and rolled to her stomach. She wanted to go back to sleep. Sometimes if she woke up in the middle of a dream, she could think about it and get herself back there.

"Mom!"

Not this time.

Cleo rolled to her back, tossed off the Peter Rabbit covers, and sat on the edge of the bed a moment. The digital clock read 6:30. She rubbed her face. How come kids liked to get up early, but adults never wanted to get out of bed? What happened there? Was it because kids thought of each new day as a wonderful adventure, while adults knew the truth?

Barefoot, wearing plaid flannel pajamas, she left the room, almost colliding with Adrian in the hallway. "Go back to bed," she told him.

His eyes were barely open, his hair sticking out in all directions.

"You were up late. I'll take care of the girls."

"Thanks," he mumbled, turning around and shuffling back to the bedroom he shared with Mavis.

In the living room, the girls were still fighting.

"What's going on in here?" Cleo demanded.

Wrong question. Macy jumped to her feet and immediately started pointing at three-year-old Carmen. Carmen was sitting on her hands—or rather, sitting on the remote control she held in those hands.

"Mommy and Daddy were up late last night. They need their sleep," Cleo said. "Instead of watching TV, let's go see what we can find for breakfast."

No argument there. Carmen pulled out the remote control, turned off the TV, and ran for the kitchen. "Fruit Loops. I get Fruit Loops."

Cleo had told Adrian he shouldn't let his kids eat that sweet stuff. Without thinking, he'd replied, "Just wait till you have kids." Realizing what he'd said, his face dropped. "Oh, hey. I'm sorry."

"That's okay. And just because I can't physically have children, that doesn't mean I won't have some of my own someday." But being married, having children, a house, a home, a car, a dog, going to PTA meetings and softball games—all of it seemed so unlikely. Cleo didn't feel it in her future. There were her nieces, though. She would watch them grow. And she would try to make it to some of their school programs. Maybe she would take them ice skating, or to the zoo. Maybe they would come and visit her occasionally, so Adrian and Mavis could have some time to themselves. But it wouldn't be the same. Of course it wouldn't be the same as having children of her own.

The kids dragged out boxes of cereal while Cleo got the milk and orange juice. In the two months that she'd been at her brother's, Cleo had gained ten pounds. She could actually look at orange juice without gagging, but she didn't think she'd ever be able to drink it.

"I'll pour the juice," Macy said, getting out three glasses.

"Cleo wants milk," Carmen said. "'Cause of her problem."

"I know that."

"No, you don't."

"Yes, I do."

"Daddy said it's a secret."

"Come on, girls," Cleo said, breaking in. "Don't argue. If you're quiet, I'll take you to the park later."

Instant transformation. They began attending to business like a couple of miniature nuns. Bribery probably wasn't the way to go, but Cleo had watched her brother and sister-in-law in action, and bribery seemed to be the child-rearing method of choice.

When they finished eating, they cleaned up after themselves, then watched cartoons for another hour. After that, they changed clothes in preparation for the park, with Cleo helping Carmen with her little pink Polartec hooded top and tiny hiking boots.

"Are you going to live with us forever?" Carmen asked solemnly, looking directly into Cleo's eyes. "I want you to."

"Ah, sweetie, I can't. I'd like to, but I can't."

"Where are you going to go?" Macy asked.

"I'm not sure. Maybe to San Francisco. But I'll come to visit. And you can visit me."

Outside, footsteps sounded on the wooden porch. The mail slot in the door opened, then clanged shut.

The familiar sound galvanized the girls into action.

"Something for you, Aunt Cleo!" Macy flapped the envelope in the air, then handed it to Cleo with a flourish.

There was her name, printed in strong, slanted handwriting. She checked the return address. D. Sinclair.

Daniel.

The dream still clung to the edges of her mind. Now, seeing his name, seeing handwriting that must be his, brought the mood of the dream back to her.

She knew what the envelope would hold. The ring. The ring she'd left in Daniel's bedroom that night. The ring Jordan had given her.

She opened the envelope. Inside was a piece of folded notebook paper, the edges ragged. She unfolded it to find not only the ring but a money order for five thousand dollars. Why had he sent it? She'd told him she didn't want the money.

He'd written something on the lined paper.

Cleo,

I'm enclosing a money order for five thousand dollars. The town council voted on it and unanimously decided that it should be sent to you. By the time you get this letter, Beau will be a married man. He and Matilda, the manager of Tastee Delight, are getting married this afternoon. I will be the best man, and Premonition is the ring bearer.

In two weeks I'm leaving for Scotland, and that's what this letter is really about. I have a friend there who bought a castle and is in the process of turning it into a museum. He's had some break-ins, and asked for my help in securing the premises and retrieving a valuable painting that was stolen. Which leads me to the point of this letter. We are in need of a psychic. Would you be interested?

What followed was his flight schedule.

If you would be interested in this job, meet me at Chicago O'Hare. If you aren't interested, then please use the money toward making a new start.
Daniel

"Come on, Aunt Cleo! Let's go to the park." The children were jumping around her feet, tugging at her, trying to pull her out the door.

Scotland.

"Okay, okay," she said, laughing. "But after that, Aunt Cleo has a lot of things to do."

She put everything back in the envelope, then put the envelope on the dresser in Macy's room. She'd never wear the ring again, but she would always keep it, always cherish it.

29

Daniel had deliberately arranged his itinerary so that there would be a three-hour layover in Chicago. Now his flight to Scotland would be leaving soon and there was no sign of Cleo.

She wasn't coming.

Disappointment rocked him, made him feel brittle and weary. He wondered why he was going to Scotland at all. For years it had called to him, for years he'd dreamed of going back, but now it all seemed so empty. For the last two weeks, whenever he thought about being there, those thoughts included Cleo. When he imagined landing at Heathrow Airport, Cleo was there. When they took a train from London to Glasgow, Cleo was there. He'd even packed his kilt, made of the red and green plaid of his ancestors, and his beret that bore their crest. He'd wanted to wear the plaid for her.

He should have called.

No, this way he would know it had really been

her choice, with no pressure. And if he'd called, he might have said too much. He might have scared her away. He knew how she was about commitment. He knew that she didn't want to get close to anyone.

He was a patient man, though. He didn't need to tell her he loved her. He only needed to be near her. For now, anyway, that would have been enough. But he hadn't really considered how it would be if she didn't come. He hadn't been prepared for the disappointment, the pain.

Restless, he picked up his green duffel bag and went back through the X-ray area, to a row of phones. There he put in a call to Beau, telling his brother that he'd call again when he landed in England. As he was hanging up, he saw her.

Cleo.

His heart began to hammer. His palms began to sweat.

Slowly he let go of the receiver. He could see her, hurrying along, her eyes scanning the mass of people. Her hair was different. Then he realized it was just cut evenly.

She was every bit as beautiful as he remembered. Every bit as exotic, wearing her red lipstick, dangling earrings, and a straight black wraparound skirt that stopped just above her rose tattoo.

Finally her eyes connected with his. Her face lit up. She waved. He couldn't move. He shoved his hand deep into the front pockets of his pants so that she wouldn't see how it trembled.

• • •

Cleo saw Daniel and gave him a huge wave. He didn't wave back. He didn't come to greet her, to meet her halfway. And when she caught up to him, he didn't look surprised or even glad to see her. He just stood there, one hand shoved deep into the front pocket of his cargo pants, the other gripping a large duffel bag that was slung over his shoulder. He was wearing his shirt with the pink flamingos, the one he'd had on the day they met. He looked maybe a little thinner, his hair a little longer, his eyes a little bluer.

"My plane was delayed," she said breathlessly. "I was afraid I was going to miss the connection."

"Our flight's probably boarding." He began moving in the direction of the X-ray machines.

What was going on? This was so strange. Or had she let herself read something into his offer that wasn't there? The dream—had the dream caused her to think there was more to their relationship than there was? Wasn't he just acting like someone who was waiting for an associate?

"How's your arm?" she asked.

"Almost a hundred percent."

"That's good." Small talk. The talk of strangers.

They got in line for the X-ray machine. "I don't know if I'm the one for this job," she said. "I couldn't even find the key, remember? So why did you ask me? Why not get somebody who's already in Scotland?"   •

"I wanted you." He put his bag on the conveyor

belt. She did the same with her backpack. They passed through the metal detector.

"We need to see the contents of your bag," one of the inspectors told Daniel. He unzipped it.

"What's this?"

"A fog machine."

"Fog machine?"

"Yeah."

"What's it for?"

"It makes fog."

Cleo stared at the contraption in the duffel bag.

"Are you in a band?" the inspector asked.

"No."

"Then what do you need a fog machine for?"

"I just like fog."

The inspector shrugged, then zipped up the bag and shoved it at Daniel.

They hurried to gate three, where boarding was underway. The line was short, most of the people having already boarded.

"Why'd you bring the fog machine?" Cleo asked at the door of the jetway, where an airline employee checked their tickets. She wanted him to open up to her, to make some kind of connection.

"I thought it might come in handy."

"Is that why you asked me along?" Now they were walking side by side down the ramp. "For sex?" Since he hadn't seemed in the least happy to see her, it was the only conclusion she could draw. And it broke her heart.

They stepped into the jet. "Middle section," the flight attendant said.

"Among other things," Daniel said, moving down the aisle, the duffel bag in front of him.

"I didn't come along for your amusement," she said.

"Why did you come, Cleo?"

She'd come because she loved him, but she'd be damned if she'd tell him that now. She tried to think of a scathing, Cleoesque reply, but she was too hurt. Her brain was too numb.

Their seats weren't together. *Thank God*, Cleo thought, squeezing in between an elderly woman and a businessman. But Daniel's seat was directly behind hers.

She should get off the plane. She should just get off the plane and go—where? Where would she go? She had no home. She thought for a moment and decided she could go to San Francisco. Yes, she could find work somewhere, reading palms and tarot cards. She could tell people about all the wonderful things she saw in their future while her own lay before her like an empty swimming pool.

She finally decided to stay on and go to Scotland. When she got there, she didn't have to stay with Daniel. It wasn't as though she'd signed a contract.

Oh, shit, she thought as she realized she was crying. *Damn. Damn him.*

She wiped at her cheeks.

Something kicked in, and air began to circulate in the cabin. Her ears rang.

There was a lot of movement in the aisle. She looked up through blurry eyes to see Daniel taking the seat next to hers. Somehow he'd convinced the woman to trade with him.

Cleo stared straight ahead, as if she were taking in every word of the cabin crew's safety instructions. Then the plane was taxiing out, coming to a stop near the end of the runway to wait its turn.

She felt Daniel's elbow prodding her arm. She looked down to see that he was handing her a napkin.

Did he know she was crying? God, she hoped not. Was that why he'd handed her the napkin? She was about to tuck it away when she noticed the handwriting on the back.

In strong, sharp, slanted handwriting was a question: *Why did you come?*

She stared at the napkin. Cleo wasn't afraid of flying. She loved it. But she also knew how unfair life could be. She knew how quickly someone could be taken from you. She knew that the plane could crash and Daniel would never know how she felt about him.

She took the pen Daniel was holding out to her, and wrote beneath his question: *Because I love you.* She folded the napkin but didn't pass it back.

At that moment the plane's engines went to maximum power and the noise in the cabin increased. They began to roll forward.

A lot of people were afraid at the moment of take-off, but for Cleo it was the best part. There was nothing so incredible as the moment the plane's wheels lost contact with the ground and you became airborne.

As the plane shuddered along, picking up speed, she handed the napkin back to Daniel. She watched him as he read it, watched as the disbelief in his face blossomed into joy, his expression telling her what words had not. Daniel Sinclair loved her.

There was no way to be heard above the roar of the plane.

He reached for her, grabbing her hand, threading his fingers through hers. She smiled at him and looked at his beautiful hair, his beautiful blond hair with its dark roots, his beautiful blond eyebrows, into his eyes, into his blue, blue eyes that were damp and shining, and thought, *How did I ever find you? How did this miracle ever happen?*

He kissed her hand, kissed her knuckles, kissed her palm. And then she saw a to-hell-with-everybody expression cross his features. He boldly took her face in his hands and kissed her mouth with a kiss that was a mind-blowing combination of exquisite tenderness and passionate desire. And when he pulled away enough to look at her, they were both laughing through their tears.

He mouthed the words *I love you*.

At that very moment the plane broke free from the bonds of earth, and they were suddenly gliding, soaring, unfettered, transcending.

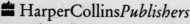